Archie could see tha━━━━━━━━━━━━━━ clothes.

The intruder's skin was almost the same grayish color as the stone statues, except for the face and hands and feet, which were strangely brown. When Archie was within a yard or two of the fountain, he realized that the brownish color was not a suntan, as he had fleetingly thought it would be. It was dirt— dirt ground into skin that had not been washed for a very long time.

Then Archie saw the darker brown stain on the man's chest—the clotted blood from a bullet hole that had crusted over.

———————————— ★ ————————————

"Ms Coker should get at least an Edgar nomination for this one."

—*Mystery News*

CAROLYN COKER
APPEARANCE OF

WORLDWIDE®

TORONTO • NEW YORK • LONDON
AMSTERDAM • PARIS • SYDNEY • HAMBURG
STOCKHOLM • ATHENS • TOKYO • MILAN
MADRID • WARSAW • BUDAPEST • AUCKLAND

APPEARANCE OF EVIL

A Worldwide Mystery/December 1995

First published by St. Martin's Press, Incorporated.

ISBN 0-373-26185-3

For Helen and Bert Holmes

Also, special thanks to the many LAPD officers who shared their stories, and who "Protect and Serve" a city that does not always appreciate their bravery and compassion.

PROLOGUE

"I COULD GET KILLED."

"You won't fall."

"I could fall off this sonofabitchin' fence and they'd find me here dead."

"You can do it. I climbed over—and with a bottle of Jack Daniel's in one hand."

When he heard the voices and saw the two figures clumsily scaling the fence into the botanical garden, he quickly looked for a place to hide. He, too, was an intruder. He had come over the same fence not long before.

The pale fourth-quarter moon gave just enough light to see that the newcomers were not the police.

"All right. Here I come, ready or not, dead or alive." The trespasser who was afraid of falling tumbled drunkenly to the ground, but managed to get to his feet and stood inside the garden now, though unsteadily. *"Las' time I climbed that sonofabitch was in high school."* He stumbled forward, breathing heavily. *"Les' stop here."*

"Keep your voice down." The second figure spoke in a whisper and moved easily up the incline, beckoning, urging the other one toward the statuary garden.

"'Sfar enough." He stood swaying with his feet far apart for balance.

Hiding close by, the listener in the deep shadows could smell the alcohol on the man's warm breath in the chilly night air.

"Come on up here." Near the fountain, the other one laughed and held the bottle of whiskey by the neck, then unscrewed the top and took a drink. *"Come on. Have a little more Christmas cheer."*

"'S season to be jolly..." he sang in a halting whisper.

Not daring to move until the drunken singer stumbled on across the silvery, moonlit grass toward his companion, the other intruder kept to the back of the tall azalea and camellia bushes. Then slowly, careful to stay on the smooth dirt path where his feet would not rustle through fallen leaves, he crept toward the slope where he had entered the garden.

"Fa la la, la la..." The inebriated voice was bolder this time.

Just as he jumped down safely onto the street side of the fence, he heard the song cut short by the sound of the gun. There was no mistaking it. And in terror, he ran as fast as he could to get away from the sound.

ONE

THE VANDALISM in the statuary garden of the Huntington Library was almost as shocking as the discovery of the dead body.

Henry E. Huntington's library, art gallery, and botanical gardens—bequeathed to the city of San Marino, California, on his death in 1927—occupied two hundred prime acres in the center of the quiet, gilt-edged community. Surrounded as it was by expensive homes with their private security systems and patrolled around the perimeter by local police, the Huntington was considered to be insulated from the harsher elements of the rest of Los Angeles County.

There were times, even when Henry Huntington still lived in the mansion that now was the art gallery, when the grounds were invaded late at night by local high school students who could not resist the challenge of locked gates and high walls. But no property had ever been destroyed. No damage had been done then, or since, when succeeding generations of teenagers (always believing they were treading where no foot had trod before) discovered how easy it was to scale the fence on the downhill section of Euston Road, the property's southern border. With a sort of pole-vault action over the top strand of barbed wire, it was easy enough to make a soft landing on the grassy upward slope inside.

The major buildings at the Huntington were protected by a sophisticated electronic security system. Almost as a formality, the grounds were also patrolled by a handful of men and women whose uniforms and badges identified them as guards, though they did not carry guns and had very little training in thwarting crime. For the most part, they were retired residents of San Marino—former business and professional people—who volunteered their services. As a matter of courtesy, they were paid a minimal salary and honored with an annual banquet at the Athenaeum on the Caltech campus. Being a guard at the Huntington was like being a member of an exclusive club. Ordinarily, the most that was asked of the members in their blue uniforms was to answer visitors' questions and, at night, simply to be there to notify the police in case there was any hint of real trouble. And there never had been.

In early November, before the discovery of the vandalism and the unidentified body, there had been an incident in the Japanese section of the botanical gardens that brought a few curses instead of the usual winks from the guards. But even then, there was apparently no malicious intent. Someone struck the bronze temple bell with such force that the antique wooden striker splintered and snapped in half as a deep *bong, bong, bong* was heard for blocks around.

Archie Chambers, the first guard on the scene, chased a giggling group of youngsters in the dark through the wisteria arbor, across the rose garden, and down the hill, where they made their escape the same way they had come in, over the fence on Euston Road.

Later that month, Archie transferred to the morning schedule. To his surprise, he found that chasing pranksters in the middle of the night was not nearly as disturbing as patrolling the grounds the next morning and finding the debris they left behind. During the first week of his new assignment Archie strolled through the Australian garden, taking in the scent of dusty eucalyptus and thinking of nothing so much as the need for rain in the milder-than-usual California winter. As he dodged around a spiky flowering acacia that hung across the path, he squinted against a cheerful sunburst reflected in the shiny metal of several scattered beer cans. With a "boys will be boys" feeling of resignation, he stooped to toss the cans into the nearest trash container.

It was then that Archie made what he felt was a scandalous discovery. There on the ground, in full view, was a pair of lacy, pink panties. Archie's face flushed with embarrassment as he picked up the garment with two fingers. Suddenly, he had the horrifying thought that some young girl had been raped on the spot the night before. He quickly searched the area for signs of a struggle. The grass was flattened next to the path, but that was all. There was no indication that anything but an act of mutual consent had taken place. For some reason he could not explain, he had a feeling of deep sadness. He wadded the satiny fabric into an unrecognizable ball and stuffed it beneath the beer cans in the trash container.

He supposed he should mention what he had found to the captain of the guards, but he was too embarrassed. He knew his face would turn red. He would probably stutter. And for all he knew, this was the only time such a thing had taken place in the botanical gardens. If it happened again, he would say something. If there was a next time, he definitely would report it. For now, he made a determined effort to forget the incident.

Archie Chambers had filled out an application to be a guard the same week he retired as manager of the Los Angeles reservations office of British Airways. To him, the Huntington epitomized the best of both his worlds: Southern California, where he had lived most of his adult life, and East Anglia, England, where he had been born and where, as he remembered without regret, he had squandered much of his youth in his father's boat-rental dock on the banks of the Stour River.

He felt a proprietary pride in the Huntington's botanical gardens, which lavishly demonstrated the hospitality of California's soil and climate. Roses and delicate varieties of herbs flourished as consistently as did the dangerous devil cacti, the bonsai trees in the Zen garden, and the massive mesa oaks that were the first to claim the land hundreds of years ago. With each changing season, flowering perennials and neat beds of annuals added dazzling color and heady perfume.

Archie loved the gardens, but still closer to his heart was Henry Huntington's mansion, which now housed the philanthropist's art collection. On the east wall of the main gallery was a landscape painting that Archie felt was a rendering of his own boyhood. The title was *View on the Stour, near Dedham*. The painter was one of East Anglia's most famous sons, John Constable. Still, the painting was almost overpowered by the rest of the collection. Here was the finest assemblage of British full-length portraits existing anywhere. Reynolds, Lawrence, and Romney all were represented, but the most famous portrait—the one that most visitors came to see—was the larger-than-life oil painting on canvas by Thomas Gainsborough titled *The Blue Boy*.

The likeness of the stripling boy with wispy brown hair holding a plumed hat and wearing a blue satin suit with knee britches had been reproduced thousands of times. It was featured on calendars, match covers, candy boxes, cocktail napkins, and even the backs of playing cards.

Usually, Archie gave *The Blue Boy* only a passing glance, and that simply because Gainsborough—like John Constable and Archie Chambers—was a native of East Anglia. But this morning, after finding evidence in the botanical garden of what must have been an illicit teenaged liaison, he was drawn to the comforting innocence in the face of the boy in the painting.

Later that same week, on Thursday, Archie arrived thirty minutes before opening time for his assignment in the statuary garden of the north vista. It was a warm December day with a view of the San Gabriel Mountains that was unmarred by smog or haze. On each side of the garden's wide expanse of plush bermuda grass, tall palm trees cast geometric patterns of shade on waxy-leafed camellia bushes and dwarf azaleas that filled the spaces between two rows of seventeenth-century Italian statues flanking a magnificent Renaissance fountain.

The moment Archie passed the far corner of the library and crossed the sidewalk in front of the north vista, he sensed something was wrong. From the farthest corner of his eye he saw a discordant splotch of red. He turned to see what it was, then stared, first in disbelief, then disgust and indignation.

Red paint had been splashed on the chest of the stone likeness of an Italian nobleman. It dripped like blood into the folds of his stone waistcoat, giving the impression that the dandified gentleman still bravely stood atop his pedestal, though mortally wounded.

For no accountable reason, the first clear thought that came to Archie's mind was that he should have reported finding the girl's panties.

Next, it occurred to him that the culprit might still be somewhere nearby. He quickly glanced around the garden, but there was no movement, not even a breeze.

Looking beyond the statue to the far end of the garden, Archie saw that something else was amiss.

The north vista stretched almost the length of a football field, and even to someone with keener vision than Archie's, it would have been difficult to identify exactly what was propped against the fountain. Yet, there was something—something that was not usually there.

Hesitantly, he started across the lawn. His first impression was that the vandal had knocked one of the statues from its pedestal. But the color was slightly wrong. And the position was half reclining; all the statues stood straight.

The closer Archie got, the more certain he became. He had suspected from the first that it was a man. Someone ill, or unconscious, or drunk. He thought suddenly of the beer cans.

Two more steps and Archie could see that the man was wearing no clothes.

The intruder's skin was almost the same grayish color as the stone statues, except for the face and hands and feet, which were strangely brown. When Archie was within a yard or two of the fountain, he realized that the brownish color was not a suntan, as he had fleetingly thought it might be. It was dirt—dirt ground into skin that had not been washed for a very long time.

Then Archie saw the darker brown stain on the man's chest—the clotted blood from a bullet hole that had crusted over.

TWO

A FEW MILES closer to Los Angeles proper in the predominantly Latino community of El Sereno, the sounds of gunshots and police sirens were not unfamiliar, and vandalism—though it produced outrage in some residents—did not come as a surprise.

On the morning when Archie Chambers made his grisly discovery in the statuary garden, Los Angeles police detectives Eduardo Lopez and Tina Roberson were headed back to Hollenbeck Division in their unmarked Plymouth after completing a domestic violence investigation in El Sereno. Detective Roberson was driving. As she began a left turn off Calle Calesa onto Huntington Drive, a battered VW van ran a red light in front of her. The driver clipped the curb as he traveled south, then overcompensated, cutting a wide arc toward the oncoming lane as he made a leisurely right onto Farrel, a narrow industrial street lined with warehouses. Detective Roberson slapped the bubble light on top of the car and turned on the siren.

"What are you doing?" Detective Lopez, who was slouched in the seat beside her and very nearly asleep, straightened and gave his partner a look of astonishment.

"I'm going to nail that creep."

The car in front was traveling at an easy speed, bouncing in the potholes of the blacktop road. Tina turned off the siren but continued to flash the light, signaling for the driver to pull over.

"You're not a patrol officer anymore," Eduardo said. "Call it in. Let one of the black-and-whites take him."

Technically, Tina was a detective trainee, though she had the workload of a detective and the privilege of the title. The pay raise and the change in status on the official roster would not be forthcoming until she passed the oral exam, and the exam was not scheduled for another six months.

"The way he was driving, he could kill somebody by the time a patrol car got here."

"Who's he going to kill on Farrel Street?" Eduardo made a big production of looking out the windows at the bleak corrugated metal and stucco buildings. There was no one in sight—the street was deserted. "You think someone's going to come out of one of those warehouses and leap off the loading dock in front of him? That's about the only way I can figure he'd hurt anyone. A pedestrian could outrun that beat-up wreck."

The van pulled to a stop next to the broken sidewalk. The driver, a middle-aged Latino man in an olive green coverall stuck his head out the window and glared at the two detectives.

"He's not going to like you," Eduardo said.

"Then I won't ask him to go dancing." Tina knew that what Eduardo had said was more than a casual remark. A black female police officer could expect to be about as popular in El Sereno as Eduardo would be in Watts. Tina unclipped her badge from her gunbelt, and approached the parked vehicle from the rear. As she identified herself and looked through the window of the van, she saw an empty wine bottle in the seat beside the driver.

"What'd I do?" The man growled at her. "Why'd you stop me?"

Until she saw the wine bottle, she had planned only to give the man a warning ticket. Now, she would have to give him a street sobriety test. "Would you exit your vehicle, please?"

"Look, lady... I just live three blocks from here. Whatever I did, I'm sorry. Why don't you just let me go on home?"

"Exit your vehicle, please." From the corner of her eye, Tina could see Eduardo watching her as he leaned on the front fender of their unmarked Plymouth. Instead of the amusement she had expected to see on his face, there was a scowl, and he motioned with a quick nod of the head toward the opposite side of the street.

Suddenly, there, from the open doorway of a warehouse, someone yelled, "Hey, Raul! Is that black gal trying to kidnap you?" The speaker and three other men stood laughing. "Better be careful man, she's got a gun."

Someone else said, "Yeah! No telling what she'll make you do." There was more laughter. More jeering faces joined the others. Five or six men jumped down from the loading dock and started across the street.

"Please exit your vehicle." Tina's voice did not waver, even though she was beginning to regret that she had not called a patrol car instead of making the stop herself. Eduardo was right. She was a detective now, not a traffic cop.

"Lady, just let me go home—"

"Officer, I know the driver." A man of about sixty wearing a red bandana around his neck had come from the warehouse on the same side of the street as the van. "He lives only a few blocks from here. Why don't you let him go on home?"

"I can't do that," Tina said. She was concentrating on what she had been taught at the police academy. When you meet resistance, there is no need to explain, apologize or make excuses. Just do your job. But, good God, where had all these men come from? When she got out of the car, there had been no one in sight. Now, there must be fifteen truck loaders and warehousemen coming toward her from both sides of the street. She looked toward where Eduardo had been standing, but several hulking men in white coveralls were moving in between them. For a moment, she caught a glimpse of her partner. Beside him now was the man wearing the red bandana who had been shoved out of the way. He was speaking in animated Spanish to Eduardo and making wide gestures with his arms toward Tina and the driver.

Someone had a foot on the rear bumper of the van and was rocking it back and forth. Someone else tugged at the back of Tina's leather belt. She quickly put her hand on her gun so that no one could take it and turned to confront the culprit behind her. As she did, a young man with slicked-back black hair and a bad case of acne reached out of the crowd and tried to grab her breast. The faces around her were no longer good humored, but menacing. It had all seemed to happen in a second. Cold panic knotted her stomach, and her hand tightened on the gun at her waist.

Suddenly, her partner was beside her, speaking calmly in Spanish to the excited group. Tina had no idea what he was saying, but the men moved back. Several of the younger ones laughed and nodded good-naturedly at Eduardo, then turned to cross the street once again.

Eduardo opened the door and helped the driver out of the van. "Get the keys out of the ignition," he said to Tina.

She quickly did as he said and handed the keys to her partner, gladly letting him take charge.

"Raul—that's your name, isn't it? Raul?"

"Yes. Raul."

"Well, Raul, your friend is going to take you home." Eduardo motioned toward the man in coveralls and the red bandana. "I was going to make you walk, but your friend says you've got a gimpy leg."

"From the war in Korea." Raul knocked proudly on his left shin with his fist. It made the sound of rapping on a tabletop. When he straightened, he said with a frown, "But my van—"

"We'll lock it up, and your pal can bring you back to get it later." Eduardo gave the keys to the man beside him. "Go sleep it off, Raul. And stay out of that van when you're drinking wine. You understand?"

Raul nodded and limped off beside his friend to get in a black Ford parked at the far corner of the warehouse loading dock.

"Are you just going to let him go?" Tina's question was a reflex. She was grateful to her partner for stemming what could have been a very ugly situation. If she had been by herself, God knows what would have happened. But Raul *was* a drunk driver. He could have killed someone. "Eduardo, we can't just let him go."

"Get in the car."

Tina started to protest again, but Eduardo took her arm and guided her toward the passenger side. She could see that several of her tormentors still were standing by watching them, and smiling approval at her partner's tactics.

Eduardo had turned the unmarked Plymouth around and driven the half-block back to Huntington Drive before either of them spoke.

"You can call this in to dispatch now." He took a folded piece of paper from his inside coat pocket and handed it to her. Raul's full name, address, and the license number of the van were written down. "A black-and-white can probably get to his house before he does."

"Thanks," she said, unable to think of anything more to say, but knowing that that was enough. They were partners. They took care of each other. She pressed the speaker button on the radio and called in the information.

Afterward was always the same. After a volatile incident all the "what ifs?" started racing around in her brain. What if she had been there alone? What if the crowd had not listened to Eduardo? But the biggest "what if" was what if she had panicked and used her gun? What if she had killed that creep because he made a grab at her breast? She could remember his face, and realized now that he was hardly more than a teenager. But with all those men making lewd remarks and laughing at her, she had focused on him as the most immediate threat. The thought sent a chill through her. Dear God. She might have killed a boy over a DWI stop when he wasn't even the driver. Her worst fear was that sometime she would have to draw her gun—and actually use deadly force.

They were within a block of division headquarters before she could trust herself not to sound hysterical. She turned toward Eduardo and asked the question she knew he had been waiting for. "What did you say to those guys, anyway?"

"I just told them about you."

"What? Some macho lie? On second thought, I don't want to hear about it."

Eduardo grinned at her.

Tina didn't care. Whatever he had said, it had gotten the goons to move away from her. Seriously, she asked Eduardo as her senior partner, "Was what I did stupid?"

"No. Once you had the guy stopped and could tell he had been drinking, there was nothing else you could do. However—"

"Oh, yeah. Here comes the however."

"Considering the makeup of the crowd that had gathered, and the fact that the driver of the van had a wooden leg..."

"How the hell did I know he had a wooden leg?"

"I'm just saying that a field sobriety test might not have worked too well—under the circumstances."

He wasn't actually laughing out loud, and she had worked with him long enough to know that he wouldn't mouth the story around the division, though he would be sorely tempted. "Whatever you told those idiots, I'm sure, was not one of the recommended approaches from the department's book on crowd control."

"I keep telling you, partner, the best way to be a good detective is to forget everything you learned at the police academy. You can't do this job by the book."

That was one of the areas where Tina and Eduardo still did not quite agree.

THREE

ARCHIE CHAMBERS hurried back to the security office at the Huntington. No one was there when he entered. There was no one to tell about the dead body he had discovered in the statuary garden. The morning supervisor—a retired senior vice president of Thurman and Forstman Investment Consultants—had left a reminder among the thumbtacked Christmas cards on the bulletin board that he would be late, as he had been invited to be the guest speaker at a breakfast meeting of the Assistance League.

With fingers palsied in agitation, Archie punched in the number of the San Marino Police Department.

The two officers from the small police force who were assigned to investigate were almost giddy with the challenge. This was the first murder to occur within the city limits in the past ten years.

San Marino was one of eighty-four municipalities of varying sizes that made up the area loosely described as Los Angeles. Of these, the most famous—and the one with the highest per capita income—was Beverly Hills, where the movie and television stars clustered together with the industry moguls. Running a close second in the amount of money ascribed to its average resident, San Marino was much less well known. The small city in the center of the San Gabriel Valley was anonymous by design.

The community had much in common with its namesake, the tiny republic of San Marino in the northern mountains of Italy. There was the same disdain for intrusion from outsiders. Although the California San Marino did not have a wall around it, as did the European city, it discouraged interlopers just as effectively by giving them no reason to be there except by invitation.

San Marino, California, was almost entirely a residential community, but with no condominiums, apartment houses, or other multiple dwellings. Of the 13,000 people living within the fewer than four square miles of the city limits, an amazing number were company presidents, board chairmen, newspaper owners, and other assorted titans of business and industry.

To protect the privacy of the citizens, no door to door solicitation of any type was allowed. There was no industry and no civic center or distinctive city hall. The one business street was notable for what it did not have. There were no bars or other on-sale outlets of alcoholic beverages, no bookstores, no theaters, no automobile dealers, and only two restaurants that could seat more than a dozen people—both of which closed at nine P.M. In short, the businesses that operated within the city were only those that provided services for the residents: dry cleaners, florists, pharmacies, real estate offices, bank branches, a few specialty food markets, and exclusive dress shops.

At one time, the city paid for the services of an official "city trapper," whose duty it was to deal with any gophers or moles that had the temerity to invade the landscaped lawns of the citizens. Though that particular public service was no longer available, the current city employees were equally dedicated to making life marvelous for those who lived in San Marino.

Chief among the local civil servants were the twenty-four sworn members of the police department. High on the list of their major responsibilities were security checks on all the homes, particularly when the residents were out of town. Then, too, there was the ongoing problem of keeping transient automobile traffic moving. Unfortunately, the main street extended beyond San Marino a short distance in both directions. Huntington Drive was a major thoroughfare between downtown Los Angeles seven miles to the south, and Santa Anita Race Track in the neighboring city of Arcadia, one mile north.

The proximity of both these undesirable areas explained a lot to the more experienced of the two police officers assigned to investigate the murder at the Huntington. It was disappointing that this case was not to be a cause célèbre. But it seemed obvious that the grungy victim was not a visitor to the museum, and certainly not a resident of San Marino.

"But what was he doing in here, and with no clothes on?" The younger officer stood from examining the body and brushed blades of grass from the knife-pleated pants of his uniform.

"I doubt that he climbed the fence that way." The senior officer did not bother to look at his partner. "It would take a hell of a brave man to climb over that top strand of wire with no pants on."

"Oh. I guess whoever shot him thought we might be able to identify him by his clothes." The young police officer stared at the mountains, having already seen more than he cared to of the body, "But what was he doing here in the first place?"

"He and his pal with the gun were probably drunk and wandered in by mistake."

"By mistake? What do you mean?"

"They probably thought they were at Santa Anita."

"You think they mistook the Huntington for the racetrack?"

"Sure. It was dark, they were both probably drunk— from the smell of this one—they saw the empty parking lot and the buildings behind the fence..."

"But they don't have nighttime racing at Santa Anita."

"No doubt they had more in mind than just saving the price of admission."

"You think they were going to try to rip off the racetrack?"

"You got a better idea?" The older officer irritably swatted at a fly attracted by the stench of the corpse.

"Constable," Archie Chambers, who had been standing well back from the examination, lapsed into British English as he always did in times of stress, "I say, Constable." The nearest uniformed man looked at him quizzically. "Sorry. I mean, Officer." He gestured toward the paint-splattered statue. "They must have been vandals. Did you notice the red paint? That wasn't there yesterday. It had to have been done last night."

The slamming of automobile doors in the parking lot momentarily distracted the three men. Between two azalea bushes they could see that the backup police car which had been summoned and the paramedic van had both arrived (without sirens, so as not to disturb the neighborhood).

As they walked toward the gate to admit the newcomers, the younger man said in a low voice to his superior, "Maybe the killer was a graffiti artist who thought he had been caught in the act. Some of those guys from Los Angeles are always looking for new territory to mess up. Have you seen that sign above the Pasadena Freeway?" He warmed to his story. "I mean, here's this freestanding traffic sign twenty-five feet above one of the busiest freeways in the country. There's no way to get up there. No ladder, no walkway. The freeway maintenance guys have to use one of those trucks with a cherry picker on it to do any changes or repairs. But somehow, someone managed to write gang symbols right between the arrow pointing downtown and the off ramp to Chinatown."

His partner grunted his disagreement.

"No, I don't suppose it could be anyone like that." The young officer shook his head, dismissing the theory. "Graffiti freaks don't carry guns; they carry cans of spray paint."

"Hell, half the people in Los Angeles carry guns."

"I meant young kids."

"Them, too."

The paramedics unloaded a gurney from the back of the van.

Archie Chambers, eager to be involved, hurried off, jangling the key ring excitedly to unlock the gate.

When he was gone, the officer in charge said confidentially to his younger partner, "Look, this has nothing to do with us."

"What do you mean?"

"It *happened* here, but I'd be willing to bet that neither the victim nor the perpetrator had any connection with San Marino. By tomorrow, the chief will be on the phone to the LAPD."

FOUR

As HUNTINGTON DRIVE stretched south beyond the bronze, set in stone CITY OF SAN MARINO sign, the wide, divided street began to lose its well-tended appearance. Six miles on, in the community of El Sereno, instead of carefully cultivated rose beds in the median strip, there were only patches of cracked concrete with tufts of brown grass poking through. The earlier shopping area of discreetly buff-colored buildings with brass name plates and carved-wood signs gave way to fading pink, red, and turquoise peeling paint on stuccoed walls. Wrought-iron grills protected the doors and windows of the small businesses with Spanish names.

And instead of the BMWs, Jaguars, and Mercedes that politely made room for each other as they purred out of the main stream of traffic onto tree-shaded residential streets named Oak Forest, Shakespeare, or Hampton Court; in El Sereno, low-rider Chevys, jacked-up pickups, and motorcycles with duel-exhaust pipes screeched and scraped against each other as they whipped onto Pueblo Avenue, Tampico, or Portola Street toward tiny wood-frame houses or over-crowded apartment buildings.

El Sereno, unlike San Marino, was not a city in itself, but one of the many diverse sections of Greater Los Angeles, and was dependent on the giant municipality for basic services, including police protection. On the map in the police chief's office, El Sereno was near the center of the Hollenbeck Division.

Later the same week as the discovery of the body near the vandalized statue in the garden of the Huntington library, El Sereno businessman Armando Estrada, the owner of El

Fenix restaurant, called the Los Angeles Police Department to report the theft of two fifty-pound cartons of chorizo sausage and to complain about the graffiti on the wall next to the front door of his establishment. Plainclothes detectives Eduardo Lopez and Tina Roberson were sent to investigate.

Detective Lopez had been with the LAPD for five years. While still a patrol officer in his blue uniform, his picture had been used in a recruiting brochure that targeted the Latino community. He had been proud of his uniform, but he preferred his current assignment.

To Eduardo, "plain clothes" meant a two-piece suit altered to nip in at the waist and a pastel dress shirt open at the neck. He carried his gun in a shoulder holster because he was convinced that it was easier to reach than hanging from his belt, and, tucked under his arm, it did not destroy the cut of the jacket. At an inch or two over six feet, and with an added two inches on the heels of his gray lizard cowboy boots, Eduardo did not go unnoticed anywhere in the Hollenbeck Division.

His partner, Detective Roberson, tended to be more casual in her choice of clothing. Her taste ran to mid-heel pumps, cable-knit sweaters—loose enough and long enough to cover a gun belt, though she sometimes carried her Beretta in her handbag—and straight skirts vented in the back (for ease of running). But being a black female assigned to a predominantly Latino area drew attention, nevertheless.

Tina would have preferred to wear a warm-up suit and running shoes as her work clothes, and almost always wore them off duty. They said as much about her as Eduardo's tailored suits did about him. She had been a competitive runner since high school, and had a collection of trophies for her effort.

When Tina was eligible to become a detective trainee, she had been transferred to the Hollenbeck Division and Eduardo Lopez had been assigned as her senior partner.

From the first, they had been wary of each other. Tina believed in a literal translation of the department Bible—the LAPD Manual—and rejected deviations with the same fervor as a Creationist rejects the theory of evolution. Eduardo found room for interpretation. He also found that the manual was just the right size to prop up the short leg of his desk.

They had come to a tenuous working agreement based on grudging mutual respect. Tina was amazed at the number of people in the community that Eduardo knew by name, and the easy manner in which he dealt with them. Eduardo was impressed with Tina's athletic prowess and her ability to keep a cool head—for a female. Most useful for each of them in dealing with the other—and with the tedium and frequent pathos or horror of their profession—was a shared slightly quirky sense of the absurd.

IT WAS AFTER midnight before Eduardo and Tina were able to follow up on the call from El Fenix restaurant.

"The restaurant is just a few blocks beyond where Mission runs into Huntington Drive," Eduardo said. He had reluctantly agreed that it was Tina's turn to drive their unmarked green Plymouth.

"Who would want to steal two fifty-pound cartons of chorizo sausage?"

"It's an acquired taste." Eduardo leaned forward and pointed a finger at the suspended traffic light in the center of the street. "Red light."

"I can see the stoplight, Eduardo." She already had her foot on the brake.

"Sorry." He grinned at her. "You've been through the academy more recently than I have. I couldn't remember whether the training covered streetlights or not."

"*Oh* yeah. We learned all about red, green, and orange," Tina said. "Of course my early training watching 'Sesame Street' was a help."

"Good, good." When the light changed, he pointed again. "Green."

Tina drove through the intersection.

"You got those colors down, all right."

Tina quickly changed lanes to avoid rear-ending a panel truck that had veered in front of them from a side street.

"El Fenix is on the corner of Huntington and Guardia Avenue."

"Another one of your hangouts, Eduardo?"

"I drop by occasionally. Just to keep my restaurant-rating system up to date." Eduardo had grown up in nearby East L.A. "On my five-star system the El Fenix gets two stars for their fajitas and another star for serving Tecate beer on tap."

"When you conduct this survey of yours, I'm sure you always pay your own tab." Tina Roberson looked at her partner accusingly.

"The owners of the restaurants on my list would be insulted if I insisted on paying. Armando Estrada, the owner of El Fenix, is a good example. One order of fajitas and a glass of beer costs him next to nothing, and it makes him happy to have a member of the police department on the premises."

"How much it costs him is not the point. If you accept a stick of Juicy Fruit from a citizen, it's a gratuity, and it gives the appearance of evil."

"Now that's where you're wrong. It's good public relations on Estrada's part. It's just his way of showing that he appreciates the protection of the LAPD."

"That's a bunch of bull, and you know it."

Eduardo laughed, and pointed to the left side of the intersection they were approaching. "That's Estrada's place there on the corner."

The restaurant was closed although a green neon sign that said El Fenix still hissed and blinked above a red and white striped awning. Armando Estrada peered through the iron grating of the diamond-shaped window in the front door,

but made no move to let them in until Eduardo stepped beneath the dim overhead light and held up his badge.

"Ah! Detective Lopez." He smiled, which caused the
edges of his mustache to turn upward. After a pause that
was filled with the clanking of the slip lock and the creak of
the dead bolt, he flung open the door and stepped aside for
Eduardo and Tina.

The two officers were ushered through the dining room,
which smelled of beer and refried beans, into the dimly lit
cantina where a sullen bartender stood wiping spilled drinks
and cigarette ashes from the bar with a damp sponge. Above
his head was a red banner proclaiming "Feliz Navidad."

Also behind the bar was a shapely young waitress in a
short red skirt and a white peasant blouse. She was obviously more interested in tall, black-eyed, black-haired Detective Lopez than in the margarita glass she kept drying
over and over.

Estrada began to rapidly describe what had taken place.

Eduardo rocked back on the heels of his cowboy boots as
he listened sympathetically to the restaurant owner's complaint. Tina sat at a small cocktail table and took notes.

"Tonight it was sausage," Estrada raised the palms of his
hands in helplessness and shook his head. "Next week it
could be worse. I'm expecting a big delivery of frozen tur-
keys. People expect turkey on the menu at Christmas—and
I have several banquets booked." He let his voice drop, and
spoke confidentially to Eduardo, then hurried over to ad-
monish a busboy for the job he was doing in clearing tables.

"Sorry." Tina looked up from the notepad at her partner. "What was that he just said?"

Eduardo grinned and leaned toward her, both hands
braced on the small cocktail table. "We're invited to come
by for a turkey dinner."

"The señorita over there would be glad to see *you*, at
least," Tina said, just above a whisper. "Is she one of your
many friends?"

"We've met." Eduardo's grin widened.

Armando Estrada returned to continue his complaint. He said that after signing a receipt for the delivery man who had set the boxes down on a counter just inside the kitchen, he had been called into the dining room for a few minutes. Unfortunately, he had gone without first closing the back door. When he returned, the boxes had disappeared. He hurried outside, but the only person he saw was someone running down the alley with a can of spray paint. *"Un adolescente."*

"... a teenager."

Oh yeah. That narrows it down, Tina thought. She made the same notes at different locations several times during each shift she was on duty. Almost every business building in El Sereno was marked with gang names or obscenities. If there was a description of the perpetrator at all, it was a teenager with a can of spray paint.

"I ran after him," Estrada said, "but he was too fast. When I looked at the wall next to the kitchen door, there was a face there."

"What do you mean, 'a face'?" Eduardo asked.

"He had drawn an outline—a profile—of a face."

"Did you get a good look at the kid?"

"No. I just caught a glimpse of him. And he was wearing a mask."

"Like a ski mask?"

"No, one of those half-masks that just covers the eyes. Like Zorro."

"At least that was different," Eduardo said. "Did you recognize the tagging?"

"Tagging" was the symbol or individual mark that each gang used to identify its area. As Eduardo described it, it was like dogs pissing on buildings to mark their territory.

"No. I think I interrupted him before he had a chance to sign it."

The phone was ringing in the kitchen. Estrada excused himself and went to answer. Eduardo wandered into the dining room and began a conversation with the busboy in Spanish.

Tina stayed where she was. She knew from experience that the local residents spoke more freely to her partner when she was not around.

From working with Eduardo, she was beginning to pick up enough street Spanish to ask the fundamental questions, although she did not always understand the answers.

Just as Eduardo moved freely and naturally in El Sereno, she had the advantage in the black communities. In her first undercover job, she had been selected simply because she looked young enough to pass as a teenager—and because she was black.

Her instructions were to enroll in a Watts high school in order to get information about the owners of a nearby crack house. However, her cover was blown when, after she had set up her first buy, the runner turned out to be her fourteen-year-old cousin.

Although she had not told the lieutenant, she was glad to be taken off that assignment. She hated the thought of snitching on teenagers and bringing them in on a first offense. To the department, any drug bust was a plus. And God knew it was an unending problem. But she could not help but believe that some of those kids could pull themselves out of the muck if given half a chance. Almost none of them did if they had a police record.

Another advantage of no longer having to pretend she was a teenager was that she could get out of those funky clothes and do something normal with her hair. As soon as she was transferred to Hollenbeck, she had made an appointment at a Pasadena salon to have her hair styled; cut as short as a man's in back, and long enough on the sides to be full around her face and cupped under at the ears.

"You're an Egyptian goddess," her enthusiastic hairdresser had announced, complimenting his own work.

"No, honey," she had stated flatly. "But I'm a pretty damn good lookin' black cop."

"Damn good lookin' black cop" had been one of the phrases used by the *Playboy* photographer she had met when she worked patrol in the Hollywood area. "Sexy" and "frisky"—she had thought "frisky" was an original touch—were other descriptive words he had used when he tried to convince her to pose for a photographic layout wearing only her L.A. police officer's hat and dangling a pair of handcuffs. She had laughed it off, and refused on the grounds that she was not allowed to wear any part of her uniform or carry department equipment while off duty.

"Jorge in there"—Eduardo nodded toward the busboy as he came back to the table where Tina sat—"said he never heard of the masked marvel before. He must be a lone hombre. At least, none of the local gangs wear masks."

Tina closed her notebook and stood. "Come on. Let's go take a look outside."

Eduardo led the way from the cantina to a back hallway that opened into the kitchen. As they passed the service island, the scantily clad waitress was waiting near the linen closet. She reached out and touched Eduardo's shoulder.

"*Buenas noches,* Eduardo."

He took her hand and kissed the palm. "See you soon, *querida.*"

As they stepped out into the alley, Tina asked, "Is there any girl in El Sereno that you haven't been out with, Eduardo?"

"Some of them are not of age yet."

As the door closed behind them, it was dark except for a single low-wattage bulb that shone dimly through the dirty kitchen window and the defused light of a street lamp half a block away. Tina stopped to reach into her shoulder bag for a flashlight. She heard the gritty sound of Eduardo's metal heel taps against the ancient dirt on the narrow brick alley as he walked ahead of her toward Huntington Drive. She had looked away for just a second—less than that. When she turned back, there was the scuffling sound of two sets of feet, and she saw a second silhouette, smaller than

Eduardo's, holding him by the arm. There was also the un-mistakable outline of a gun pressed against her partner's head.

"Empty your pockets," the man said in accented English.

Instead of the flashlight, Tina pulled her clip-loaded Beretta from the bag. Instinctively, she shouted the words she had never used since she graduated from the academy. "Police! Drop your gun!"

The thief had not seen her before. His head spun in her direction.

Tina realized he still had the advantage. She was facing the dim light from the street. All she could see of him was his outline.

After a moment of surprise, he laughed. "Hey! Look at the bitch with the gun!"

"I'm a police officer." She took a step forward. "Drop it! Don't get yourself in more trouble."

There was anger in the man's voice now. "*You* drop it, or I'll blow his head off!"

"For God's sake, Tina." Eduardo shouted. He was try-ing to sound calm—authoritative—but she heard the qua-ver in his voice. "Do what he says."

Behind the two figures she could see the brief flash of headlights, then red taillights as a car sped north on Huntington. A moment later she heard the siren of one of the black-and-whites from Hollenbeck chasing the speeder. There was no time to get out her radio. No way to flag them down. She held her gun steady and took another step for-ward.

"Do you want to see his brains splattered all over this fuckin' alley?" There was uncertainty in the man's voice, but he pressed the gun harder against Eduardo's head.

"Tina! Do what he says!"

She shut out the sound of Eduardo's voice. "Listen, creep! If you shoot him, I shoot you. There's no way you can get us both." One more slow step.

"I'll kill him! I swear to Jesus."

"If you do, *you* die tonight."

Suddenly there was the sound of a second siren going north on Huntington.

The police car did not slow, but continued pursuing a speeder. Still, just its presence could have been the reason the man released his grip on Eduardo and ran to jump into a waiting automobile that sat idling at the curb of the darkened street.

The gunman undoubtedly told himself that was why he ran. Never, he would never admit to himself or to the driver of the car that a black female with a gun had faced him down.

Tina unclipped her Rover radio from her skirt belt and was calling in the description of the attacker and the direction the car was headed as she ran toward Eduardo. She did not make it to the entrance of the alley soon enough to see the license plate. It was too dark, at any rate.

"Good God, Tina." Eduardo was slumped against the wall of the alley.

"Are you all right?"

"Jesus God."

"I'm sorry, Eduardo."

"No. You were right."

"It's just— He could have killed us both if I'd dropped my gun." Her throat was raw and she felt she was gasping for air between every word.

"I know." Eduardo straightened and put his hand on her shoulder.

"I couldn't have been much help to you if I was dead."

"Yeah. I know, I know."

Her body was quivering all over. What if she had gotten the shakes when she was holding the gun?

Eduardo put both arms around her to hold her steady. "You were right. You did the right thing."

She sobbed, deeply, once, into his shirt front. "At the academy they kept pounding into us, Never drop your gun! Never give it up!"

"I guess it's a good thing one of us goes by the book, huh?" Eduardo tried to laugh. He was the strong one now, the protector. He smoothed her hair comfortingly, then gently pushed her away and reached in his pocket for a handkerchief. "Good God, woman, you're getting my shirt all wet."

FIVE

In London, without the Thanksgiving holiday to get through first, the Christmas decorations had been fully in place since the middle of November.

As her final project of the year for the Victoria and Albert Museum, Andrea Perkins had restored and overseen the display of hundreds of Victorian Christmas cards and tree decorations. Naturally enough, the V and A made a big thing of the fact that Prince Albert introduced the Christmas tree—a tradition of his native Germany—to England and the rest of the English-speaking world. Candlelit fir trees decorated to Victorian excess were on display in every area of the museum. Because of the fire laws, the candles were artificial, but the garlands and ornaments were all authentic nineteenth century. The cards, mounted behind protective glass, were typically lace-trimmed depictions of apple-cheeked children, adorable kittens surrounded by gift-wrapped packages, and snow scenes of sleigh rides or scarf-draped carolers bunched together under street lamps.

The one card that rated a solo display case with overhead pin-lights was the least extravagant and, in Andrea's view, the most charming of them all. It was a pencil sketch of two ice skaters hand in hand. The woman was short and a bit chubby with large, adoring eyes that smiled up into the stern face of her slim, handsome partner. The drawing with the handwritten greeting "Merry Christmas to your family from ours" was signed by the artist: Victoria Regina.

Since Andrea's restoration and identification a year before of the drawing of the Balmoral Nude, she was more conscious than ever of the innumerable paintings, drawings, and photographs of Queen Victoria at the V and A.

Some of them seemed to look back at Andrea with a scathing reprimand; others, she could have sworn, were on the verge of a conspiratorial grin.

With one final inspection of the Christmas exhibit, Andrea headed through the V and A's labyrinthine hallways to her own small office. Henry March, her scruffy young assistant, had finally been entrusted by the museum with his own assignment, which had taken him to Scotland. Andrea missed him. Still, in less than a week, she, too, would be gone.

The phone was ringing when she entered her office and threaded her way through the clutter of picture frames, paintings and small sculptures to her equally disorganized desk. She reached the phone on the third ring. "Andrea Perkins here."

"My goodness, you sound British," a tinkling female voice said.

"I do?" Andrea was taken by surprise. In England, she was teased about her American drawl. Though how someone born and brought up in Boston could have a drawl, she could not imagine.

"At least to someone from California you sound British. This is Georgene Dodson. I wrote to you about staying in our guest house in San Marino while you're working at the Huntington Art Gallery."

"Of course, Mrs. Dodson!"

"Georgene. Please."

"Georgene." Andrea lifted the Edwardian clock she used as a paperweight to hold down a stack of correspondence as she searched for the letter from Georgene Dodson that had arrived a few days earlier. Glancing at the clock—it was just past eleven A.M.—she said, "Good heavens. What time is it there? It must be the middle of the night in California."

"I suppose so. But I'm here in London." Georgene Dodson laughed. "It was a spur-of-the-moment thing. My husband is here on business, and I decided to come over and surprise him. It was a good excuse to work in an excursion of my own to Harrods and Sotheby's to do some Christmas shopping. From him—to me.''

"Well, then, welcome to England.''

"It's rather like coming home. I lived here, briefly, a few years ago. My husband's company has a British branch. And although he's technically retired now and has excellent people in charge of his import business, he still feels he has to make an appearance over here from time to time to make sure everything is running properly.'' Georgene Dodson paused with an indulgent sigh at her husband's inability to let go of the reins. "At any rate, I'm looking forward to meeting you, and I called to say that if I were going to be in San Marino when you arrived, I'd probably meet you at the door with a glass of our California Sonoma Valley wine. But here I am in England. So, how about tea instead this afternoon at my hotel?''

"Well, yes. I'd love to, Georgene.''

Georgene Dodson's hotel was the Savoy. It was too far to walk. Andrea made that decision the moment she left the cheerful artificial snow scene at the V and A reception desk and was confronted on the doorstep with the very real freezing rain and slushy sidewalks. Pulling the turtleneck of her sweater up beneath her ears and tucking the loose strands of her red hair inside the hood of her well-used raincoat, she hurried toward Kensington Gore, across from the Albert Memorial, and hailed a cab. As she huddled in the backseat of the taxi, the thought of California sunshine—and more important, the possibility of being with Aldo Balzani again—generated an inner warmth that stopped her shivering.

Since Andrea first met the transplanted American, Aldo Balzani, in Florence, the time they were able to spend together was limited by his responsibilities as chief of detectives of the Italian city, and her assignments—wherever they happened to take her—in the world of art. Now, barring last-minute changes in either of their schedules, they were going to be in the same city at the same time.

Leaving the cab and entering the Savoy Hotel's chilly lobby, the first thing that caught Andrea's eye was the latest official photograph of Queen Elizabeth II. Encouraged by the royal stiff-upper-lip expression, Andrea grudgingly left her warm coat with the cloakroom attendant.

The Savoy Grill was quite comfortable in contrast with the entrance to the hotel, where each new arrival or departure was accompanied by a blast of cold air. The small alcove to which she was ushered after giving the name of her hostess to the maître d' was warm and cozy. Andrea appreciated the fact even more when she glanced out the window at the frozen slope of the Victoria Embankment Gardens and noticed that the icy rain had turned to snow.

"Snow! Don't you just love it?" Georgene Dodson smiled at her like a child with a new sled that she could hardly wait to try out.

Andrea thought for a moment she had been shown to the wrong table. The vague mental picture she had formed of the wife of Mr. Dodson, the retired businessman, included gray hair and a lumpy figure. Instead, the woman who rose to greet her was a beautiful young woman—possibly a year or two younger than Andrea herself.

"You forget how beautiful snow can be when you don't see it for a while." Surprisingly, Georgene extended her left hand, rather than her right to grasp Andrea's fingers briefly with a little fluttery motion.

"One or two days a year like this are fine." Andrea gratefully accepted a steaming cup of tea from the white-gloved waiter. "But I'm looking forward to your famous sunshine."

Georgene Dodson was a sleek blonde with a hint of winter suntan. She was a stunning example of the tall, athletic, fair-haired beauties pictured in ads for beachwear. She was not of the glossy blue-eyed variety, however. The contrast of her dark eyes—so dark they seemed to have no iris—and the pale shade of her straight, shoulder-length hair made her beauty truly unique. The combination seemed a genetic impossibility. But what heredity had been unable to provide, Andrea decided, an accomplished hairdresser had.

"You'll love San Marino," Georgene told Andrea as the waiter placed a silver basket of scones on the table. "It's one of the three or four safest cities in California. Nothing like Los Angeles, even though it's only a few miles away."

Andrea found it strange that safety was the number-one attribute Georgene had come up with to recommend her hometown. The official of the Huntington who had offered Andrea the contract to examine and restore the famous *Blue Boy* painting before accompanying the masterpiece back to England for a Gainsborough exhibition had written in praise of the Southern California weather and the quiet of the estate area where she would be staying. He had also described the spacious work room provided for her. But there had been no mention made of the local concern for personal safety in San Marino.

"Not that you'd have anything to worry about. The house has an electronic burglar alarm, plus we employ a private security company to patrol the grounds."

"Georgene, it's very kind of you to offer your hospitality, but a hotel would be—"

"It's my pleasure!" Her dark eyes gleamed like onyx marbles. "Every one of the board members of the Friends of the Huntington wanted you as a houseguest, but I spoke up first."

"Still—"

"Actually, there has been a change. My sister from Kentucky has decided to move back to California with her ten-year-old son and they'll be staying in the guest house until they decide where they want to land permanently. You and your friend—he'll be joining you from Italy, didn't you say?"

"Possibly. We hope so. If he can get away."

"The two of you will be in the main house."

"Really, Georgene. I hope you didn't vacate your house on our account. I appreciate your offer, but a hotel would be fine."

"No, no. As I told you, with my husband already here in England, it was a perfect excuse for a giant shopping spree. And as to your staying in a hotel, there *aren't* any in San Marino. The nearest decent ones are in Arcadia, and they're booked a year in advance for the winter season at Santa Anita Race Track."

"But your sister and her son—surely they should have the house."

"Sarah *asked* to be in the guest house. She thought it would be nicer for Benjamin—the pool is right outside, and there's a giant TV screen with video games in the recreation room next door." Georgene stirred her tea with quick little motions, then lightly tapped the tiny spoon twice on the rim of the china cup before returning it to the saucer. "You needn't worry about Benjamin being a problem. For a ten-year-old boy, he's the quietest child you can imagine. Sarah says that sometimes he goes two or three days without saying hardly a word. Frankly, I don't know how she copes." The tinkling laugh again. "There's no question that she's better equipped to be a mother than I am."

As Georgene continued to nullify any further reasons why Andrea and Aldo should not look upon the Dodson home as their own, Andrea found herself only half listening. She became fascinated with the California beauty's hands. As she talked, Georgene held them clasped beneath her chin, the left cupped over the right. They were smooth and had the same well-cared-for sheen as creamy porcelain. The nails were perfectly manicured in the French style—the half moons and rounded tips were white with silvery polish between. When she reached for a scone, her nails glinted with the same tiny metallic flashes of light as the tea knife she used to spread cream and jam. With both hands exposed, Andrea could see that the last two fingers of her right hand seemed to be the same length. It was as though her little finger was missing. Andrea mentally counted them and came up with the proper number, but there was something out of kilter—there was a prominent scar opposite the last knuckle. She was not quite perfect after all, Andrea thought.

"And your friend who is meeting you in California—"

Andrea forced her attention back again to what Georgene was saying.

"—how romantic that he's coming all the way from Italy to be with you."

Andrea had no intention of discussing Aldo Balzani with this woman whom she barely knew. But in explanation, she added, "If he can get away. There are some meetings in Los Angeles that he hopes to attend." That was true, but Andrea had very little knowledge of what they were—something to do with international law enforcement, she thought. If he had told her, she had forgotten. The one important thing she remembered from their last telephone conversation was that he would be arriving in Los Angeles shortly before she did. That was, if he was able to be there at all.

To Georgene's credit, she did not press for more information. Instead, she said, "We old married ladies sometimes long for a little romance." This was prefaced with something that sounded more like a teenaged giggle than a laugh.

Andrea felt no need to protest Georgene's reference to herself as old, because she obviously was not. Further, lacking romance, having a husband who would finance a European shopping trip that included Harrods and Sotheby's Auction House would not seem a hardship to most women. But Andrea was saved from having to come up with an inane comment by her hostess's skill in hurrying on to another topic.

"Here are the spare keys to the house." Georgene tossed a key ring on the table. "I'll make a list of what each of these is for." The silver and white fingertips unfastened the clasp of a black leather handbag, took out a small notepad and a pen, and began to write.

Watching the strangely beautiful hands again, Andrea suddenly knew who it was this woman reminded her of: Anne Boleyn. Georgene Dodson was a twentieth-century version of Hans Holbein's portrait of Henry VIII's second wife. The black eyes, the hair—in its natural state—probably the same color as her eyes, and the fair skin. But it was the hands, or rather the one hand with its last two fingers the same length, that suggested the comparison. She wondered if Georgene, like Anne Boleyn, had been born with a sixth finger. If poor, tragic Anne had known Georgene Dodson's hairdresser and orthopedic surgeon, she might have looked very much like this woman from San Marino, California.

"I'll send you more detailed information." Georgene snapped shut the notepad and dropped it with the pen back in her handbag. "But anything you want to know—like the best dry cleaners, hairdressers, pharmacy—that sort of thing, you can ask my sister. We both grew up there." She stirred two circles with the tiny spoon again, then laid it on the saucer. "The town hasn't changed much since then."

There was an edge of bitterness in the last remark that Andrea thought seemed out of character for the self-confident Mrs. Dodson.

"And, Holly! I forgot about Holly."

Georgene's ebullience was back, but Andrea had no idea what she was talking about. Vaguely, she found herself glancing at the Christmas decorations in the Savoy Grill.

"Holly is Sarah's cook. If she'd just keep her nose in the kitchen, she'd be a marvel, but she tends to want to mother the world." Georgene hurried on, "She'll want to cook for you. She'll probably insist, and she's truly miraculous with pots and pans and spoons and spatulas and that sort of thing— But then, that's up to you."

"This is all very kind of you," Andrea said, "but I can't help feeling I'm disrupting your household."

"Nothing of the kind. We're delighted you're going to stay in our home."

Nevertheless, Andrea resolved to investigate the hotel situation for herself once she got to San Marino.

When the two women left the dining room, Georgene walked with Andrea across the hotel's lobby.

"There's one thing you're bound to hear about as soon as you check in with the people at the Huntington," Georgene said as they waited for the cloakroom attendant to locate Andrea's coat. "The body of a man who had been murdered was recently found on the grounds—in the statuary garden."

"What?"

"It was an isolated incident. It's not as though they find a dead body at the Huntington every day. He was a derelict, apparently, who just wandered onto the grounds by mistake."

"How awful."

"I felt I had to mention it, but I don't want you to think that San Marino is in the midst of a crime wave. It's really a lovely little city—strictly a residential and estate area. Nothing like murder—well, at least not the murder of an outsider—has ever happened there before. You'll be perfectly safe. But I did want you to know about our security system."

"Here you are, Miss." The uniformed cloakroom girl handed Andrea her raincoat, still wet from the freezing rain.

SIX

AN HOUR LATER, in the Pacific time zone, the early-morning sun was settling in to give Los Angeles another record-breaking day. The weather was the warmest it had been for the month of December in a decade. Daytime temperatures were in the high eighties. The nighttime lows meandered into the fifties, and were chilly but not cold. It was also the driest year in some time, with the average rainfall several inches below normal. Since late summer, jovial TV weathercasters had been optimistically pointing out on their high-tech weather maps a succession of storms as they formed in the Pacific and swirled toward shore in the northern part of the state. In the San Francisco area, they unleashed their rain with abandon. But always, by the next day, the clouds had started to dissipate when they got as far south as Bakersfield, and by the time they reached Los Angeles, they were merely thin trails of white vapor, if they had survived at all.

The mayor urged L.A. residents to conserve water and predicted compulsory water rationing. But the officials delayed carrying through on the threat because of the enormous problems of policing such an action. And so, the sprinkler system that kept the wide lawn in front of City Hall lush and green all year round continued to turn on automatically each morning at 5:30 and shut off at 6:15. Across the street in the city mall, the palm trees and tropical shrubs were equally well tended.

The only area in the city complex that suggested an effort toward water conservation was the starburst fountain in the center of the mall. It was no longer in daily operation. Most of the people who had reason to pass by the fountain thought of its inactivity as a regrettable but necessary measure toward water economy. Instead, it was the result of a call to the public works department from an irate city councilman.

The councilman happened to cross through the mall on the way to his office earlier than usual one morning and was shocked at what he saw. "One of those goddamn street people that congregate around the fountain was doing his laundry and hanging it on the back of a public bench to dry. And as if that wasn't bad enough, another one was standing in the middle of the fountain buck naked taking a goddamn shower! Even if we can't get rid of the goddamn creeps, we can sure as hell get rid of the fountain. Shut the goddamn thing off!"

A further call resulted in having the signs that were already posted replaced with new ones that said the same thing, only in larger letters: THE MALL AREA IS CLOSED TO THE PUBLIC BETWEEN 7:00 P.M. AND 6:00 A.M. EVERY DAY OF THE WEEK. TRESPASSERS WILL BE PROSECUTED UNDER PENAL CODE SECTION 602k.

The warning was of no consequence to Rainbow, a winter resident of the mall who spent his days sleeping on one of the benches. During the summer, he slept on the cool grass in the shade of a liquid amber tree on the City Hall lawn. But he made it a rule never to bed down in either place until the buildings were open and the city employees started showing up for their jobs. It was not safe to be asleep before daylight. If you were smart, you kept moving until the sun came up and the police came out to protect the working people.

Anyone who would try to sack out at night just had not been on the street long. The newcomers were the ones who got their shoes or their wine stolen. They were the ones who ended up with broken heads or a knife between their ribs.

Rainbow's name had nothing to do with color. His pants and—depending upon the season—the number of layers of shirts, sweaters, and jackets he wore all seemed to be the same shade; just lighter than black. Goochie, his friend on

the street, had hung the name on him. He said Rainbow's
eyes reminded him of the rainbow trout he used to catch
when he was a boy. "I'll bet you could see great underwa-
ter. Your eyes don't ever seem to close—they don't look like
they even have any lids."

You had to be careful, that was all. You had to watch
what was going on.

Rainbow's daily routine was to be in line for breakfast
when the bell rang at the Union Rescue Mission. Afterward, he checked all the trash containers between there and
the mall for aluminum cans. When his plastic Sav-On
Drugstore bag was full, he took the cans to the cash-back
machine and crushed them. It usually took a couple of trips
before he had enough money for the next bottle of Cuca-
monga wine. When the money was safely inside his shoe, he
headed for his bench in the mall.

Slatted wooden benches were set in concrete every few feet
along the sidewalk. Rainbow always tried to get the bench
nearest the tall clock opposite the fountain. Not that he had
any special interest in time. It was just that the early-
morning sun hit that corner first and dried the disinfectant
that was sprayed on the benches, the concrete steps, and the
stone patio every morning before the mall was open. When
Rainbow kept track of time at all, it was by the length of his
hair. It took about three weeks between cuttings for the hair
at the nape of his neck to get inside his collar and become
bothersome. He and Goochie knew that three weeks must
have passed when Rainbow asked to borrow Goochie's nail
clippers.

It was about that time now. Rainbow's neck was beginning to itch. As he wrapped his tattered blanket around him
before he lay down, he looked around for his friend who
usually took the bench next to his. The bench was empty
again. Rainbow began to wonder how long it had been since
he had seen his buddy. A day or two—maybe a week—since
that TV guy gave Goochie ten bucks.

One morning just before it was light, while Rainbow and Goochie were still cruising the streets, some big trucks pulled up and a bunch of guys jumped out and started unpacking lights and stringing camera cable across the lawn in front of City Hall. TV and movies were always filming scenes around the city center. There wasn't anything new about that. But that morning one of the guys in jeans and a T-shirt with a movie logo gave Goochie ten dollars. And it was all because of his shoes—and the fight.

The way it happened, Rainbow was getting ready to count up the aluminum cans he had collected from the trash barrels and head for the can-crushing machine. As he started in that direction, Goochie folded his copy of that day's edition of the *L.A. Times* under his arm and sat down on a bench next to the TV remote truck. (Every morning on their way back to the mall, Goochie stopped by the Times building and picked up a discarded copy in the alley. He said the world could go to hell in a hand-basket for all he cared, but he liked to read Jim Murray's column on the sports page and check out the handicapper's predictions when the horses were running at Santa Anita.)

"Let's sit here a minute and see what these TV guys are doing," Goochie said.

It was okay for Goochie to goof off if he wanted to. He had his newspaper to look at, and he still had a good three inches left in his wine bottle. Whereas Rainbow was already down to his last two swallows. Beside that, he was sleepy, and anxious to stake out his regular bench. But he was feeling mellow, and joined his friend.

There wasn't much to see. As usual, the guys from the truck would spend an hour or so screwing the cables into the cameras and setting up the lights. Then it would take thirty seconds to shoot a scene for some TV lawyer show of a guy in a suit with slicked-back hair or a blonde in a short skirt carrying a briefcase walking up the steps of City Hall. Rainbow's attention wandered. He glanced off toward First

Street and watched two of the downtown regulars approaching. "Here comes Smokey and Tiddles," he said.

Goochie grinned. "Maybe they want to get on TV."

Smokey was big and black and scary. Tiddles was a scrawny little guy who wore his blond hair in a ponytail. The two of them were always together, and nearly always holding hands.

The twosome stepped up on the sidewalk and headed next to the City Hall steps where they usually crashed during the day. As they crossed the lawn, Tiddles tripped on one of the cables and almost fell face down.

"You pushed me!" Tiddles, who was well known for becoming belligerent by this time in the morning, accused his companion in a whiny voice.

"No, I never." Smokey reached out with one of his beefy hands and tried to hug the smaller man, but Tiddles squirmed out of reach.

"Did you push me?"

"Naw, Tiddles."

"You did! You pushed me!" He was drunk and aggressive.

"Aw, Tiddles, you know I never."

Tiddles swung his fist upward at Smokey's chin. Smokey, leaning down to catch Tiddles's wrist and stop the blow, instead caught the force of the small fist on the side of his nose. When he straightened, blood was streaming down his face.

"Stop it now, Tiddles. You've given me another nosebleed," the big black man whined.

"Ain't nobody, not even you, that's going to push me!"

"I never pushed you. Ain't never pushed you in my life."

It wasn't really a fight. Tiddles kept swinging and Smokey kept dodging out of his way. They were thrashing around, tripping on the cables, and suddenly Smokey backed into a camera and knocked it on its side.

When that happened, a wild-eyed young man wearing white coveralls and a headset came rushing out of the back of the TV remote truck and stood on the tailgate. He yelled at the cameraman—a husky young man even larger than Smokey—who had stepped well out of the way of the confusion. "For God's sake, stop those two," the man in white coveralls said.

The cameraman, keeping a wide distance between himself and Smokey and Tiddles, came next to the truck and spoke in a loud whisper. "Are you crazy? The big guy's bleeding."

"If you have to, get someone to help you, but stop those idiots. Do you know how much that camera cost?"

"Listen, jackass, I've got a scratch on my hand. I'm not touching either one of them. *You* stop them, if you want it stopped."

The man in coveralls paused a beat, taking in the significance of what the cameraman had said, then yelled at no one in particular, "Call the police!"

The duo was now dancing and dodging between the TV remote truck and the bench where Rainbow and Goochie sat watching.

As Tiddles jumped in the air, flailing his arms in an approximation of throwing punches, Goochie stuck out his leg and tripped the small man. Tiddles did fall this time, face down in the grass.

The excitement was over. Tiddles sat up, crying. Smokey, his face and shirt smeared with blood, scooped up the cocky combatant and half-carried him to their spot near the City Hall steps.

"Hey, thanks," the man in coveralls said to Goochie.

Goochie shrugged.

Rainbow knew that Goochie had not tripped Tiddles just to help out the TV crew. If Tiddles had come straight down after that last jump in the air, he would have landed on Goochie's feet. And Rainbow's pal was particular about his shoes.

But the man on the remote truck didn't know that. He reached in his pocket and took out some money, then jumped down from the edge of the tailgate and offered a paper bill to Goochie.

Goochie took it. He would not have asked for anything, because Goochie *never* asked for handouts. The guy just gave it to him.

As a precaution though, the guy in the white coveralls had rolled the money lengthwise into a cylinder and held it by one edge before offering it to Goochie. No doubt this was a protective measure so that their hands need not touch.

Ten bucks.

"I'm going to turn this ten into a thousand," Goochie had said later when Rainbow got back from the can-crushing machine. He did not say how he was going to do that, but it must have had something to do with horse racing, 'cause he had been studying that page of the newspaper.

Rainbow didn't remember much about what happened next. He was stretched out on his bench and half asleep when Goochie shook him by the shoulder and promised he would come back and buy his friend a steak dinner and a bottle of first-class red wine when he had made his thousand.

That was the last time Rainbow had seen Goochie.

Rainbow scratched his neck where the hair was curling down beneath his collar. He missed his friend and wished he was there with his nail clippers.

The benches around the fountain were beginning to fill. Most of the people were regulars. There was one new woman with a scroungy poodle in a Von's Supermarket shopping cart. Rainbow was glad to see that she picked a bench on the other side of the mall. He didn't want to have to listen to a yapping dog.

Where could Goochie have gotten to? he wondered. Rainbow tried to think about that day, the last time he had seen him.

Goochie had said something about the Oak Tree Meet at Santa Anita. Then he started laughing. Now that was different, right there. Rainbow had never heard his friend laugh before.

"This is my lucky day, Rainbow, old fish," he'd said. And that was when he said he was going to turn the ten bucks into a thousand.

No, that came earlier.

Goochie had looked at the daily lineup on the racing page—as he always did. Then he turned the page. That's right, he turned the page and didn't say anything for a while. Then *that's* when he laughed. He had the racing lineup in his hand, then he made a little mark on it with a pencil stub he always carried in his pocket. He folded the paper up, real neat like, and put it in his pocket.

"Nope, forget about the thousand dollars," Goochie had said. "This ought to be good for much *more* than that."

Rainbow now felt sure that Goochie had gone to Santa Anita Race Track. Maybe he *did* get lucky. Rainbow hoped he had. But the one scrap of faith in human nature he had left was stuck to his friend Goochie. If Goochie said he would be back to buy dinner, he would have been back—and before now.

Rainbow stretched out as far as he could on the bench, keeping his feet flat against the metal armrest so no one could mess with his shoes without his knowing. He pulled the bill of his greasy Dodger cap down low on his forehead. Before he closed his eyes—he really could close them, no matter what Goochie said—he decided that if his pal was not back when he woke up, he would go across Los Angeles Street to the police headquarters at Parker Center and talk to Tina Roberson.

Something must have happened to Goochie. Detective Roberson ought to know about it.

SEVEN

THE SERGEANT at the front desk eyed Rainbow coldly when he came through the double glass doors of Parker Center.

"I want to speak to Officer Roberson." Rainbow smoothed his hair back from his forehead as though the single gesture would take care of any deficiencies in his appearance.

"Who?"

"Officer Roberson. She does nighttime patrol across the street."

"We don't have anyone by that name assigned to the mall."

"Roberson. She's a girl. Tina's her first name." Rainbow knew he remembered it right. She had kept a gang that hung out around the Dorothy Chandler Pavilion from mugging Rainbow and Goochie one night. She had scared them all off—five or six guys—by just yelling at them. And he was sure about her name: Tina—because she looked like a teenager—and Roberson—because she'd scared off the robbers. That's how he had remembered. She told him and Goochie that if they had any trouble to ask for her. "Tina Roberson," Rainbow repeated to the desk sergeant.

"Oh, yeah. She's been transferred to Hollenbeck division."

This was something unexpected. It had not occurred to Rainbow that she wouldn't be there, and he couldn't think what to do next.

"Anything else?" The sergeant was making it plain that he had other important things to do.

"Tell her Rainbow wants to talk to her."

DETECTIVE ROBERSON was off duty the day Rainbow came by to see her. It was sometime later before the scribbled message from the Parker Center desk sergeant would catch up with her. She was spending her time off studying for semester finals at the University of California in Los Angeles.

Tina had entered the university on an athletic scholarship in track. She had started running competitively in junior high school under the tutelage of her father, who was a Pasadena high school athletic director. His aim had always been to groom her for the Olympics. But that was his aim, not hers. She had been determined to become a police officer since grade school when a ten-year-old classmate who lived in the next block was shot and killed in a drive-by shooting.

To please her father, she had done well enough as a long-distance runner to fill a shelf with trophies and win a UCLA scholarship. But when, in her second year at the university, her father suffered a fatal heart attack, she decided to let his dream for her die with him. She changed her major from education (she had enrolled with the vague idea of becoming a high school teacher/coach) to criminal justice. And when she reached the minimum age of twenty-one, she filled out an application to join the LAPD. Since then, she had taken courses whenever she could work them in. A college degree was not a requirement of the police department, but it could move a personnel file from the big stack to the little stack.

Tina knew she was good at her job and deserved recognition for performance of duty alone. For that reason, she no longer resented the fact that her file was coded female/black. If being a member of two minorities would help speed her promotion, so be it. Tina wanted all the help she could get. Her long-range plan was to take the lieutenant's exam, but her immediate goal was to move up from detective trainee to detective I.

Tina was hired a few years after the Los Angeles Superior Court had approved a consent decree that required the department to increase the number of women employees until 20 percent of its sworn work force was female. The same decree required an increase in the percentages of blacks and Latinos.

When she joined the department, she more than met the minimum qualifications: she was twenty-one, she was more than five feet tall, and though all that was required was a passing grade in the high school equivalency test, she had already completed two years of college.

The recruiter who had met her at the door of his office at Parker Center had short-cropped, brown hair and a pattern of tiny broken veins across his nose and cheeks. He took a firm grip on her upper arm, pressing the backs of his fingers against the side of her breast, and led her to a chair across from his desk. She would be a shoo-in, he had told her, grinning, as she filled in the small white blanks on the single sheet of the application. He would guess—he winked at her—that she would do fine on the psychological testing. As to the physical, there sure as hell didn't seem to be anything wrong with her physical condition. His pursed lips and raised eyebrow made it clear that he would like to conduct that particular examination himself. Plus, he added, she was lucky enough to qualify in *two* minority categories.

He called her sweetheart when she had finished the application and stood to leave. "Don't worry about the written and oral examinations, sweetheart," he had whispered, standing so close beside her that his hot breath fluttered the collar of her dress. "Adjustments—if you know what I mean—are made in the scoring so that the department can fill its minority requirements."

When she left the office, she could feel him watching her as she walked down the hall. She was so intent on keeping her hips from swaying that she almost stumbled before she reached the lobby that opened onto Los Angeles Street. As the doors closed behind her, she heard the uniformed man say, "Don't hesitate to call me if I can ever be of help."

She hated herself for wanting to be a police officer so badly that she had let the creep get by with his slimy tactics. It was some consolation a few months later when Tina learned that her recruiter had been charged with sexual harassment by a tall blond female whose father was a captain in the department. As a result, specific nondiscriminatory guidelines that all recruiting officers were required to follow were reinforced. Still, Tina wished the jerk who had interviewed her could see the results of her tests. She had scored several percentage points higher—in both the written and oral exams—than most of her male Caucasian classmates at the police academy, and she could run faster than any of them.

The memory of those pudgy fingers against the side of her breast and the hot breath on her neck were among the reasons she had worked so hard to be accepted as a detective trainee and to get her college degree.

For the past six months, Tina had been assigned to the Hollenbeck Division.

The day Rainbow came looking for her she was at the UCLA library. The captain had given her a week off after the ordeal with the gunman in the alley—of course she had the time coming, anyway. But Eduardo's report had made her sound like a hero, and prompted the captain to recommend her for a commendation. She was touched by her partner's praise on paper, though neither of them would ever mention the incident to the other one again. It had happened. It was over. Eduardo had reacted the same way she probably would have if someone had a gun to her head. Who could say what they would do until it happened?

Tina had gladly accepted the time off. She needed it to study for semester finals. She should have told the captain she was going on vacation to Hawaii or Mexico. He might not have been so quick to pull her back on duty if he had thought she was out of town. But just staying at home and sleeping late was the only vacation she had in mind. Even that was not easy in the house where she lived in North Pasadena.

She was the head of a household that consisted of her mother and her sister's two kids, who had been dropped off five years earlier and never collected. Noise was as much of a staple at Tina's house as peanut butter.

"Sorry, Tina," the captain had said when he telephoned personally to apologize for bringing her in three days early. "At least we spared you the briefing meeting. Lopez can fill you in when you get there."

Tina did not usually question an assignment, but the Huntington was not even in L.A. "Why can't San Marino handle its own homicides?"

"They asked for our help, and you and Lopez were the logical choice."

"Why? Did they specify a gorgeous female of the darker hue and a guy who thinks he's the Latin Warren Beatty?"

"They think the victim and/or the perpetrator may have wandered in from Hollenbeck. In which case, this would be your assignment anyway." The conciliatory tone was gone from the captain's voice. "Nine A.M. tomorrow at the Huntington. Lopez will meet you in the loggia at the front of the art gallery."

"The *LOW-gee-a* of the art gallery," Tina said as she put down the receiver. "Hell, yes. Lopez and I will feel right at home in the *LOW-gee-a*."

The next morning, with no unauthorized persons yet allowed inside the Huntington's high wrought-iron gates, the only sounds were the hum of the lawnmowers, the splash of the fountains, and the songs of the birds. The sun shining through the leaves of the oak trees scattered bright spots like gold coins on the sidewalk in front of the art gallery. A light breeze carried the mingled fragrance of more than a thousand species of roses. Except for the roses, Tina was not impressed.

Nor did she give more than a second glance to the art gallery that looked like an English country estate that had been dropped down in California. Undoubtedly, many of the visitors who toured the Huntington indulged in the daydream of what it would be like to own this mansion, which was built by Henry Huntington, the wealthy railroad tycoon. Tina did not. She dealt with reality. If such a flight of fantasy had occurred to her, it would have been followed by the thought of her mother complaining about going up and down all those stairs with her arthritis. And if it came to a choice between a Gainsborough painting and a big-screen TV, Tina would take the big-screen TV any day. At least that would help keep her sister's kids quiet.

But the roses were different. She liked the roses. She even decided to stop by the Armstrong nursery and pick up a bare-root bush on her way home. December was as good a time as any to plant the bare-root ones, and there was a spot between the garage and the alley that could use a little color.

"Tina!" Eduardo Lopez stood leaning against a French sculpture of Diana, the Huntress. Eduardo was in as good physical condition now as he had been eight years earlier when he spent a season sitting on the bench for the San Diego Chargers. He had been fast enough but not big enough to compete with the breed of monsters coming out of college football. When he joined the LAPD, he was surprised to find that he liked police work even better than football. For the most part, it was not as dangerous. But more than that, he was proud of his profession. He liked to think he truly did "protect and serve," as the department motto stated.

"Hey, Lopez." Tina hung her sunglasses on the leather gun belt she wore under the loose-fitting jacket of her lavender wool-blend suit. "Get away from that naked girl," she said sternly, pointing a figure at the placid goddess as she joined Eduardo in the loggia.

Eduardo made a kissing sound toward the nude statue and patted her bronze behind, then sat on an ornate wrought-iron bench, leaving room for his partner.

"So, fill me in. What are we doing here?"

"Waiting," Eduardo answered.

"Who are we waiting for?"

"The guard who discovered the body."

Tina raised her eyebrows in boredom, prepared to wait until her partner was ready to give her a full answer.

Tina and Eduardo read each other well. The male/female ground rules had been set their first week out. Tina was as realistic about sex as she was about everything else in her life. There had never been much time for dating when she was in school fulltime. Her father had seen to it that she kept to a strict regimen as a competitive runner, and when she was not training, she was studying. When she entered the police academy, she had, for a while, a heart-paralyzing crush on her Criminal Law instructor, but he was married, and although he was willing to overlook that technicality, she was not. Now, at twenty-three, she was somewhat surprised to find herself still a virgin.

It was her most closely guarded secret—like being a closet drinker. In the first place, people would not believe her if she told them—but it would be worse if they did. She could imagine the teasing she would have to endure, especially among her fellow cops, if anyone knew. This was particularly true because her partner was Eduardo Lopez and accepted by all as the Hollenbeck Division Romeo. If Eduardo knew, he would make her life unbearable with advice, suggestions, and lewd jokes. As it was, he had gotten the vague idea that she was involved with "some jock"—another competitive runner. When he tried to weasel information about her love life, Tina simply refused to discuss it.

Eduardo considered himself a romantic, which, he said, accounted for the fact that he kept getting married. He was currently in the middle of his third divorce. Since puberty, he had known that women found him attractive. Somehow, he felt it was his duty to make a pass at every female who came close enough. When he casually dropped a hand on Tina's knee one morning as she was driving their unmarked car, she said, "If you don't move your hand, you'll never have to get another manicure, 'cause you won't have any fingers left."

They both laughed and were both secretly relieved that sex was never going to be an issue between them.

"Actually," Lopez said now, shooing away a bee that had diverted its attention from a camellia bush to the two police detectives, "the department sent us here because they thought you could use a little culture, and they knew I'd be willing to show you around."

"*Oh* yeah. Well, you're certainly the right man for the job."

"Just promise me one thing, Tina."

"Anything at all, Eduardo, darling."

"Please don't embarrass me by telling the guard that there's a guy at your neighborhood Mobil station selling pictures out of the back of his van just like the ones they have in there."

"I appreciate what you're trying to do for me"—Tina pinched Eduardo's cheek—"but I'm afraid it's going to be so boring for you."

"I don't mind. Anything for a partner and a *compadre*." He gave her a one-upmanship grin.

"But the thing is," Tina said, "I don't think the Huntington specializes in the kind of art where you qualify as an expert."

"Oh, no?"

"I'll bet there's not a single painting in there on black velvet of a nude woman with purple nipples like that one you admire so much in Pepe's restaurant."

Eduardo's laugh gave notice of capitulation. "That's an amazing picture, you have to admit."

"*Oh* yeah. Now would you please tell me what this is all about?"

"Murder and vandalism."

"San Marino doesn't want to do a nasty old murder?"

"This one was in such poor taste," Lopez said.

"What was the cause of death?"

"A chest problem."

"A bullet-in-the-chest problem?"

"Um."

"Who was the victim?"

"They haven't been able to I.D. him."

"No fingerprints on file?"

"Nope," Lopez answered.

"No clothing labels?"

"No clothing."

"None?"

"None."

Tina said, "Maybe he was a wood nymph out galloping through the gardens."

"Could be. His feet were dirty enough."

"Oh?"

"Feet, hands, ankles, face, hair, and neck—all the normally exposed parts of the body—were extremely dirty according to the report."

"No wonder San Marino wants to give him back to L.A."

"They've had murders in San Marino before," Eduardo said. "But I think it was the vandalism that really set them off. They figure graffiti and spray paint had to come from Hollenbeck."

"Oh, God. Graffiti again. Do you think we're destined to spend the rest of our lives tracking down graffiti artists?"

At that moment, Archie Chambers hurried up, apologizing for being late. "I always stop by the office and read the report of the night guard who has just gone off duty before I do anything else," he said.

Tina extended her hand. "That's all right Mr. uh . . ."

"Chambers. Archie Chambers." Archie shook hands with each of them. "I want you to know that nothing like murder has ever occurred at the Huntington before."

"Yes," Tina said. "We've been told that."

Archie added with a shudder, "And I had to be the one to discover the body."

"I'm sure it was a shock," Eduardo offered.

"It was the second truly disturbing discovery I've made since I've worked here."

"Oh, what was the other?" Tina was aware that they were through with the preliminaries. She waited to let Archie tell his story naturally. It was always possible to get information if you just let a witness talk, if you let him tell his story in his own way.

"It's embarrassing to discuss." Archie's eyes were directed toward his neatly trimmed and buffed fingernails. "But under the circumstances, I suppose I should tell you everything."

"Yes, it's important. And I want you to understand that at this point everything you say to us is confidential," Tina assured him.

"Well. One morning when I arrived early, I was making my rounds through the gardens," Archie began. With a good deal of hesitation, he was able to relate the incident of finding the pair of girl's panties by the side of the path, and his efforts to determine if there was any indication of rape.

"Sounds like a couple of high school kids just found a nice private place to make out," Eduardo offered.

"Yes. Yes, I decided that was the case," Archie concurred a bit reluctantly. "I don't suppose there's any connection. But I admit I wondered—you don't suppose there's some sort of teenage sexual cult involved in all this."

"Oh, I don't think so." Tina hurried to reassure Archie and help him past his painful embarrassment.

Eduardo started to laugh, but with a freezing look and a jab in the ribs from his partner, he was able to convert a guffaw to a fairly respectable cough.

"Maybe if we walked over to the statuary garden . . . That's where the crime took place?"

"Oh, yes. It's just across the service road. If you'll follow me."

Tina and Eduardo followed the purposeful stride of the guard who led them to the perfectly designed and maintained garden. On first seeing the statuary garden, most visitors responded to the aura of serenity.

"Nice place," Tina said.

Eduardo agreed. "Nice quiet place for a murder."

EIGHT

THAT NIGHT, he climbed the fence again on Euston Road and ran through the grounds of the Huntington to the statuary garden. The moon was even smaller now, pale and misshapen, but bright enough to make the stark white of the statues gleam in the darkness.

In one hand he carried a can of Glengarrif Green spray paint; in the other, a gun.

The gun felt like dry ice in his hand—frozen, stuck to his sweaty fingers.

Once and forever, he must get rid of the gun.

The night was still. The only sound was the hum of traffic on the distant Foothill Freeway. Then, suddenly, there was a rustling noise near the azaleas by the fountain.

He stood motionless, barely breathing, not daring even to hide as he squinted into the shadows. For a moment nothing moved. Then, the lower branches of the largest bush began to tremble, and the rustling noise increased. The sound stopped as quickly as it had begun as a large gray rabbit hopped noiselessly onto the open lawn.

A rabbit. It was only a rabbit. He almost laughed.

Shoo! Back in your hole or wherever you belong.

The rabbit skittered off toward the art gallery and disappeared behind an Australian flame tree.

Placing the gun and spray paint carefully side by side on the grass, he began to dig with his hands in the soft soil at the trunk of a sturdy azalea bush. When the hole was wrist deep, he dropped in the gun. Carefully, he covered it, then crawled behind the flowering shrub and was sick. He continued to retch long after there was anything left in his stomach.

Weak and trembling, he pulled his body out onto the open lawn. Lying face up with his eyes closed, he willed thoughts of the gun—memories of its sound—to the back of his mind. At last, he was able to summon the silence of white. White first, white that spread and closed off his mind, and then he could see the spectrum of color. Color was his salvation. When he visualized color behind his closed eyes—first the primaries, then the shades and gradations—he could blot out thought. Finally, when his hands were steady and his legs would support his slight weight, he grabbed the spray paint and leaped to his feet.

The sun would be up soon. Already, the east side of the San Gabriel Mountains was tinged with pink.

Shaking the can and listening to the comforting ping of the metal ball as it mixed the viscosity of the paint, he strode between the rows of statues. Stopping in front of the likeness of a seventeenth-century Italian gentleman, he climbed to the pedestal and began to spray-paint the statue's terracotta tunic a bright and cheerful shade of green.

NINE

A FEW HOURS LATER—Greenwich mean time—Andrea Perkins boarded a Los Angeles-bound British Airways plane at London's Heathrow Airport. She checked one bag through, and stowed her carryon in the compartment above the first class window seat that had been reserved for her by the public relations department of the Huntington. Her briefcase and the canvas tote bag that held her equipment she put under the seat in front, where she could see them.

As always during takeoff, Andrea looked for ways to keep herself busy. She read the hieroglyphics on her ticket, and leafed through the airline magazine trying to ignore the ominous changing pitch of the engine and the clank of the wheels retracting. Once the plane was in the air and seemed to be flying in a straight line, her heart dropped from her throat to its proper place in her chest and she allowed herself to raise the window shade and look down.

Each time when she arrived or departed London, she was in awe of the view. Sir Christopher Wren's master work, St. Paul's Cathedral, stood staunch and solid at the center of the city. The aerial view of its massive dome compounded the impression of indestructibility. This formidable house of worship gave the appearance of having evolved over eons and forcing its way up from the earth like a mountain. By contrast, the Houses of Parliament, with their fragile-looking towers and spires, seemed to float precariously at the edge of the Thames, as though they were in constant danger of breaking loose from their moorings and drifting down the languid river.

"Do you live in London?"

Andrea was startled to hear a voice close to her shoulder. She had paid little attention to her seatmate, a balding man with a ponytail wearing an Irish tweed sport coat.

"No," she answered.

"Andy Nash." He leaned sideways and extended his right hand. Andrea shook it and introduced herself. They gave each other faint smiles of appraisal.

"In L.A.? You live in Los Angeles?"

"No." She was not being intentionally evasive; it was just that she would be hard put to name the place where she actually lived. In the last few years, because of her assignments as a restorer and authenticator of art, she had been briefly a resident of Florence, Ferrara, Venice, and most recently, London. Boston was still the place she gave as her permanent address, but that was where her parents and her sister lived. "This is my first trip to California," she answered.

"Where are you going—I mean, what part?"

"San Marino."

"Ah! Equityville East. My broker lives in San Marino," Andy Nash said. "Nice little upscale community. If you're into peace and quiet, you'll love it there. Harv, my broker, is always bragging that it's one of the safest cities in California."

It was interesting, Andrea thought, that both Georgene Dodson and Andy Nash placed safety at the top of the list of things to recommend San Marino.

"Is this trip pleasure, or business, or none of my business?"

"I'll be working at the Huntington Art Gallery. I'm an art restorer."

"Um. That must be interesting." His frown apparently was meant to convey sincerity. He seemed to search for a follow-up question with no success, then headed for firmer conversational ground. He told her about himself. "I'm in the arts, too. I'm a booking agent—hard rock, mostly. I've been in Manchester auditioning a group called The Terminals, and, believe me, they sounded like they were. There's nothing new anymore. All these kids are derivative. Over and back in three days to listen to that.'' He pressed the palm of his hand against his forehead in a display of agony. "I'm going to be suffering mondo jet lag by the time I get home."

Andy Nash closed his eyes and Andrea thought he had gone to sleep until suddenly his eyes opened again and he turned to look at her. "The Huntington—that place with the gardens and the library and all that?''

"That's right."

"Yeah. I thought that name rang a bell, as it were. That's the place Harv said they found a dead body last week. Some guy with no clothes was stretched out on the lawn with a bullet in his chest." Then, thinking better of what he had just said, Andy Nash patted her hand apologetically. "Sorry. I shouldn't have mentioned it. The only reason it's newsworthy, Harv said, is because things like that just don't happen there. It's the tranquility capital of the San Gabriel Valley, according to Harv. You'll love San Marino." He adjusted the seat to a reclining position and closed his eyes again. "Don't worry about it."

Andrea did not intend to. She looked into the gray cloud bank that was undoubtedly dropping chilling rain or snow on the earth below and thought of California sunshine. Sunshine, and the fact that when the plane landed in Los Angeles, Aldo Balzani would be there to meet her.

SHORTLY AFTER SUNSET Pacific time, the captain announced that they would be arriving in Los Angeles, where it was clear and a balmy seventy-five degrees, in approximately forty-five minutes.

Andrea rose from her seat next to the window, and stepped across her sleeping seatmate, whose head had landed on her shoulder several times during the flight.

In the aisle, she reached into the overhead compartment for her raincoat and her carryon bag, then quickly made her way to the lavatory, which, for once, was not occupied.

She felt smudged and rumpled, and in spite of the cramped space, was determined to redo her face and change clothes before landing.

Aldo Balzani's flight was scheduled to arrive at LAX an hour earlier than hers. The last time he phoned from Florence, they had agreed that while he waited, he would arrange for limousine service to take them to the Dodsons' house in San Marino. He would meet her, he said, as soon as she had gone through customs. He had repeated all of this several times, as though she might be tempted to wander off with a stranger.

They had not seen each other since October, and then only for a brief weekend in Brighton. This trip was to be as close to a real vacation as they had ever had together.

In the lavatory, Andrea peeled off the turtleneck sweater, suede boots, and heavy woolen slacks that had been so comfortable when she left the snow of London. Feeling like a contortionist in the tiny cubicle, she squirmed into the major new addition to her wardrobe: an almost weightless orange Day-Glo bikini.

It had seemed like such a good idea when she bought it: to change on the plane, and be wearing this next-to-nothing absurdity underneath her raincoat when she met Aldo in the terminal. What could be more appropriate for a vacation in California? But in the blue neon light in the airplane rest room, she was beginning to feel a bit ridiculous. Nevertheless, she persevered, adjusting snaps and straps.

Her plan was that when she met Aldo in her buttoned-up raincoat and boots she would appear to be dressed like most of the other women arriving from London. Then, when they got in the limo, it would be wonderful to hear his laugh when he discovered what she was wearing underneath.

Shivering, with the air-conditioning vent blowing frigid air down the back of her neck, she had to stretch her arms above her head to slip them through her coat sleeves, then banged an elbow against the wall as she tied the belt around her waist. After pulling her boots back on, she combed through her thick red hair and dabbed on a bit of eye makeup. She wanted to make sure that the moment Aldo saw her, he would be convinced that his long flight from Italy had been worthwhile.

Andy Nash was still asleep when she returned and settled back into her seat. Holding her hands above her eyes like a visor, she peered through the window at the darkening landscape below.

With the exception of the Pacific Ocean, it was difficult to know where Los Angeles began and ended.

Arriving by plane after dark in great cities such as Paris, London, and New York, Andrea always felt awed by the view that dazzled in the way a skyrocket dazzles with its central core of color, flash, and glitter. But coming into Los Angeles was more like looking down at a gigantic tangle of mismatched Christmas-tree lights. Each interconnected strand was slightly different from the next, but together they spread across the floor of the desert and trailed up the sides of the mountains in a seemingly endless jumble.

The area loosely described as Los Angeles was not one Great City, but a hodgepodge of eighty-four municipalities, she had been told. Each had its own city government, and its own individual character.

The plane set down smoothly. In her eagerness to see Aldo Balzani, Andrea, for once, forgot her fear of takeoffs and landings.

Andy, wide awake now, grabbed his gear from under the seat. "Come on," he said, "I'll run interference in the terminal."

Andrea followed behind, holding her carryon in front of her and clutching her briefcase and canvas bag of art supplies in the other hand.

Once inside, Andy was soon several passengers ahead of her and was lost in the crush of tired, disgruntled, and excited travelers.

When she had finished her dealings with the customs officer, she cinched the belt of her coat and hurried through to the waiting area. Her knees felt weak and her heart was pounding as she searched the crowd for the sight of Aldo's dark eyes and curly black hair.

Because he was taller than average, she was looking above the heads of most of the new arrivals and the friends and relatives who had come to meet them. She had glanced around the entire area twice before she lowered her gaze and spotted the sign.

A boy of about ten was holding a large piece of white cardboard with "Andrea Perkins" written on it.

"I'm Andrea Perkins."

"Miss Perkins." A woman standing next to the boy stepped toward her. "I'm Georgene Dodson's sister, Sarah Anderson. And this is my son, Benjamin."

"How do you do, Sarah—and Benjamin." Andrea glanced at them quickly, but continued to search the crowd for the face she wanted to see. "Forgive me for seeming startled," she said, "but I wasn't expecting to see you until I got to San Marino. Someone else is supposed to meet me."

"Oh, yes. There was a telephone call. And this telegram." Sarah took a yellow envelope from her purse and apologetically handed it to Andrea.

Andrea knew what it said—or approximately—before she opened it. Aldo had been detained. Something had come up. He would call and explain. He loved her.

"I'm sorry," Sarah Anderson said.

Andrea tried to fight off her disappointment. "This is always happening to us." Her smile was so brief, it might never have been there. "If it's not my work that gets in the way, it's his."

"Mom! There's our limo driver!" Benjamin waved at the uniformed man and energetically motioned for him to join them.

As the two women and the boy stood on the sidewalk waiting for Andrea's bags to be stowed in the trunk of the spotless white vehicle, Andrea had trouble fighting back her tears.

"You saw Georgene in London—" Sarah said.

"Yes." Andrea cleared her throat. "We had tea at the Savoy."

"I'm sure she's fine."

"She certainly seemed to be."

As Sarah explained that Georgene's sudden trip to England was typical of her sister, Andrea mentally compared the two women.

Sarah's hair was a natural light brown, whereas Georgene's was a professionally done glistening silvery blond. They both had dark eyes and slim figures. And though Andrea suspected that Georgene was older, Sarah's face had tiny lines around the mouth and eyes—worry lines, Andrea's mother would have called them.

"Benjamin and I are in the guest house and we'll stay out of your way—"

"Oh, no, please," Andrea protested. "I probably won't be at the house much, anyway." If Aldo was not going to be there, she was determined to finish this assignment as quickly as possible.

"Benjamin has an art tutor, but they'll be in the recreation room or out by the pool—"

"There's no problem, no problem at all."

Benjamin was a skinny little boy. He had light blond hair, and the same dark eyes as those of Sarah and Georgene, but in his small face they were so large, they seemed to leave very little room for his other features.

"All ready, ladies"—the driver slammed down the trunk lid and smiled at Benjamin—"... and gentleman."

As Andrea bent to climb into the automobile, a breeze flapped the tail of her coat and chilled her bare legs. Thinking with embarrassment and disappointment of her quick-change routine in the lavatory of the airplane, she clutched the coat tightly around her.

"And there's Holly," Sarah said. "Technically, she's my cook—but she's more like a mother hen. She has the maid's quarters—a couple of rooms and a bath in a wing off the kitchen."

The limo ride to San Marino seemed to take forever—which would have been fine if it had been Aldo in the backseat with Andrea.

TEN

TINA ROBERSON and Eduardo Lopez sat in the winter sunshine on a low concrete-block wall next to the car wash at LAPD headquarters. The outside of the unmarked Plymouth was merely dusty. The inside, however, along with the usual clutter, had dried mud and some evidence of duck shit on the floorboard beneath the front seat. The car was in that condition because of an incident that had occurred the night before.

TINA HAD BEEN driving. They were on their way back to Hollenbeck on Huntington Drive where it splits and becomes Soto Street, going south, and Mission Road, going west toward Union Station. Tina automatically took Mission. She and Eduardo had driven this route at least once every day since they had been assigned as partners.

The nighttime street was all but deserted except for Pepe's Cantina near the city park, Plaza de la Raza. Pepe's small parking lot was filled and mariachi music throbbed through the bar's cranked-up speaker system.

"Look! There's another one. Looks like the face on El Fenix restaurant." Tina pointed through the car window toward the park across the street. Two of the vapor lights in the park were out, but one near the public pavilion lit the side of the building where a large profile-drawing of a face—possibly meant to be an Aztec warrior—had been freshly painted with spray paint. At least, the two detectives had not seen it there that morning.

"I'd like to catch that little bastard," Eduardo said.

"How's your fencing technique? If this is the guy who think's he's Zorro, he probably wields a mean sword."

"These kids make me sick," Eduardo said. "No pride. No respect."

Tina could tell that her partner was winding himself up to make the same speech she had heard from him many times before.

"They come up here from Mexico and join gangs and bring dishonor to their families and—"

This was the part, Tina knew, that truly rankled with Eduardo.

"—they give all Latinos a bad name."

"This guy shows some originality, at least. His drawing is not half bad," Tina said. "If he's not Zorro, he's the Lone Ranger, because he sure doesn't seem to belong to a gang. There's never any tagging."

"Slow down." Eduardo stuck his head out the window and squinted into the darkness.

"Why?"

"I saw someone in the headlights coming out of the men's toilet."

"That's not exactly breaking the law." Tina slowed the car to a crawl and tried to see what her partner had seen.

"I'd swear the guy was wearing a mask." Eduardo had his hand on the door handle. "Take the road into the park next to the railroad tracks. Follow me in the car. I'm going to chase that sonofabitch down."

"Eduardo!" Tina shouted, but her partner was already out of the car.

"Stop! Police!" Eduardo sprinted across the grass. At the sound of his voice, the slim figure several yards ahead of him broke into a run and veered toward the duck pond.

Tina could tell that they were quickly going to be out of her line of vision. She pulled to the curb and stopped the car. Unfastening her seat belt, she flipped the automatic door locks and started running after the other two.

"Damn you, Eduardo," she muttered, "I ought to write you up for this."

The words of the academy instructor rang in her ears. *Never separate from your partner. Never try to follow in a car if your partner's chasing someone on foot. A car can't run upstairs. A car can't climb a fence.*

The boy was faster than Eduardo and had increased the distance between them. The two of them had a considerable start on Tina, but she was faster than either of them and was gaining ground. The boy disappeared down a shallow slope toward the edge of the pond. Eduardo followed like a rabbit down a hole.

As Tina neared, she heard a splash first, followed by the frantic quacking of a frightened duck. Next, she heard Eduardo shouting a stream of profanities at the culprit who had led him to the water's edge. When she reached the slope, Tina saw her partner scrambling up from his knees where he had stumbled in the mud. Eduardo regained his footing and hurtled after the boy who had neatly skirted the pond and shifted course toward the railroad tracks.

"Eduardo! Give it up! He's going to go over the fence."

"Stay out of this, Tina!"

Fired by his anger, Eduardo picked up speed and was running smoothly behind the boy. Tina cut across the top of the incline and was rapidly catching up. From her higher elevation she suddenly saw what the other two could not: the headlight of a train in the distance.

The boy leaped to grab the high horizontal support strip of the spiked iron fence and swung his body over the top.

"Train! A train is coming!" Tina's last words were blotted out by the heavy, harsh horn of the train as it sounded a warning in advance of the underpass on Mission Road.

Eduardo was now straddling the top of the fence, off balance, and had no choice but to drop down on the other side. Tina scaled to the top moments later and landed in the loose dirt beside her partner just as the boy dashed in front of the oncoming train and scrambled up the embankment on the opposite side. In the fleeting glimpse of the boy's face—the part that was visible beneath the half-mask—he appeared to be about fourteen years old.

The two detectives stood with their backs to the fence, holding to the iron stakes for support as the long Southern Pacific freight train lumbered by.

"...you stupid jerk!...*never* leave your partner..." Only part of what Tina was screaming at Eduardo was audible over the sound of the train. "...that kid could have been killed—*we* could have been killed!...how was I supposed to follow you into the duck pond in the car?...ought to write you up for this...don't you remember anything they taught us..."

When at last the red light on the caboose passed by, Tina and Eduardo walked silently to the corner where there was a break in the fence and climbed back up to the side street off Mission Road where the green Plymouth was parked.

Tina was breathing heavily—more from anger than exertion. Eduardo was as contrite as it was possible for him to be. Tina took the keys from her pocket and unlocked the door. "*You* drive. You won't be able to get out of the car so fast and go chasing through the park if you have to fight with the steering wheel first." She turned and saw her partner with his report book open, reaching in his breast pocket for a pen. "What are you doing?"

"Sorry, Tina. I'm going to have to write this up."

"What are you talking about?"

"Turn on the headlights, then come here, and I'll show you."

Puzzled, she did as he asked.

"I know that in cases of emergency we are authorized to ignore the rules that apply to ordinary citizens. I learned that at the academy," he said with emphasis. "But as you so politely pointed out when we were about to be swept under the freight train, what we were doing there could not really be classified as an emergency."

"You're damn right! Chasing a teenage kid who's carrying nothing more dangerous than a can of spray paint through the park—the middle of the night—is not what the captain is likely to concede is an emergency."

"As always, my beloved, you are right."

"Eduardo," it made her shiver to think what might have happened, "somebody could have gotten killed."

"I know. I'm sorry." He said it sincerely. "That's why, starting right now, I'm going to do everything strictly by the book."

"*Oh* yeah. Well, we'll see." Tina started toward the passenger side of the car.

"Wait. Just wait a minute. I want to prove to you I meant what I said." Putting his report book on the hood of the car, Eduardo reached for the flashlight at his waist. "Since we both agree that this little episode was not an emergency, then there's no justification for disobeying laws that the rest of the citizens have to abide by, is there?"

"No." She knew he was setting her up. She did not know how, but he was doing it to her again.

"Sorry, Tina. I'm going to have to write you up for this." Eduardo focused the flashlight first on the red stripe of the curb and then at the sign that stood beside it: NO PARKING ANYTIME.

The adrenaline was still pinging around in her body and it suddenly seemed to congeal in her right fist. She wanted to punch Eduardo's glittering white teeth down his throat.

Furious, Tina got into the passenger seat and slammed the door.

Contrite, Eduardo pulled the car back onto Huntington and drove sedately for a block or two. Suddenly, he rolled down the window. "Jesus! What's that smell in here?"

In the light under the dashboard, Tina could see her partner's lizard cowboy boots were covered with mud and a black and white slime across the toes and heels. "My guess is duck shit," she said.

Eduardo looked at her, mystified.

"Look at your stupid boots!" There was no way Tina could have kept from laughing.

Once Eduardo understood what she meant, there was no way he could continue to drive, he was laughing so hard.

He pulled over to the curb and stopped the car. Neither of them spoke, but they alternately—and together—laughed at the absurdity and danger of their run through the park.

Finally, Eduardo took off his boots and put them in the trunk. Tina was still giggling while he was gone. She knew their laughter was probably a form of hysteria. But, dear God, how could you do this job if you couldn't laugh? Somewhere in the recruiting literature, she thought, there should be a warning to the effect that because of the danger, the responsibility and the frequent horror of being a police officer, no one without a sense of humor need apply.

THE NEXT MORNING as they waited at the LAPD car wash, Eduardo went inside Parker Center for a few minutes. When he returned, he asked Tina, "Do you know someone named Rainbow?"

"Who?"

"What do you mean, who?" Eduardo removed his sunglasses and squinted at her in the bright morning sunshine. "Do you mean—who?—you didn't hear me, or—Rainbow who?" He was pretending to make a big thing of it.

"Yeah, I know him," Tina said, not going along.

"I see. You heard me, but it took you a moment to figure out which one of your many acquaintances named Rainbow that I meant? Is that it?"

"I know him, I know him." Tina was impatient. "What about it?"

"He wants to see you." Eduardo reached in the pocket of his sports jacket and took out a pink slip of paper with "While You Were Out" printed on the top, and a handscribbled note beneath. "He came in yesterday looking for you."

"I wonder what he wants?"

"I've given you all the information I have." Eduardo handed her the note. He was no longer interested.

"Where did this come from?"

"Front desk." Eduardo pointed with his glasses toward Parker Center. "They *might* have gotten around to faxing our messages to Hollenbeck sometime, but I thought as long as we were here—"

"Thanks, Eduardo." With a sigh, Tina said, "Somebody probably stole his shoes."

"Who is this mysterious Rainbow person? One of your super-jock running friends?"

"No. He's a poor old guy who hangs out on one of the benches in the mall." She stood and brushed dust from the concrete-block wall off the seat of her skirt. "Since we're waiting around anyway, I think I'll run across the street and see if I can find him. Okay?"

"Okay. If they finish with the car before you get back, I'll pick you up in front of City Hall in twenty minutes."

"See you there."

Eduardo watched her as far as the corner. He considered going inside Parker Center to wait, but just hanging around was frowned on no matter what the reason. It was not time for lunch, and he had already had three cups of coffee, but he headed for the Kosher Burrito—a favorite hangout for Metro Division cops. Some of the guys he knew were bound to be there.

The Kosher Burrito was across the street and a half block down from City Hall. In giving the location of any business or building in the civic center, the starting place was always City Hall: "It's two block west of—" or, "It's just around the corner from—" or, "It faces the rear entrance of—"

City Hall first became the hub of the city—the strategic locater—because for many years, at twenty-seven stories, it was the tallest building in Los Angeles.

If Los Angeles were to build a new City Hall, the result would probably be a high-rise monolith balanced on a modern teeter-totter sort of foundation. The experts have guaranteed that contemporary California skyscrapers will easily shift and sway and survive atop the state's unstable earth. It is not clear, however, who would collect on the guarantee after an eight-point-plus earthquake if the experts were wrong.

In the mid-twenties, when the City Hall was constructed, such innovative foundations had not been introduced. At that time, there was little optimism about tall buildings being able to withstand the perennially predicted "Big One." The arbitrary theory was that thirteen stories was about as high as a building ought to go.

City Hall was the one exception to the thirteen-story limit. This exception was granted as the result of a general election. The citizenry voted for permission to build a slim tower that would rise twenty-seven stories above the sprawling city. The existence of at least one tall building appealed to civic pride. And, the electorate may have been influenced by the thought that if anyone had to go in an earthquake, it might as well be the local politicians.

The architectural plan that was chosen was a combination of Greek and Roman with a pyramidal peak at the tower. The impression it gave—and gives—was that it was constructed with giant Legos.

Like everything else in Los Angeles, city government grew faster than anyone could have predicted. Early on, more space was needed to house a variety of municipal offices. As a result, two additional buildings (both boxlike and under the thirteen-story limit) were constructed across the street and given the utilitarian designations of City Hall East, and City Hall South. The personnel department was assigned to City Hall South. Interviews for prospective police officers are still conducted there.

The day Eduardo Lopez was scheduled for his first interview as a prospective member of the LAPD (some five years before his partnership with Tina Roberson and their current assignment to investigate the murder and vandalism at the Huntington), he circled the block three times before deciding to keep the appointment.

In El Sereno, the nearby suburb where he lived, it was common practice to avoid the men in blue uniform whenever possible. A large part of the general wariness was a language problem; neither group making a sufficient effort to understand the other.

In Eduardo's own family, the distrust of the police was a carryover from his father's experience with the Mexican Federales in Guaymas. The senior Lopez had owned and operated a small fishing boat there before he fled with his wife across the border to Mexicali. Eduardo never knew whether the threats and intimidation from the machine gun-wielding Federales was due to the cargo his father imported, or a cargo the Federales wished him to import. Whatever the disagreement, the hatred that Señor Lopez nurtured for all uniformed authority had been passed on to Eduardo's mother, four sisters, and his idolized older brother, Umberto. Still, it was because of Umberto—the way Umberto had died—that Eduardo had talked with a recruiting officer at the Los Angeles Police Department.

The day he had been scheduled for an appointment, he was still undecided about whether he would go in and take the exam. As he turned right on Los Angeles Street for the third time, Eduardo spotted a parking space less than a block from City Hall South. This was a bit of unexpected luck. Then, when he left and locked the low-rider Chevy he had inherited from his brother, he discovered the parking meter had forty-five minutes remaining. It had to be an omen.

Eduardo was a secret believer in omens and signs. The convenient parking space with almost an hour of free time was a minor twist of fate, but potent enough to make him straighten his shoulders and propel himself down the sidewalk toward the personnel building.

There had been other, more dramatic omens in his life that he would never forget. There was the shattered bottle the night Umberto was ambushed and killed outside La

Raza Cantina on Lower Huntington Drive by marauding Calzado gang members.

Eduardo had planned to go with Umberto. He would have gone—in which case he would have been dead now, too—if it had not been for the broken bottle of after-shave.

It had all been a stupid accident and bad timing. Umberto had threatened to leave without him. In his hurry, Eduardo dropped the bottle of Canoe in the sink. When he tried to clean up the glass, he gashed his hand.

Eduardo protested, but Umberto drove him to the hospital and shoved him out of the car at the emergency entrance.

"Go get some stitches in your hand."

"It's all right! I've got a handkerchief wrapped around it," Eduardo insisted.

"You'll get blood on my seat covers." Without a backward look, Umberto had driven off to La Raza Cantina alone.

Hadn't Eduardo's life been spared for some reason? Wasn't he meant to avenge his brother?

And then, a few years later, there had been a mysterious intervention on Eduardo's behalf with a priest. It had happened in the confessional. When Eduardo and Angelina had been married for only a year, his feelings of guilt had forced him to go to church and confess his adultery. Wasn't what happened then a sign, too?

His sin had weighed heavily on him. Eduardo and his bride were both seventeen when they took their marriage vows the Sunday before Valentine Day. He had sworn to lifelong fidelity and he had meant it with all his heart. But how was he to know about Felicia? How could he have known that near the end of the scorching summer when he was working as an installer for Supremo Carpets in a row of tract houses that the contractor's vulgar wife would scheme to be alone with him?

He was on his hands and knees that day tacking down the last corner of Misty-Heather-Plush-Nylon in the master bedroom.

"I decided to bring your check to you this week instead of mailing it," Felicia said, standing close behind him.

He was startled. He had not known there was anyone else in the empty house. When he twisted around to a sitting position, his face was level with her knees. She was wearing a short, wraparound sundress. Before his eyes rose to meet hers, he caught a glimpse beneath her skirt of smooth rounded thighs and a flash of white lace panties at the top of suntanned skin.

Her face was unremarkable with small, walnut-colored eyes, and her bleached short hair was dry and frizzled from too much sun. She was the kind of woman who would never get a second look bundled in woolens, but who thrived in a warm climate where bikinis and sunglasses can be worn most of the year.

Before Eduardo realized what was happening, the contractor's wife had dropped to her knees beside him.

"Here's your check." She leaned forward, taking an envelope from her purse that had fallen to the carpet beside her. As she did, the top of her dress gaped open and Eduardo could see most of the rest of her tan.

"Gracias." He was excited, but still not sure of her intentions. A moment later, there was no doubt.

"And this week, I think you deserve a bonus." As she said that, she reached to the side of her waist and untied the single bow knot that held her dress together.

Eduardo hated himself later. His feelings of guilt were so intense that he knew he must visit the church and seek absolution.

The sanctuary smelled of varnish, and the only sound was the moist whish of a painter's brush as he touched up the well-worn pews in the front of the church. Head bowed, Eduardo entered the tiny cubicle of the confessional. He sat, contemplating his deed for a moment before he began to speak. Soon, he heard a muffled cough from the other side of the screen, which he interpreted as impatience.

Hesitantly, he said, "Forgive me, Father, for I have sinned."

The priest coughed again. It was a rasping sound this time.

Eduardo waited, but the coughing did not stop; it grew louder and became a gagging sound.

In a strangled voice, the priest managed to say, "Sorry, my son. It's the paint fumes. Continue."

Eduardo tried to confess his sin, but he could not. The coughing continued, and compassion for the priest forced Eduardo to say, "I'm sorry, Father. I'll come back tomorrow." And he hurried from the confessional, closing the door softly behind him.

Wasn't that a sort of Divine intervention?

Why had God sent the painter to the sanctuary on the very day that Eduardo decided to confess his fall from grace? Didn't that mean that He understood? Wasn't that forgiveness without penance? Wasn't it a sign that though He could not forgive adultery in everyone, He knew that some men—like Eduardo—meant no harm? They merely had greater needs than others?

Eduardo never went back to confession. He clung to the belief that God would always understand and forgive his adultery (although later, when Angelina found out, she did not forgive him—nor did his second wife after a similar incident).

The day he went for his interview with the Los Angeles Police Department, Eduardo's confidence ebbed and swelled. There was the free parking meter, but could he really call that an omen? It was hardly a guarantee that he would pass the exam.

But what if he did pass?

Could he take the derision of his friends in El Sereno if he became a police officer?

At the corner of First and Los Angeles streets, he glanced at his reflection in the glass-enclosed bus stop and smoothed his black hair. When the streetlight was green, two young women who were coming from the opposite way in the crosswalk smiled at him as they passed. Eduardo smiled back, but for once, his thoughts were elsewhere. He was nervous and unsure of what lay ahead inside the characterless building with its lawn of short winter grass that glistened like lime Jell-O.

"...great eyes," he heard one of the girls say.

"...great buns," the second girl said.

Eduardo raised his chin and straightened his collar as he confidently took the marble steps of City Hall South.

Room 202, where he was instructed to wait until his name was called, was large and spare with dirty windows. There were four rows of bolted-down seats separated by bolted-down tables that held outdated copies of *Newsweek* and *Reader's Digest.* Two receptionists were seated behind stacks of applications and various color-coded forms, and on the front of each of their desks was a large sign that read ALL CONVERSATIONS IN THIS ROOM ARE BEING RECORDED. As a result, there was no conversation at all.

Eduardo glanced around at the other applicants who were waiting to be interviewed. There were three Marines in uniform, two young men in suits and ties, one cowboy type with longish brown hair wearing boots and a denim vest, a young woman with a pockmarked face who looked as though she could lift the row of chairs out of its bolts with the Marines still sitting there, and a petite blonde wearing spike heels, a pink suit, no makeup, and a gold chain with a large cross that glistened at the neck of her white lacy blouse.

All of them had their eyes fixed on the large clock that was suspended in the center of the room.

From time to time, one of the receptionists would stand and read off a name from a card in her hand, then lead the candidate down a long, narrow hallway. When at last it was Eduardo's turn, he was escorted to a closed door that had a metal number *8* tacked at eye level and, taped beneath it, a sheet of typing paper on which DO NOT ENTER! was handwritten in red.

The receptionist opened the door. Reading from the card, she announced Eduardo's name to two men in business suits who stood from behind a small desk when he entered. One of them, a kindly looking black man with graying hair, extended his hand and said his name was Abraham Hempstead, and that he was with the city personnel department. He introduced the other man as Sergeant Arnold Rossiter, who also shook Eduardo's hand.

Mr. Hempstead indicated a wooden chair across the desk. "Have a seat," he said.

The room was small, windowless, and unadorned. On the desk in front of Eduardo's application were nameplates for the two men, some scattered pencils, a stack of scoring sheets, and two red-bound notebooks. It was a moment before Eduardo noticed that an ugly, black microphone hung from the ceiling above the desk. He had been warned that the interview would be recorded, but the sight of the microphone—hanging like a snake in front of him—made his throat contract in apprehension. Who would be listening to him, and why?

"Don't let the microphone bother you," Mr. Hempstead said in a soothing voice. "All interviews are taped so the department has a record of what we say, as well as what you say." But he did not explain why the department thought this was necessary. Eduardo guessed that the tape would be used as evidence in case someone contested their score.

"Now then, Mr. Lopez," Mr. Hempstead leaned forward and smiled, "is it okay if I call you Eduardo?"

Say, "yes," not "jes," he warned himself.

"Yes," Eduardo answered. Mr. Hempstead's kindly manner was helping him relax a bit.

"Eduardo, the first thing we'd like for you to tell us is why are you interested in being a Los Angeles police officer?"

Because my brother was killed by the Calzado and I want to see the bastards put in jail. Death was too good for them, his father always said. Eduardo believed that, too. Jail was worse than death.

Eduardo sat straight in the chair with his hands on his knees—this was the proper attitude for an interviewee, he had been told. Hoping his expression was thoughtful, he did not answer immediately. He had attended the police department seminar to prepare for the oral exam, and he had read the brochures handed to him when he left. He knew the answers they were looking for.

"I want to be a Los Angeles police officer," he said, "because I'm concerned about the drug and gang problem in our city, and as a police officer, I feel I could do something positive for my community. Also, because I speak, read, and write Spanish, I think I will be able to relate to a large segment of the population who do not speak English."

"Eduardo," Mr. Hempstead did not exactly sigh, but there was a note of resignation in his voice, "after you took your written exam, did you stay for the police department seminar and participate in a mock interview?"

"Yes, sir."

"Good," Mr. Hempstead said, but his eyebrows went up a fraction as though he were inviting Eduardo to just answer the questions.

Don't give in, Eduardo warned himself. Tell them what will sound good when the tape is played back.

"I see you've been working as a carpet installer for the past three years." Mr. Hempstead was reading from Eduardo's application.

"Yes, sir."

"And the jobs you had before that—at McDonald's and Taco Bell—"

"Those were part time, while I was in high school, sir."

"Did you consider going to college after you got out of high school?"

College? How the hell could I go to college? I was married when I was seventeen. We barely had enough money to pay the rent.

"Yes, sir. I thought it was important to get some work experience first, but I plan to enroll next semester at East Los Angeles College and get a bachelor's degree in Criminal Justice. Eventually, I hope to go on to get a master's. I realize how important an education is to anyone who plans to advance in this profession."

Mr. Hempstead all but yawned as he asked Eduardo in more detail about his work experience, his leadership qualities, volunteer work he had done in the community, and what he expected to be doing during an average day as a police officer. Eduardo was confident that he aced every question.

"Thank you, Eduardo. Sergeant Rossiter has some questions for you now."

Sergeant Rossiter was red-haired and freckled, and obviously physically fit. But he looked more like an accountant in his blue suit and subdued tie than like a police sergeant—except for the shoulder holster beneath his open jacket.

He had been staring out the window through the dirty slats of the venetian blind while Hempstead questioned Eduardo. Now, he leaned forward and opened the red-backed book to a page marked with a paper clip.

"Eduardo, I'm going to ask you some situational questions—give you some hypothetical problems to solve. Do you know what I mean?"

"Jes." *Oh, God.* "Yes."

"I want you to answer them just using common sense. We know you do not have any previous training as an officer, so just do the best you can. Do you understand?"

"Yes."

Sergeant Rossiter read directly from the book. "Your partner, whom you consider to be a good friend and an excellent police officer, has been reporting to duty with a mild odor of alcohol on his breath lately. What do you do?"

Tell him to chew some gum.

"I'd ask him if he's having a personal problem that I could help him with. If he doesn't want to talk to me, I'd tell him there's counseling service available in the department and try to get him to see a professional."

"Would you go on duty with him?"

It depends on whose day it was to drive.

"No, sir, I wouldn't. I'd tell him to sign himself out sick. But first, I'd advise him to go explain to the sergeant, and if he refused, I'd tell him I'd have to report him myself."

Sergeant Rossiter's expression was noncommittal. Without looking up, he went on to the second question.

"Okay, you've got your partner safely off duty, and you're sent out with another officer you've never worked with before. You get a call that there's a robbery in progress at a local convenience store. You're only a block away, and when you arrive, the perpetrator is still at the scene. You and your new partner disarm him with no trouble and handcuff him. All of a sudden, the man you have arrested starts yelling obscenities at your partner. Your partner becomes enraged. He hits the man you have in custody in the face with his open hand. What do you do?"

I'd remind him that you never know when someone's out there with a video camera.

"First, I'd separate them. I'd get the guy that's handcuffed locked in the backseat, then I'd talk privately to my partner and get him cooled down. And when we got back to the station, I'd make a written report of exactly what happened, and I'd probably go in and have a talk with the sergeant, too."

There were some other questions about how Eduardo handled personal conflicts and about athletic activities he had participated in.

Finally, Mr. Hempstead asked if there was anything additional that Eduardo wished to say that had not already been covered in the interview.

The instructor at the seminar had said to expect this question, and Eduardo had rehearsed his answer.

"I'd like to thank you both for this opportunity. I just want you to know that to be a police officer is something I've wanted all my life. My family has taught me to respect the law and encouraged me in my choice of a profession. If I am selected to be a member of the Los Angeles Police Department, I would consider it a great honor, and an opportunity to give something back to the community."

And there's Umberto!

Eduardo was told to wait in the reception room and that Mr. Hempstead would be with him shortly.

Ten minutes later, Mr. Hempstead walked with him out into the main hallway and handed him a white card with instructions to report to the fourth floor to make an appointment for his physical and psychological examinations.

He passed. Within a month he would be a member of the next training class at the academy.

When Eduardo left the building, he almost ran to his car in his excitement. As he put his key in the lock, a feeling of dread spread over him as though he had misread a signal— a sign, an omen. The arrow on the parking meter was pointing to red, and there was a ticket on the car window underneath the windshield wiper.

ELEVEN

WHEN TINA REACHED the L.A. Mall, the stone patio and steps were still wet from a daily hosing down with disinfectant. A residual sweet, astringent odor hung in the morning air. At City Hall East and City Hall South, the glass doors that opened onto the public courtyard were kept swinging by office workers arriving for the start of another midweek workday.

Tina spotted Rainbow just ahead of a city cleanup crew in orange vests. He was checking the trash bins for empty aluminum cans before the debris from the previous day was hauled off in giant biodegradable bags.

"Hey, Rainbow." Tina had not seen him for several months. He looked older than she remembered. She had no idea what his age really was; he could have been anywhere from thirty to sixty. There was no way to tell under the layers of dirt and disillusion.

"Rainbow." She said his name again as she walked slowly toward him, stepping around a greenish puddle of disinfectant.

He turned and scowled suspiciously at her.

"It's me. Officer Tina Roberson."

There was still no sign of recognition. His eyes were as bright as a fish's, and had the same absence of expression.

"I got a message you wanted to see me. Have you got a problem?"

Rainbow picked up his plastic shopping bag filled with discarded soft-drink cans and put them on his usual bench under the pedestal clock. "You're wearing a skirt," he said.

"Yeah. I'm not on patrol anymore; I'm on a new assignment where I don't wear a uniform."

"You look nice in a skirt."

"Thanks." At least he remembered who she was. She wondered if he could remember why he wanted to see her.

Rainbow shoved the plastic sack next to the armrest and sat protectively beside the bounty of his morning scavenging. Tina leaned against the base of the clock.

"How are you doin'?" Tina looked at Rainbow's feet. At least stolen shoes was not his problem. His canvas basketball high tops were filthy, but comparatively new. No doubt he had gotten them in the recent grab-bag giveaway sponsored by an overstocked sporting goods distributor.

As he tied together the handles of the sack full of empty cans, he asked in a confidential tone, "You remember my friend Goochie?"

"Umm huh." She remembered that Rainbow had palled around with some other street guy, but that was about all. Rainbow was the one who always sought her out and talked to her. His friend held back and seemed suspicious of everyone. "What about Goochie?"

"Have you seen him?"

"No. But like I said, I'm not on patrol in Metro anymore."

"He's gone. He never did come back."

"How long has it been, Rainbow? Did he say where he was going?" He could be anywhere, Tina thought. Anywhere he could get to by walking.

"He said he knew where he could get some money, and he promised to buy me dinner and a bottle of wine, but he never came back."

Tina did not respond. She could think of a number of reasons why Goochie had disappeared, and none of them would be of any comfort to Rainbow. The first and most likely explanation was that if he had money, he probably spent it all on wine for himself.

"He would have come back," Rainbow insisted stubbornly in an effort, it seemed, to convince himself.

"How long since you've seen him?"

He pulled thoughtfully at the bill of his L.A. Dodgers cap as though the cap itself was the key to his memory. "A few days. Maybe a week—two weeks."

"Where was he going to get the money to buy dinner and a bottle of wine?"

"At the track, I guess."

"The racetrack?"

"Yeah."

"Where did he get bus fare to the track and enough money to place a bet?"

"Some guy from a movie company gave him ten dollars."

Tina felt like she was trudging through sludge to get any information, but she continued to prod Rainbow with questions until she was able to piece together the story of Goochie's good fortune. Rainbow gave her a fragmentary account of the way his friend had stopped the fight in front of a TV remote truck between the well-known lovers, Smokey and Tiddles. And how, when Goochie interceded, a man wearing coveralls and a headset had dashed out of the back of the truck and rewarded him with ten dollars.

"Goochie weren't no hero." Rainbow laughed in a high, squeaky way that sounded as though he were hyperventilating. "It was just that Smokey and Tiddles were pushing each other around in front of the bench where he was sitting. When they got too close, Goochie stuck his foot out and tripped Tiddles to keep him from steppin' on his shoes." Rainbow laughed again, remembering. "Goochie was always particular about his shoes. They was leather. He said those leather shoes was all he had left from before he landed down here on the street."

Tina asked, "Did a lot of people see it happen?"

"What?"

"The fight. And the man giving Goochie ten dollars."

"I guess."

If other people from the street had witnessed Goochie's windfall, the money could have disappeared in worse ways than in a liquor store. Ten dollars was reason enough for murder in that part of Los Angeles.

"I'll see what I can find out about him, Rainbow." The morgue would be the first place she checked. "Describe him for me."

Rainbow pulled the bill of his cap an inch or two to the left. "He was about as tall as me. He had black pants and a sweatshirt. He didn't wear no hat, so he was kinda sun-burned. For a while there he had a Von's Supermarket cart, but it got stolen. I think he was glad. One of the wheels always ran sideways. And all he had in it was some card-board boxes, anyways." Rainbow's eyes shifted and fixed vacantly on the inactive sunburst fountain in the center of the mall.

"Anything else?"

Rainbow straightened his cap again. "He knew a lot about horses."

"Racehorses?"

His face screwed up and his eyes darted to Tina with something akin to a twinkle. "Yeah, racehorses. He weren't no cowboy."

Tina returned the grin of the unkempt man who sat on the wooden bench in front of her.

"He used to pick up a newspaper from behind the Times building every day and read the racing page," Rainbow said. "He'd sit there and study the daily lineup and write stuff in the margin, like he was going to place a bet on every race. When he got through doing that, he'd look up the results from the day before. 'Rainbow,' he'd say, and then thump me on the back. 'I'd have made fifteen thousand dollars yesterday.' Or more likely, he'd shake his head and tell me he would've lost twenty-five thousand. I told him it was a good thing he didn't have no money. At least that way he came out even."

Tina was becoming more than routinely interested in the details of Rainbow's story. If the facts had been simply that a street person who was known to be carrying money had disappeared, the outcome would be depressingly predictable. But the mention of Goochie's fondness for horses and the approximate time of his disappearance made her wonder if the San Marino police had been onto something after all.

She had not taken their theory seriously before. It seemed unlikely that the dead body in the statuary garden, and whoever killed him, had mistaken the Huntington for Santa Anita Race Track. But the local attitude seemed to be that there was no other explanation of why a derelict would have been found within the city limits unless he had come there by mistake.

Even assuming they were right, there was no real reason to believe that the murdered man was Goochie. But what other lead did they have?

Tina asked, "Rainbow, are you sure that Goochie was going to the racetrack the day he got the ten dollars?"

"That's what he said. And one thing about old Goochie, you could believe what he said."

"Try to remember. This is important. Tell me exactly what happened—what Goochie told you after the man gave him the money."

Rainbow pulled his cap down over his brow so that Tina could no longer see his eyes, but by the set of his mouth she could tell that he was making an effort to conjure up the memory of the last time he had seen his friend.

"He was holding the ten in one hand and the sports page of the paper in the other," Rainbow began. "And he said, 'Rainbow, I'm gonna turn this ten dollars into a thousand, and when I come back, I'm gonna buy you dinner, and a bottle of good red wine.'" Rainbow's mouth snapped shut and he was silent.

"Did he say anything else?"

Rainbow scratched the back of his neck and seemed to have drifted off somewhere.

Tina glanced at her watch. It was almost time to meet Eduardo. She was afraid that all Rainbow was going to be able to remember about Goochie's disappearance was the unfulfilled promise of an evening meal somewhere other than the Union Rescue Mission.

"He tore the racing page out," Rainbow surprisingly continued, "and threw the rest of the newspaper in that trash can." He pointed toward the bin where he had earlier been scavenging for empty soft-drink cans. He was silent again, but he left the hat pulled down.

"Rainbow, is there anything else—"

"Then," he interrupted in an almost animated tone, "he looked down at the racing page and laughed." Rainbow's fingers danced across the bill of his cap. "He said—like to himself—'Well, I'll be damned.'"

"Why did he say that?"

"Don't know. He just slapped the pocket where he'd put the money and he said, 'Rainbow, I've got a feeling I just might be able to get more than a thousand dollars for this ten.'"

"Do you think he knew something about one of the horses?"

"He didn't say. He just left."

Rainbow pushed the cap to the back of his head and yawned.

Tina tried to hold his attention a while longer. "Is there anything else you can tell me about Goochie?"

Rainbow thought for a moment, then said, "He didn't like oatmeal."

"No, I mean about his appearance. The way he looked."

"His hair was brown. Guess his eyes were, too."

"How old was he?"

"Forties, maybe."

"Where did he come from?"

"Down by Union Station. Said he used to have a refrigerator carton out by the Amtrack car barn."

"Where did he live before that? Where did he live when his leather shoes were new?"

"I don't know. We never talked about that."

"What was his name, before?"

"He never told me."

"Why'd they call him Goochie?"

"He *did* tell me that." He fingered the bill of his cap again. "But I don't remember."

He stood and picked up his sack of aluminum cans. "Guess I'll go on over to the can crusher." Then he turned and grinned at Tina. "If you find old Gooch, tell him I'm still waiting for dinner, and I'm getting hungry."

"Sure, I'll tell him." But Tina knew that if she found Goochie, the chances were that he would be beyond hearing anything she had to say.

"Wait a minute, Rainbow." Tina reached in her purse for her billfold. She quickly looked around to make sure no one was watching before she took out a ten-dollar bill. In a low voice, she said, "Here. Go buy yourself that dinner and bottle of wine tonight."

Rainbow snatched the bill from her hand, not out of rudeness, but to shorten the time the money was exposed to sight. "Thanks," he said without looking at her.

He sat down on the bench he had just vacated and unlaced one of his high tops and pulled it off. Folding the bill into a tiny square, he pressed it into the toe, then put the shoe back on and tied the strings in a double-bow knot. When he stood, he picked up his sack of empty cans again, intent on taking them to the crusher and turning them to coins.

"Well, I'll see you around." Tina started back across the mall.

She knew better than to get personally involved in a case. Every time she did, she got this same lump in her throat, and the same feeling of helplessness.

Her training officer, Max Sutherland, a fifteen-year veteran on the force, had warned her over and over while she was on probation. "Don't get involved. You can't solve all the problems in the world by yourself. Just do your job." Max, she learned later, was not the best person to give that advice. During the five years when he was assigned to Juvenile Division, he and his wife had adopted three abandoned children.

Tina secretly hoped she never had to work juvenile. She was not sure she would ever be strong enough to deal with cases like some she had heard about. When she worked the precinct desk, it was hard enough just to read through some of the reports. The last one before she was transferred to detective trainee, she remembered, was about an unapprehended woman who had delivered her own baby in the rest room of a Taco Bell. And left it there. And the impersonal black-and-white pictures of battered and maimed children were impossible to forget. She knew you had to be able to get past all that in order to be a good cop, but she was not sure she would ever be able to.

Eduardo was just pulling up and parking in the bus stop in front of City Hall South when she came through the front doors from the mall. She hurried down the steps and jumped in beside her partner as a City Transit Company bus honked at them to move and the driver yelled angry obscenities through the open side window.

Tiny rivulets of water still ran down the windshield of the three-year-old unmarked Plymouth from the recent servicing and washing, and the interior had been cleared of debris and vacuumed. Tina stretched her legs in front of her under the dashboard—an area which, for the time being, was free of taco wrappers and empty plastic soft-drink cups.

She asked, "Where are we headed?"

"The Huntington," Eduardo said. "The graffiti artist struck again. One of the statues is now wearing a green vest."

Tina felt deflated. That did not fit in with her new theory. How did the spray paint fit in if Goochie was the victim and the perp was someone from the street who had followed him for the ten dollars? But that didn't jibe either. The time was wrong. The murder had apparently occurred late at night. Goochie had left the mall during the morn-

ing. If he was at the Huntington by mistake, what had be
been doing, and where had he been all day? And was it even
the same day? That would be easy enough to trace. She
could check city permits and find out who had been filming in front of City Hall the day before the murder victim
was discovered. Then she would contact the camera crew to
see if any of them remembered the incident of the ten-dollar
bill. It was worth a few telephone calls.

"At least there was no dead body left behind this time,"
Eduardo said.

"I wonder if they're really connected?"

"What?"

"The vandalism and the murder."

Eduardo shrugged. "It makes as much sense as the
guard's theory that it was a teenaged sex cult."

"Come on now, Eduardo, I'm doing serious work here."
She jabbed her partner gently in the ribs. "Why do we think
they're connected?"

"We don't know that they *are* connected. All we know is
that there's never been any vandalism—or a murder—at the
Huntington before, and they both took place on the same
night."

Eduardo took First Street across the overpass of the
Harbor Freeway, then veered off past Olivera Street to
where it dead-ended at Union Station. Before he could turn
left onto Alameda, they were stopped by a red light.

"But this time we have vandalism without murder," Tina
said. "The most important thing we have to do is identify
the body."

"Any suggestions? We've run prints and come up empty.
And unfortunately, he wasn't wearing any clothes that
would give us a clue."

"I know, but I may have someone who can make an
identification." Despite all the inconsistencies and unan-
swered questions, the possibility that the nude body at the
Huntington was Goochie seemed stronger the more Tina
thought about it.

"Did you get a lead from your friend Rainbow?" The light changed and Eduardo turned left on Alameda, then right on Macy.

"Maybe. His buddy, who was a big horse-racing fan, is missing, and he'd just had a very public ten-dollar windfall."

"So?"

"So, he had money, and Rainbow said there was something on the sports page that day that he was especially interested in. Maybe he knew something about one of the horses. He used to pick up a newspaper from behind the Times building every morning to read the racing lineup. Betting on the horses is probably why he ended up on the street. Who knows about gamblers? But one thing is for sure—they always think *this* time they're going to win. Seems logical that he planned to take his money to the track and get rich."

"Okay, but then why did he go to the Huntington to get himself killed?"

"I don't know." Tina slid further down in the seat.

They drove a block farther before Eduardo said, "What the hell. You think we ought to go back and pick up your ole buddy Rainbow?"

"We don't have anything else to go on."

There was no place to turn around before the next traffic light beyond the railroad yards. Tina looked out the window, thinking of the refrigerator carton that had been Goochie's home.

She shivered and thought of her father and the many times he had come home with empty pockets from the racetrack. Everything in life seemed to be just a matter of degree.

TWELVE

THERE WERE NO window coverings of any kind in the master bedroom of Joseph and Georgene Dodson's house in San Marino. Dense foliage around a patio provided privacy and prevented glare. By the time the morning sun reached the flagstone terrace, the light had been filtered through the variegated greenery of palm fronds, oak branches, and hibiscus leaves until it was reduced to a pale citrus shade. The two outside walls of the room were floor-to-ceiling plate glass that extended to a corner fireplace of off-white stucco. The only reminder that the room was enclosed was a sliding glass door.

The remaining walls were the same creamy shade as the fireplace, as were the carpet, plush twin sofas, matching cushioned chairs, ceramic lamps on all-but-invisible Plexiglas tables, and a paper-mâché sculpture of a running horse with flying mane and tail that hung above the bed.

Andrea woke tangled in a puffed and downy white coverlet with no idea where she was. Facing away from the windows, her initial impression was of still being in the airplane somewhere inside a cloud bank. The only splash of color was her own red hair hanging down in front of her eyes, until she raised on one elbow and was confronted with the brilliant greenery outside. Her revised feeling was of having been dropped into a Gauguin painting. She would not have been surprised to see a tiger saunter through the lowest branches of hibiscus and stretch out on the patio's wicker chaise longue.

Reaching for her watch on the bedside table, she caught sight of her coat through the partly open closet door, and reality began to seep in. She sighed at finding herself alone in what seemed a half-acre bed and knowing that Aldo was still in Florence with no assured time of leaving. The sigh became a groan as she remembered the embarrassment of the bikini episode.

Georgene's sister, Sarah Anderson, had tried not to stare at Andrea's coat that remained tightly buttoned even inside the house. "We can adjust the thermostat if it's too cool in here for you," she had said.

"Oh, no, it's fine." Andrea was sure she had smiled. But she was also sure she had clutched the collar even closer around her neck.

"This is the room Georgene wanted you to have. The driver will be in with your luggage in just a few minutes." Sarah stood uncertainly in the doorway of the master bedroom, as though wanting to offer assistance but unsure of what kind Andrea needed. "When you get organized, I'll be in the lounge next to the kitchen. Maybe you'd like a cup of hot tea or something." And she had retreated noiselessly down the carpeted corridor.

The moment Andrea was alone, she retrieved the wrinkled woolen pants and heavy sweater from her carryon bag and hastily pulled them on over her bikini. She knew that these bulky clothes—which had been well-suited to the freezing weather of London, and, she was now convinced, would have been adequate on an Arctic expedition—would only compound the impression that she was either anemic or eccentric. Still, she decided, it was better not to even try to explain some things, and had gone to join her hostess.

But now, in the bright light of morning, the memory of the night before was decidedly uncomfortable. The thought of Sarah's solicitation and her son Benjamin's large suspicious eyes following her about was enough to get Andrea out of bed and into the shower.

There were no window coverings in the bathroom, either. A bamboo fence enclosed a tropical garden outside the sunken tub and open shower. The effect was of bathing under a waterfall on a private island, and a very long way from the tiny stall shower of Andrea's flat in London.

Stacks of white towels and a fleecy terrycloth robe had been laid out for her. She made short work of the shower and quickly climbed into the robe feeling strangely exposed with all the open space around her.

Setting her watch to Pacific time, she calculated that she had more than two hours before she was to meet Harvey Latimer, the art curator, for lunch in the tea room at the Huntington. She had been too excited to eat the evening meal on the plane the night before. Now, she was hungry, and two hours until lunch seemed torturous.

Taking care to be appropriately dressed this time, she stepped into a feather-weight wool dress of green and blue Paisley, tied her hair back with a green silk scarf, and ventured out into the hallway.

The bedroom wing of the Dodsons' rambling architectural showcase home was connected by a glass-sided hallway to the dining and kitchen area. Sarah had told Andrea the night before that she would find the housekeeper there.

A plump young woman of nineteen or twenty, with frizzed blond hair that looked as though it had the tensile strength of screen-door wire, was the only person in sight when Andrea entered the kitchen.

"Hi. Great dress," the blue-eyed girl said.

"Thanks." Andrea returned the girl's smile.

The housekeeper, if that was who she was, wore faded jeans, a red T-shirt, and a striped bib-apron, and was taking a baking sheet of something that smelled of yeast dough, sugar, and cinnamon from the oven. When she had the pan safely on a cooling rack, she said, "You're Andrea, the English artist."

"Right, I'm Andrea—but wrong, I'm not English, and I'm not an artist in the sense you probably mean."

"Whatever. The artsy person from England." She grinned, put her hands on her rounded hips, and rotated her shoulders in a suggestive parody. "I'm Holly the happy hooker." Then she shrugged and brushed floury hand prints from her jeans that conformed unflatteringly to her thighs and hips. "Don't I wish," she said.

Andrea laughed. Whoever this girl was, she liked her immediately.

"Make that happy housekeeper. But the alliteration—not to mention the fantasy—comes off better the other way." She quickly transferred a hot cinnamon roll to a small plate with her fingers. "Want one of these?"

"Umm, yes." They smelled wonderful. Andrea took the plate Holly held out to her.

"There's coffee on the counter by the sink."

A porcelain cup and saucer had been set out. Andrea helped herself.

"Sarah had an appointment with her shrink, and Benjamin's out by the pool taking an art lesson. He and his teacher, Nikki Yamaguchi, will walk you to the Huntington when you're ready to go."

"I could probably find my way, but that will be a help." Andrea sat on a pale oak stool across a large butcher-block worktable from Holly. There were no forks or napkins in sight, so she ate the delicious cinnamon roll with her hands and licked the sugar from her fingertips.

Andrea was surprised to learn that Sarah was seeing a psychiatrist. From Holly's offhand comment, it apparently was an ongoing arrangement. Andrea wondered if what she had believed was just innate shyness in Georgene Dodson's sister was instead a symptom of some more significant problem. Or, perhaps, seeing a psychiatrist was merely fashionable in California for women who could afford it. In either case, it was not something she felt she could question Holly about. Instead, she fastened on the information about Benjamin. "Does Benjamin have artistic ability?"

"Who knows? Nikki, his tutor, seems to think so, though he'd choke before he said as much. But Benjamin is already as good as Nikki, it seems to me. They're like Salieri and Mozart—did you see the movie *Amadeus?* I'm the one that suggested the art lessons. Sometimes I wonder if I made a mistake." She took a long-handled spatula from a drawer and transferred the remaining cinnamon buns from the baking sheet to a cooling rack. "Oh, well—it's only until the first of the year, then Nikki will be going back east to school. Until then, I can keep him in check. And art lessons still seem like a better way for the kid to spend his time than playing video games all day."

It was midmorning of a weekday, and Andrea felt safe in asking, "Does Benjamin need a tutor? Doesn't he go to school?"

For the first time, Holly seemed evasive. "He did, back home. But—well, we haven't been here long enough for him to get enrolled." She put a second cinnamon bun on Andrea's plate. "Here, have another." This time she handed her a paper towel. "Sticky, aren't they?"

"They're marvelous." Andrea could not remember anything that had tasted so good, and the coffee was perfect with a slight hint of vanilla. "Are you really the housekeeper?"

"Hard to believe, isn't it?" Holly grinned as she expertly patted a ball of dough into a rectangle. "I'm sort of in charge, but there's a cleaning crew that comes in twice a week and does that kind of stuff. What I do mostly is cook."

"And wonderfully well." Andrea picked up a last crumb from her plate.

"Yeah, I know." She put a glob of butter in the center of the flattened dough, and spread it evenly with her fingers. "I work for Sarah, not Georgene. When we got here three weeks ago, Georgene was between housekeepers—*again,* so the word is—and I'm just filling in until she gets back."

"I think Georgene told me that Sarah lives in Kentucky."

"Yeah. I live with her and Benjamin and go to school at Kentucky U. I'm a sort of home-grown au pair for the kid and a cook and dust-buster for Sarah in exchange for room and board."

"What are you studying at the university?" Andrea watched the big, confident girl deftly sprinkle the dough with a mixture of spices and sugar.

"General stuff. I don't think I'll finish. It's all a bunch of crap." She formed the dough into a long roll then began to slice it in inch-thick rounds. "The only thing I've learned was in my food science classes. And what I learned there was not how to cook. I think talent, in whatever form, is...innate...don't you? Is that the right word? Anyway, just having access to the big kitchen there convinced me that what I want to do with my life is to be an internationally acclaimed 'down-home' chef." She placed the unbaked buns on a baking sheet and put them in the oven. "My instructor gave me a letter of recommendation to the head cookie cutter at the Ritz Carlton. If he's smart enough to offer me a job, I may just stay here."

She wiped her hands on her apron, and went to look out the sliding glass door at the teenaged tutor and his young pupil, who were seated at a round glass-topped table at the edge of the pool. "It depends on whether the change of scene from Kentucky to California has the effect on Ben it's supposed to have."

Andrea was surprised at Holly's look of concern. The young woman made no explanation of her comment about Benjamin, and as she opened the door, she was her usual blustery, bossy self again.

"Hey, you guys!" Her voice would have carried well into the next block. "Come on in if you want one of the world's best cinnamon buns."

There was something basically unappealing about Nikki Yamaguchi. He rushed in the door ahead of his small charge and grabbed a bun without acknowledging Holly or Andrea.

"Help yourself." Holly's voice was heavy with irony.

Nikki grinned. "Thanks," he managed to say with his mouth full.

As she poured a glass of milk for Benjamin and handed him a cinnamon bun on a paper towel, she introduced Nikki and Andrea.

Nikki took the carton from Holly and poured himself a glass of milk. His opening line to Andrea was, "The kid and I have been deputized to escort you to the scene of the crime." With that, he drew himself up to his full five-foot-seven and with a demonic expression, whirled toward Benjamin with outstretched hands aimed at the boy's throat. "There was a murder committed there," he said, "and maybe the murderer is still running loose in the neighborhood."

Benjamin had not cried out, but he took several steps backward until he collided with the safety of Holly's ample legs.

Holly swung at Nikki, scoring a substantial blow to his shoulder, and causing him to slosh milk on the kitchen floor. "What did I tell you about that?"

It was Nikki's turn to retreat—which he did, with the same unsavory grin as before.

"No more of that crap or I'll knock you sideways." Holly was convincing, not only in tone of voice, but in girth and stature. "And clean up that mess." She threw a sponge at Nikki and stood over him as he wiped up the spilled milk with as much bravado as he could muster.

When Benjamin had finished eating, and taken a few sips of milk—despite Holly's urging that he drink it all—Andrea and her escorts set out for the art museum.

Outside, as they stepped down from the curb in front of the Dodsons' house, Nikki pointed to the high fence across the street. "That's the back end of the Huntington property," he told Andrea. "If you didn't have on those high heels, I'd show you how to climb the fence. It's about half as far to the art museum from here than it is if you go all the way around."

"Thanks," Andrea said. "But I'd rather stick to the sidewalk."

"Do you think you'll need a car while you're here?"

"I don't see why I would. The entrance is only about a block past the bend, isn't it?"

"Yes, but just in case…" Nikki reached in his pocket for a business card that he handed to Andrea. "This is my father." The card read "Takashi Yamaguchi, President/General Manager, Western Region Honda Motor Company." "My uncle, who is one of the founders of Honda, still lives in Japan. He sent my dad over here to take care of this part of America. Anyway, if you're in the market for a car, I can get you a deal." Nikki's expression was almost comically self-important.

"Sounds as though you're planning to follow in your father's footsteps."

"He'd like nothing better. But I'd rather be an artist."

"Are you any good?" Andrea decided Nikki's conceit deserved the blunt question.

"Yes. I'm good." Then, for the first time, Nikki spoke with a sincerity that was disturbing because of its undertones of bitterness and even jealousy. "I'm good—technically, very good. But, though I hate to admit it, that kid is better. He's really talented." He nodded toward Benjamin, who was walking several paces ahead of them, kicking at the dry leaves that had collected next to the curb.

Quickly changing the subject, Nikki told Andrea, "My dad used to bring me here to the Huntington every Sunday. He'd point out the library and the gardens and the mansion and say—all this Nikko, all this from hardware and hard work."

"Hardware? I thought the Huntington fortune came from railroads—is that what you mean by hardware?"

"Mostly railroads." Nikki was pleased to see that Andrea was interested in his story. "But he started in actual hardware—hammers and nails and all that kind of stuff. The story I heard from my father, ad nauseam, I might add, was that Henry Huntington's Uncle Collis came to California from the east coast during the gold rush. In Sacramento, Collis met up with a guy named Mark Hopkins and they went into business together. As my father put it, they sold the miners the gear including those silly sieve pans that most of those get-rich-quick johnnies used to go broke with.''

Andrea laughed. She was being pulled into Nikki's story despite herself.

''The railroad—transportation—was the point of my dad's story. Collis Huntington started developing an overland railroad because he could see a need to get more gear shipped to California. Plus, there had to be a way to bring more people to California to buy the stuff he had shipped.''

''Seems like a sound idea.''

''Then, he began to realize that he needed more help, because by now Mark Hopkins was busy with a hotel he built in San Francisco. I suppose it took a lot of time getting all those towels monogrammed. So, Uncle Collis sent for his nephew, Henry, to come help out.''

Nikki led the way through a side gate of the parking lot.

''And together they built the Southern Pacific Railroad,'' Andrea contributed, in an effort to bring the story to an end.

''Right. And they both became super tycoons,'' Nikki said. ''The moral is—according to my father—that just like Henry Huntington, who came from New York to California to help his Uncle Collis crisscross the United States with railroad tracks, my father came from Japan to California to help his brother crisscross the freeways with Hondas.''

Surprisingly, Nikki lapsed into a glum silence. The would-be artist was apparently contemplating his future in the automobile business. Somehow, being a tycoon did not seem to be such a terrible fate, Andrea thought.

Ahead was the entrance to the Huntington. A bronze, two-tiered fountain splashed gently near the sidewalk. Wide, low steps led to a covered veranda. A glass-enclosed information booth stood in the center, and in the booth was a uniformed guard. Andrea identified herself to him.

"Miss Perkins. Yes." The guard consulted a clipboard. He was a dapper gentleman of retirement age who seemed to view his role as a representative of authority at the Huntington with mixed pride and condescension. "Mr. Latimer asked me to escort you to the tea room, but..." He made a production of taking a watch from his inside pocket and snapping open the lid.

"I know I'm early," Andrea said hurriedly. "I'd be happy just to look around for a while. I'm sure I can locate the tea room."

"Not a bit of it." Having established that she had caused some small inconvenience, the guard was now prepared to be magnanimous. "I'll be just a moment while I get someone to take my place here." He exited the booth and hurried into the office building.

Nikki Yamaguchi was deep in conversation with a group of Japanese tourists who were waiting for the library to officially open. Andrea felt sure he must be giving them the benefit of his self-styled expertise in things both Oriental and Occidental.

Benjamin stood by himself, studying the cover of a brochure he had taken from a rack near the guard's station. Andrea was glad to have the opportunity for a moment alone with him. She realized she had not yet exchanged a word with the child.

"Benjamin, have you ever been through the Huntington art museum?"

Without looking up or making a verbal reply, he nodded that he had.

Except when they first met at the airport, Andrea could not recall hearing the boy speak at all. If he had said anything during the ride from the airport or even after they arrived in San Marino, she had no memory of it. But then she had been too absorbed in her own problems to pay much attention to him.

Pointing to the cover piece of the brochure, which was a reproduction of Gainsborough's portrait of a young boy in a blue satin suit, she asked, "Have you seen *The Blue Boy*?"

Benjamin gave her another affirmative nod.

"Did you like the painting?"

"Not much," he said.

"Why not? What didn't you like about it?"

"Too much blue."

Andrea laughed. "You're not the first one to come to that conclusion. A lot of experts have said the same thing." She pressed her luck. "Do you know why Gainsborough used so much blue?"

"He shouldn't have."

"I'm inclined to agree with you. But there was a reason. He was trying to prove a point. All his artist friends said it was impossible to use blue as the major color in a painting—it was too cold. Everyone had always insisted that it was impossible to come up with a cool shade that would work as the dominant color in a painting. But Gainsborough said, I can do it. They said, no you can't. He said, I'll show you. They said, put your money where your mouth is. He said . . ."

"Miss Perkins." The guard emerged from the office building, followed by his replacement. "Well, now. Almost everything is taken care of." He unlocked the entrance cubicle and began to make a notation on the clipboard. "Be with you in a moment."

At that same time, Andrea saw that Nikki had tired of the Japanese tourists—or they of him—and was bearing down on Benjamin.

"Benjamin!" He made a grotesque face and said in a fiendish voice, "While we're here, do you want me to show you where they found the dead body?"

Benjamin turned away from the older boy and ducked his head.

Andrea felt a surge of anger. "You're a real comic, aren't you?"

"It was *supposed* to be *funny*." Nikki grinned. "It was just a joke."

Leaning down so that the older boy could not hear, Andrea said to Benjamin, "While I'm here, would you like to come with me sometime and see the kind of work I do?"

He shrugged and gave a sort of half nod, then ran off toward the gate where they had entered. Nikki followed after him, not hurrying, exiting with a sort of ambling swagger.

"Sorry to have kept you waiting." The guard motioned that she should precede him through the veranda to the sidewalk in front of the library.

"I'm Archie Chambers," he introduced himself. "I dare say it will come as no surprise that I'm British. Even though I've lived in California for the past twenty years, people still say that as soon as they hear me speak, there is no disguising my origin."

Andrea thought it must have taken a lot of work to preserve his accent for that length of time.

"I'm delighted to be the first to welcome you to the Huntington. Especially as your mission here is to spruce up the masterwork of my fellow East Anglian."

Andrea made an effort to respond to Archie's account of growing up in the same area of England where Gainsborough and Constable had lived and painted. She smiled and nodded appropriately, but her attention was on the lavish beauty of the lawns and gardens.

As it was still a few minutes before the Huntington was due to be open to visitors, they saw no other people until they reached the sidewalk in front of the statuary garden.

"I'm sure you've heard about the horrible incident that happened here." Archie lowered his voice. "I won't burden you with my personal theory of who was responsible for the murder of the unfortunate man who was found stripped naked in front of the fountain. But as you can see, there is a new indication that teenaged vandals were involved." Archie pointed out the likeness of an Italian gentleman whose stone jacket had been painted a bright green.

A woman in a lilac sweater with a matching jacket thrown over her shoulders stood with two men in dark-colored business suits near the statue examining the damage.

"Ah! There's Mr. Latimer," Archie said.

A tall man of about thirty watched Archie and Andrea cross from the sidewalk. More accurately, he watched Andrea. He reminded her of someone she had known before. There was something disturbingly familiar about his black hair and bronzed skin, and his sultry eyes that appreciatively took her in from the green scarf in her hair to her shoe tops. His blatant admiration brought back disquieting memories of a modernist painter she had known when she worked on a project at the Prado in Madrid. More than known, in point of fact. For one sizzling summer season they had spent every free moment together when she lived in an apartment on the Calle de Alcala. When her work was completed and it was time for her to leave, they had both sworn that they would find a way to be together again, that nothing would keep them apart. But their resolve had faded like the summer heat and the sweet, sad sounds of a flamenco guitar.

Still, seeing the same Latin sensuality in the face of the man walking toward her made her catch her breath and shut out the presence of the man and the woman behind him.

"Hello, Archie. I see you've had a problem here again," he addressed the guard without once taking his eyes from Andrea.

Distracted, Archie was waiting for the second man and the woman to join them. "Hello, Detective Lopez," he answered, "yes, the vandal has made a return visit." Following Eduardo's eyes, he said, "Oh, sorry. Detective Lopez, this is Miss Perkins."

Eduardo bent slightly at the waist in a courtly bow. "Miss Perkins. My pleasure."

"How do you do, Detective Lopez."

"Mr. Latimer!" Archie motioned to a rather rotund, balding man whose pallor suggested he spent most of his time indoors under artificial light. "This is Miss Perkins. From England." Realizing he had committed a breach of etiquette by failing to introduce the female first, Archie said, "Forgive me, Miss Roberson," he amended. "Miss Perkins, I'd like you to meet Miss Roberson."

"Detective Roberson, actually," Tina said.

Andrea and Tina acknowledged each other with frank looks of appraisal.

Harvey Latimer welcomed Andrea on behalf of the entire board of the Huntington, and in particular the restoration and authentication curatorial staff.

Tina Roberson's face remained expressionless. She waited a moment, but her partner had still not shifted his gaze from the redhead, so she gave him a sharp jab below the rib cage. "Come on, *hermoso,* we've got work to do."

THIRTEEN

"ONE MOMENT, Tina. Before we go"—Eduardo stopped his partner with a hand on her elbow—"no reason why we shouldn't tell Mr. Latimer and Archie what we learned this morning at the morgue."

Both men reacted as Eduardo expected. They were obviously eager to hear any "inside" police information. And by detaining them—Andrea's host and her escort—he had kept her from leaving, too.

"We still have only a partial I.D.," Tina said. "We don't have the victim's legal name."

"These gentlemen may be able to help us." Eduardo spoke with a gravity that implied the input of the guard and the curator was the key to solving the crime. "One of them may have seen something, or may have some thought or knowledge about the murder that they didn't know they had."

Both Archie and Harvey Latimer nodded solemnly.

Tina rolled her eyes upward. She did not share her partner's flair for the dramatic.

Eduardo operated on the theory that most "civilians" expected a detective to be a version of what they had seen in the movies or on TV. He felt he was performing a public relations function for the department when he took on the trench-coat image.

The truth was, most of their investigations were conducted by sitting behind a desk and applying the index finger to the push buttons of the telephone.

On a simple neighborhood complaint, like the robbery of two cartons of chorizo sausage from Armando Estrada's restaurant in El Sereno, they conducted a scene-of-the-crime investigation. But more often, detective work in Los Angeles—because of the heavy caseload, the distances involved, and the vast population—was of necessity a series of endless telephone calls that were recorded, transcribed, and filed.

This was especially true when the crime they were investigating was murder. Detectives made calls to witnesses, calls to family members and friends of the victim, calls to family members and friends of the suspects, calls to forensics, and to a network of other police departments. Then there were hours spent in front of computers cross-checking the records of suspects and their known companions, consulting both city and county court records, and, sometimes, contacting authorities out of the state or out of the country.

Granted, the murder at the Huntington was somewhat different. Tina and Eduardo had been called in as consultants in a neighboring city. San Marino police facilities were understandably limited considering the small size of the affluent residential community they served. The file on known criminals could be kept in one folder.

"Why don't you tell them what we discovered this morning at the morgue, Tina?" Eduardo was determined to draw her in.

Harvey Latimer and Archie Chambers looked at Tina expectantly. Andrea had the expression of someone who has walked into an animated conversation midway.

With an impatient glance at her partner, Tina said, "This morning, an acquaintance of the deceased positively identified the victim as a resident of the street who was known to inhabit the City Hall area and who went by the name of Goochie. Other than the fact that he was a Caucasian male in his mid-forties, that's all the information we have."

"I knew it," the guard said quickly. "I knew he didn't belong here. When I first saw him"—Archie was not likely to let anyone forget that it was he who discovered the body—"even though he was lying there with no clothes on, when I saw those filthy hands and feet and face, I knew immediately that he had no business in San Marino."

"Detective Lopez—" Harvey Latimer began, but the words were drowned out by the sudden sound of a leaf-blower being wielded by one of the gardening staff. The man in green coveralls seemed determined to banish every twig and fallen leaf from the area around a nearby nineteenth-century marble statue of a bewinged toddler placing a scarf over the eyes of a comely young woman. The plaque on the pedestal read "Cupid Blindfolding Youth."

Latimer motioned toward a group of tables on the patio in front of the snack bar, indicating that the small group should reconvene there. Then, leaning close to Andrea and raising his voice above the annoying sound of the gasoline motor, he said, "I hope you won't mind a slight delay before lunch."

"Not at all." She was early for their appointment at any rate, and she certainly was not hungry after two of Holly's cinnamon buns.

The five of them crossed the grassy open space of the statuary garden. On the sidewalk, only two people could walk comfortably side by side between the rows of marigold and chrysanthemum beds. Eduardo had contrived to lead the way next to Andrea. "Do you live near here, Miss Perkins?"

She told him no, that this was her first trip to California, and that she had arrived only the night before.

"Are you here on a visit?"

"No. I'm going to be working here."

"In San Marino?"

"Here at the Huntington."

"That sounds pleasant." Eduardo guessed that if he flat out asked where she was staying, he would get a vague answer or no response at all, and so he said, "I don't know where you're staying, but you'll probably have to commute, and the freeways here can be kind of tricky. If you need any maps of the area, the police department has—"

"Oh. No, thank you. That's very nice. But I doubt that I'll be doing any driving."

Eduardo could not immediately think of a way to get a specific answer to where she was staying, and so he said, "Are you doing research in the library?"

"No, I'm here to work on an art-restoration project."

"Fascinating. I have a great interest in art."

Tina, who was walking behind them next to Harvey Latimer and in front of Archie, said, "It's true, Miss Perkins. He's what you might call an untrained connoisseur." Sweetly, to her partner, she prompted, "Eduardo, tell her about that painting you admire so much in Pepe's restaurant. The girl with the purple—"

"I didn't get your first name," Eduardo hurriedly broke in.

"It's Andrea."

"ANN-drea." He contemplated the sound of his own voice. "ANN-drea... it has a softness, a lilt. It suits you."

"Would everyone like coffee?" Harvey Latimer chose a round table in the sunshine for the small group.

Archie Chambers, taking the cue from the curator, did not wait for an answer. He scurried off to give the order, then hurried back so as not to miss any of the conversation.

Eduardo held out a chair for Andrea. The others seated themselves. Harvey Latimer made an attempt to assist Tina, but she already had impatiently dropped the strap of her shoulder bag over the back of a different chair.

"How did you track down this... friend of the victim?" Latimer asked when they were all settled.

"He's one of Officer Roberson's informants," Eduardo answered.

"Rainbow is not exactly an informant." Tina hastily added, "He's just a poor guy who lives on the street."

Rainbow had never been added to the list of registered informants. It was not that he would intentionally give misleading information; it was just that his memory was clouded with his own demons and fantasies and not to be trusted.

The registered informants that the detective division used on a regular basis were thoroughly checked for prior arrests and outstanding warrants before they were considered reliable. Having a record did not necessarily make them unreliable; it was just a matter of clarifying their motive for cooperating with the police department. The best informant was someone who was genuinely interested in cleaning up his own neighborhood. But there was always the possibility that the department would receive misleading information that was motivated by revenge or personal profit. One drug dealer, for instance, might inform on a competitor just to get him out of his territory. But the great danger in acting on unsolicited information was that the informant might be setting up the officer to be ambushed. He might be led into a dark alley or an empty house with the promise of damning evidence that would convince the district attorney's office to prosecute a pesky case. But when the officer got there, he might be shown the barrel of a gun pointed in his direction or the blade of a knife aimed at his throat instead. For that reason, strict department policy was that no sworn personnel were to ever meet with an informant alone.

Rainbow would never fit into any of the specified categories of informants. His only motivation in contacting Tina was that he missed his friend.

"I got to know this guy when I worked patrol in Metro Division." Tina emptied a packet of artificial sweetener into the cup of coffee that Archie set in front of her. She went on to explain briefly how Rainbow's concern for Goochie had led them to take him to the morgue to see if he could identify the body. She did not describe Rainbow's bleary fish eyes streaming with tears when he recognized his lifeless companion. Nor did she mention how her own eyes had burned and her throat had ached when she saw the grief on his face. She knew that the companionship of his friend was the only thing of value that Rainbow had left. And now that, too, was gone.

Harvey Latimer asked, "Is there a possibility that this person who identified the body might be the murderer?"

"No. For one thing, he wouldn't have had bus fare to get this far from downtown." Tina added, "Just as a matter of routine, we checked with the patrol officer on duty that night. Rainbow didn't leave the mall."

"The victim had come into a small amount of cash the day he was killed," Eduardo told the group around the table. "He said he was going to Santa Anita and get rich. That's about all the information we have, so far. We think someone downtown may have known he had some money and followed him. Or, it's possible that he did come out a winner at the track. He might have taken up with a stranger he met there who could have been the murderer."

Tina stood and retrieved her shoulder bag from the back of the chair. "I suppose we'd better be on our way. Right, partner?"

Eduardo checked his watch. "I'm afraid so."

They had an appointment in fifteen minutes with the grounds keeper at Santa Anita. When they had called him earlier, he mentioned some discarded clothes that had been found on the property.

The others at the table stood to leave as well.

"But what about the statue? What about the red paint I found on the statue the same morning I found the body?" Archie Chambers had trouble accepting the theory of simple robbery. "And then just last night, someone got into the grounds and painted another statue green. Don't you think there's some connection?"

"Archie, so far there doesn't seem to be a relationship between the statue and the murder," Tina said. "I'm afraid what you've got here is just a midnight vandal," she said. "It would probably be worthwhile for the nighttime guard to hang around the statuary garden the next few weeks and see what he comes up with."

Harvey Latimer asked Archie, "Who's on night duty?"

"I'm scheduled, starting tomorrow." Archie straightened his shoulders and gave a curt nod. "You can be sure I'll keep my eyes open."

Eduardo and Andrea were a few steps behind the others. "ANN-drea, I hope they found a convenient place for you to stay while you're here. I know the nearest decent hotels are in Arcadia and at the best of times public transportation or taxi service is not very reliable, and during racing season the traffic between here and there can be a real problem."

It was not too subtle, but it got the answer Eduardo wanted.

"Actually, I'm staying just across the fence, as the crow flies." She told him that she was a houseguest of the Dodsons—that Mrs. Dodson was a member of the Huntington board and had insisted that she stay there.

"I might need to get in touch with you again."

"Whatever for?" She laughed. "I wasn't even in this country when all this happened."

It was obvious he was reaching. What he came up with was, "But if you're going to be working here at the Huntington, you may notice something—overhear something." He stopped short of asking for her address, but handed her his card. "Just in case, this is where you can get in touch with me. Will you do it?"

"I promise that if I come across anything that even vaguely appears to be a clue, I'll let you know."

"Good. Well, then, maybe I'll see you again."

"Maybe."

The statue with the newly painted green jacket was now covered with a large sheet of opaque plastic. Two workmen had left their pickup truck at the curb and seemed to be trying to decide the best way to remove the damaged work of art.

"You men!" Harvey Latimer went running toward them with Archie Chambers close behind. "You'll need to get more help with that. Two of you can't move it. I want it taken to the workroom, and I don't want it chipped or damaged in any way!'' Over his shoulder he called back to Andrea, ''Sorry, Miss Perkins. I'll have to see how they plan to do this.''

She waved to him to go ahead.

''We're going to be late, Eduardo,'' Tina said sternly. For Andrea, she managed a small smile. ''Nice to have met you, Miss Perkins.''

''And you, Detective Roberson.''

''More than likely we'll be back to talk with Archie and Harvey Latimer again,'' Eduardo said, ''I'll look forward to seeing you then.''

Tina took his arm and they hurried down the sidewalk.

Andrea watched them leave.

Eduardo Lopez was nothing at all like the artist she had known in Madrid. There was none of the subtlety, none of the sensitivity, certainly none of the artistic temperament— that in all truth became wearing after a while. Strange, though, that at first glance she had been reminded of that summer she worked at the Prado.

The detective and the artist did have in common the lean, muscular build and the bronze cast to their skin—and the hands. They both had large, strong hands. She tried to remember. Was it only his appearance that had attracted her to the Spanish artist? Was it just his physical being that she had missed so desperately when the summer was over?

Eduardo turned and waved just as they reached the corner, then he was out of sight.

Andrea suddenly had an absurd feeling of loss.

FOURTEEN

ON DAYS WHEN the horses were running at Santa Anita Race Track in Arcadia, the four eastbound lanes of Huntington Drive were packed solid for an hour before post time. The flow of traffic moved surprisingly well once it left San Marino and entered Arcadia. Past the dividing line of Rosemead Boulevard, traffic officers in neat brown uniforms were on every corner, and the stoplights were timed perfectly to hurry the hopeful inside the gates of the "Great Race Place" parking lot. Because a large part of the city's tax revenue was contributed by the racetrack, the local officials saw to it that every courtesy was extended to those who brought their money and—as the odds were—left it there.

Tina Roberson had spent many afternoons at Santa Anita with her father as she was growing up. It had seemed to her then, as it did now, that she was entering a Hollywood movie set. The turquoise and cream grandstand with its racing stable flags flying from the turrets looked one dimensional from the front. She had always half-expected to see angled two-by-fours on the back side holding the facade erect. The infield and paddock area were spread with flawless green grass that appeared to have been tacked down just for the day and the countless beds of purple and gold pansies might have been set out minutes before the gates were open. Even the view of the San Gabriel Mountains looked as though it had been painted on a canvas backdrop that could be rolled up and stored away after the final race of the day.

The first race was in progress when Eduardo pulled the unmarked police car alongside a parking attendant and showed his identification, then drove past the general admission parking lot. Outmaneuvering a stretch limousine with tinted windows, the detective flashed his badge at the driver and angled into a reserved parking space in front of the clubhouse entrance.

Tina gave her partner a suspicious look. "Why are we going to the clubhouse instead of the grounds keeper's office?"

"He said to meet him here—for lunch. Come on." Eduardo was already out of the car and heading toward the entrance.

Tina locked her door and caught up with her partner at the turnstyle between the ticket booths. "He invited us to lunch?"

"Yeah, nice of him, wasn't it?"

"We can't accept."

Eduardo grabbed her arm and dodged ahead into the crowd, leading the way through the lines of people waiting to place their bets at ticket windows on each side of the square-columned hall.

On a covered terrace to their right were small tables with white tablecloths. The tables held Reserved signs and had been arranged as close together as possible, but in a way that would not destroy an unobstructed view of the track. Waiters in cropped black jackets were on hand to take luncheon orders and deliver Bloody Marys. Some of the clubhouse patrons were milling about; others were already seated at the tables. All of them seemed to be comparing *The Racing Form* with the predictions on the sports page of the daily newspapers and the tip sheets they had purchased at the gate as they came in.

Eduardo straightened his tie and reached in his sports jacket pocket for his notepad to double-check the name of the grounds keeper. "We're here to meet Mr. Whitestead," he announced to a blond young woman, wearing a green vest with a Christmas wreath lapel pen and a pleated skirt, who was stationed behind a stand-up desk.

"You're the detectives." She had used the plural, but she was looking only at Eduardo. "Mr. Whitestead just called and said he was going to be delayed. If you want, you can go onto the terrace and wait. Or, if you're in a hurry, he'll be in his office for about thirty minutes more if you'd rather meet him there."

"Thank you," Tina said. "We'll do that." She started back the way they had come before Eduardo could object.

When he caught up, Eduardo grinned at her. "I try to take you classy places—"

"*Oh* yeah. I'll settle for a hot dog when we leave."

As they neared the less-grand grandstand, Eduardo stopped to look at the two closed-circuit TV monitors mounted above the doorway. A rerun of the previous day's races was being shown on one; the other reported the constantly changing odds on the upcoming race and the daily double.

Tina impatiently watched her partner for a moment, then tapped his arm. "Let's move."

Eduardo glanced at her, then back at the board. "Have you been here before?"

"Yeah, I've been here." And she had seen the same excited spark in her father's eyes as he calculated the odds that she saw in Eduardo's now.

"Are you good at picking winners?"

"Apparently not," she said. "I got you for a partner, didn't I?"

"Hell, that was the luckiest day of your life," Eduardo said.

"Come on, now. Let's head 'em in and move 'em out." She started on. Eduardo reluctantly followed. "Seriously," she said, "I've spent a lot of afternoons out here with my dad."

"Is this where he brought you for training?"

"For training?"

"He was the one who trained you to be such a hot-shot track star, wasn't he? I thought maybe he sent you out through the starting gate to see if you could outrun the horses."

Seeing a break in a long line in front of one of the betting windows, Tina mumbled apologies to the crowd and cut through, motioning for Eduardo to follow. "I can do okay on a fast track."

"Damn. I'll swear to that." Reluctantly, Eduardo caught up with her. "Slow down."

Though she had been to Santa Anita often, she had not been there lately. The excited babble of the crowd and the sound of laughter echoing in the high-ceilinged hall were familiar. And the faint whiff of horses from the paddock mixed with the smell of the turf and the freshly overturned earth on the dirt track were vivid reminders of those afternoons with her father. She had pleasant memories of the rush to find a place along the fence near the finish line and the way her father waved a confident fist and yelled, "Go, baby!" as the announcement came over the loudspeaker "...and they're off!"

But there was also the prickly presence of the countless times she had seen her father's face grown ashen as he tore up a handful of losing tickets. "Just wasn't my day, Tina, darlin'," he would tell her. It had seldom—very seldom—been his day.

That last afternoon he had been here at the track, but Tina had not gone with him. She was tired of it, she told him, tired of seeing him lose. Would it have mattered if she had been there? Her mother had called from the hospital. "Hurry, darlin'. He's asking for you."

"Just wasn't my day" were the last words Tina ever heard her father say.

"Wait a minute." Eduardo had stopped and was looking at the odds on the tote board in the infield. "I'll be right back."

He started toward a short line in front of the last window as the announcement was made, "The horses are now approaching the starting gate."

Tina grabbed the back of his shirt. "No you don't."

"Let go, Tina."

"I'm not going to let you place a bet." She was speaking just above a whisper, but if she had yelled, no one would have noticed in the din of voices.

Only Eduardo heard her, and he laughed as though he could not believe what she had said. "You're not going to let me?"

"Don't do it."

"What makes you think you can tell me what to do?" Suddenly he gave up the pretense that it was a joke. He twisted away from her hand.

"I swear if you go over to that window," she said in the same low voice, "I'll report you to the lieutenant."

"Tina!" Making light of it, he said in shocked surprise, "Are you threatening me?"

"I'm not threatening. I'll just by God do it."

His voice was angry now. "I'm not in uniform, for God's sake. What the hell's the difference?"

"We're on duty just the same. What if somebody you know sees you?"

"What if they do?"

She knew how he would react to the phrase that had been pounded into her when she was a recruit at the academy, but she could think of no other way to express it. "It has the apeparance of evil."

"Oh, shit." Eduardo lurched through the crowd and all but flung himself down the outside steps that led toward the stables. His long legs carried him several paces ahead of Tina.

She easily caught up. "Even if you are my training officer, I can't let you jeopardize your job—and mine." They were outside now, away from the crowd. Since she had started, she might as well say it all. "And another thing." She took a deep breath. "We can't accept a gratuitous meal in the clubhouse, or anywhere else. And...and what was all that nonsense at the Huntington with the woman with red hair? We were there on business to talk to the guard and the curator about the vandalized statue. The way you were carrying on—''

''Had the appearance of evil?'' Eduardo spit out the words.

''Well, no. But—''

''Goddamnit, Tina, you don't have to take all that shit they taught you at the academy literally. It's all right to go by the book in an emergency, but the rest of the time''—he began to walk even faster—''we do our job. We do a damn good job.''

Tina kept pace. Her heart was pounding, not from exertion but uncertainty.

''Too bad they didn't give me a partner who could figure that out,'' Eduardo said.

Tina knew better than to push any further. They had not accepted a free lunch and he had not placed a bet. She had won on both scores. And she had said what she thought about his behavior at the Huntington. Better leave it at that.

When she became a detective trainee and was transferred from Metro patrol to Hollenbeck, Tina was apprehensive when she learned that Eduardo was to be her training officer. He had a reputation for being a maverick who put more faith in omens and his own instincts than he did in computer printouts and department procedure. Her respect for him grew when she discovered that he knew the Hollenbeck area street by street, and was recognized and held in high regard by the predominantly Spanish-speaking people who lived there.

It was not just that the people in the community counted him as one of their own; the Los Angeles Police Department, by law, had a sizable percentage of Latino officers. But Eduardo was considered *compasivo* by the older residents in the division and *macho* by the younger ones. People he questioned would give him information they probably withheld from their families. Eduardo was the best interrogator in the department. He knew it, and he liked his job.

He would be content to stay a detective the rest of his life. And that was the major difference between the partners. Tina was determined to climb every rung of the ladder as soon as she found a foothold.

Unable to take her partner's silence, Tina risked asking a question, even though she dreaded the answer. "You wouldn't really rather have a different partner, would you?" Maybe she had come on too strong.

"Goddamnit, Tina, you're a real pain in the ass sometimes," he said. "It's sure as hell not easy working with a trainee who says she wants to be a detective but acts like she's bucking for sainthood."

At least that wasn't a yes. But he was still angry. She couldn't stand it if he was going to stay angry at her all day.

Eduardo continued to walk fast and look straight ahead.

"Yeah," she said, "but think about this. You'd never get another partner who's as cute as I am." She tapped him on the shoulder, then fluttered her eyelashes at him.

Eduardo stopped and pointed a finger an inch from her nose. "Don't ever do that again."

"What?" Tina had the panicky feeling that he might hit her. It wasn't until she noticed the corner of his mouth begin to twitch as he tried to keep a straight face that she knew everything was all right.

"If you ever bat your eyelashes at me again," he said, "I'll report you for sexual harassment."

They walked on in silence.

Eduardo said, "Talk about the appearance of evil . . ."

Tina was the first to laugh.

Then Eduardo.

Then Tina again, her apprehension disappearing in a series of giggles.

Ahead, just beyond the fenced-off area where the horse trailers were parked, the grounds keeper had stepped out of his prefabricated office and waved to them.

"Straighten up." Eduardo gave her a companionable elbow in the ribs. "We don't want to give the appearance of silliness."

The sign on Aubrey Whitestead's door did not say Grounds keeper, but Landscape Architect. Nor did Whitestead conform to what might have been expected of someone whose career was involved primarily with dirt, fertilizer, and plants. It would be hard to imagine him in dirty jeans or coveralls. He was a dapper gentleman in his sixties with silvery hair and a mustache to match wearing a finely tailored houndstooth jacket and charcoal woolen slacks.

"Sorry we had to meet here. I had to wait and sign for a shipment of gardenias. The nursery driver was late. Said he couldn't find us. All he had to do was ask somebody. These are just temporary quarters, you see." Whitestead extended a manicured hand first to Tina and then to Eduardo.

"No problem," Tina said.

"My office in the main building is being enlarged. I'm temporarily camping out until they get the walls back up."

The prefabricated building was divided into two rooms of equal size. The one behind the partly open door apparently was used as Whitestead's office. The room where they stood was a reception area and was immaculate enough to have served the same purpose for a doctor's office. The polished plastic-tile floor was accented with burnt-orange throw rugs. A wood-frame couch with brown and tan plaid upholstery and two matching chairs were grouped with twin end tables with white ceramic lamps and a burnished-pine coffee table that held a neat display of magazines. Nubby floor-to-ceiling beige draperies covered two walls, giving the impression that there were large picture windows rather than corrugated metal behind them.

Considering that the building was next to the stable area, the most unexpected aspect of Aubrey Whitestead's office was the pervasive scent of lavender. This was achieved by the presence of a glass bowl of potpourri on each of the tables.

"We appreciate your cooperation, Mr. Whitestead," Eduardo said, "we'll try not to take much of your time."

As good as Eduardo's word, Tina dispensed with preliminaries. "I wonder if we could examine the clothes you said were found here at the track?"

"Yes, yes, of course. Wait here, and I'll get them."

Whitestead went into his office. Eduardo sat on the couch and thumbed through a copy of *Thoroughbred*. Tina stood impatiently flipping the clasp on her shoulder bag with her thumbnail and watched through the open door as the landscape architect pulled a large cardboard box from under a long metal table and rummaged through it.

"One of the cleanup crew found them in the drainage ditch near Huntington Drive," Whitestead said. "You wouldn't believe the things people leave here every day. Empty wallets, binoculars, wristwatches, jewelry—ah, here they are." Whitestead brought out a plastic garbage bag closed with a metal tie into the waiting room and put it on the floor near the outside door.

Eduardo left the open magazine face down on the coffee table and stood. "Mind if we have a look at it here?" He began to untwist the tie.

Frowning, Whitestead said, "Let me get some newspapers to spread on the floor." He obviously did not want to contaminate the lavender-scented waiting room, and returned in a moment with the classified section of that day's *Los Angeles Times,* which he spread on the polished floor.

Eduardo emptied the bag onto the paper. The clothes had only a dusty smell, not the perspiration and urine odor that might have been expected. The wearer had managed to keep himself reasonably clean. "Trousers . . ." Eduardo handed a pair of cotton twill slacks to Tina to examine as he went through the pockets of a frayed nylon jacket.

Three of the pants pockets had holes in them. The left front pocket held a broken comb, a pencil stub, a toothbrush with a paper towel twisted around it, and an expensive pair of nail clippers. If these were Goochie's clothes, where would he have gotten clippers like those? Tina wondered. Had he stolen them? Rainbow might know.

"Tell us again, if you would, please, Mr. Whitestead, where these clothes were found, and why you thought we might be interested in them." Eduardo had turned the jacket inside out and was unzipping an inside pocket.

"It was a big joke with the cleaning crew. Ordinarily, the man who found them would just have thrown them away. But he brought them back to the equipment barn to show us. He was laughing and telling everyone, 'I've heard of people losing their shirts at the track, but—'"

Tina broke in, "Brought them back from where?"

Her partner's raised eyebrow and Whitestead's look of annoyance told her that she should not have interrupted.

Whitestead cleared his throat. "As I told you before, there's a concrete drainage ditch that runs through the parking lot to the street and then connects with the city's underground system. They were in the ditch on the Santa Anita side of the fence."

"Approximately where along the drainage ditch, Mr. Whitestead?" Eduardo asked. "Was it up near the grandstand or closer to the street?"

"Right next to the fence by the second entrance off Huntington. Someone could have easily driven up and dropped them over the fence." Whitestead was warming to his story again. "The guy who found them said he was going to turn them into lost and found. Said he'd like to see whoever it was who came to claim them."

Eduardo laughed companionably.

"Ordinarily they wouldn't have been found right away," Whitestead continued. "But we flush the ditch out with hoses every two weeks, and the last time was a few days after the nude body was found in the statuary garden. I read about it in the newspaper. That's why I called you."

"We appreciate your help." Eduardo picked up a rumpled flannel shirt from the pile of clothing on the floor and poked his fingers in the pockets. "You'd be surprised how many people just don't want to get involved."

"It seemed to me it would be easy enough for someone to just drive up and drop them over the fence," Whitestead repeated.

"Weren't there any shoes?" Tina smoothed her skirt under her and sat on her haunches. She pushed a pair of threadbare wool socks aside and lifted the last garment, tattered boxer shorts, with a pencil.

"Yes, of course, there were shoes." Whitestead looked puzzled for a moment. Then, "Oh, yes. I had them put in a paper sack separately. Shoes are so heavy, I was afraid they'd fall through that flimsy plastic. They're in my office somewhere."

As the landscape architect went back into his temporary office to dig through the boxes and sacks stored under the metal table, Eduardo sat and picked up the copy of *Thoroughbred* again. Tina stood, impatiently tapping the pencil against the wooden arm of the couch.

"Sit down and stop racing your motor," Eduardo said.

She sat on the chair adjacent to Eduardo and leaned forward. In an excited whisper she said, "That pair of nail clippers in the pants pocket. They were good ones, not the drugstore kind—"

"We'll talk about it in the car," Eduardo said evenly. "Here. Read a magazine." He purposely left it open to the picture spread he had turned to.

She took the glossy periodical from him and glanced down, but her mind was still on the clothes that she was convinced had belonged to Goochie. The odd thing was the nail clippers. They had a gold overlay like the kind she had seen in catalogs from expensive specialty stores under the heading of *"For the Man Who Has Everything."* Of course Goochie could have stolen them. He probably stole them. But where? From whom?

Tina absently rolled the edge of the magazine page between her thumb and forefinger. Eduardo was right. This was no place to discuss whether these were Goochie's missing clothes, but she was impatient to talk with him alone.

Suddenly, she realized what she had been looking at in the horse owner's trade publication Eduardo had handed her. With a gasp, she almost jumped out of the chair, and dropped the magazine face down on the coffee table. The article was titled "New Methods of Artificial Insemination," and the double spread of photographs were explicit closeups of a manually induced technique of capturing thoroughbred sperm.

Tina prided herself on seldom being embarrassed, but she had never seen anything like those pictures before. Her face was burning. She could not look at her partner, but she could hear the trouble he was having trying to keep from laughing.

"Here are the shoes." Whitestead came into the waiting room gingerly holding a brown paper sack. "They were behind a stack of hybrid annual catalogs. If the contractor doesn't finish with my office soon, we're going to be in total chaos."

"I know what you mean," Eduardo said, bending down and dumping the contents of the sack on the floor. "I've always believed in a place for everything and everything in its place."

"*Oh,* yeah." Tina leaned next to her partner to examine the shoes and managed to swing her shoulder bag with some force against his ear. "Oh, sorry."

Eduardo grinned, but did not meet her eyes. Seriously, he said, "Tina, would you write a receipt for Mr. Whitestead, please?"

"A receipt? I don't need a receipt for these."

"It's really more for our benefit than yours, sir." Eduardo put the clothing back in the plastic bag and shoes in the paper sack. "It's a matter of keeping track of evidence."

Tina quickly read out loud as she wrote—pants, shirt, boxer shorts, jacket, shoes, nail clippers, comb, pencil, toothbrush.

"There were two one-dollar bills and seventy-five cents in change and a folded page from the sports section of the newspaper in the zippered inside pocket of his jacket," Eduardo said.

Tina added this to her list. "Would you read this, date, and sign it please, sir?" She handed the receipt pad to Whitestead to examine.

"Yes, of course." He glanced at the list, then wrote his signature and the date.

"Thanks again, Mr. Whitestead. It's concerned citizens like you who make our job easier." Eduardo held the two sacks in one hand and opened the door with the other.

"Not at all. Glad to be of help." Whitestead nodded curtly and closed the door behind them.

"Those shoes, Eduardo." Tina could not contain her excitement any longer. She bounced along beside her partner as they passed in front of the grandstand and angled toward the reserved parking area where they had left their car.

"Yeah. Not hard to guess where Rainbow's pal got his nickname now, is it?"

Tina felt just the smallest bit deflated. It would have been nice to know that she was first to realize the significance of the shoes. But the feeling was only momentary. She could hear the same enthusiasm in her partner's voice that she felt herself. They had a starting place now. There was something to work with.

"I've never been able to afford shoes like that," Eduardo said. "Even though the heels were worn down to the soles, the leather was still good, and they still had the emblem."

"Gucci."

"Yeah. Goochie."

FIFTEEN

BEFORE LOPEZ AND Roberson left the Huntington to go to Santa Anita, Andrea had begun to cast around for an excuse to refuse Latimer's invitation to lunch. She was still not hungry, and she was eager to see the gallery where *The Blue Boy* was on display so she could start making a preliminary assessment of the work ahead of her.

Then suddenly, when Latimer became so distracted by the preparations for the removal of the damaged statue, the subject of lunch became less than trivial.

"You men! I told you before! Stop what you are doing!" He had thrown his hands in the air and run across the lawn toward the maintenance crew. "Look! Look what they've done," he yelled back at Andrea and Archie, who were following behind at a slower pace.

Both Andrea and the guard were startled at the near hysteria in the voice of the curator.

The workman had backed a flatbed truck as close as possible to the pedestal. The statue was covered with a heavy protective plastic and crisscrossed with hemp rope. Using a sort of pulley arrangement, they had obviously planned to lower the statue horizontally onto a layer of woven padding, then tie the rope to the truck panels to keep their cargo from moving as it was transported. From the garden to the workroom was only a half mile ride. Andrea thought it looked like a perfectly workable arrangement.

"Who authorized this?" Latimer sternly addressed the two men in coveralls who had implemented the method of removal.

"We've got a work order." With an air of resignation, the man who was directing the operation jumped to the ground from the truck bed. He took a folded yellow sheet of paper from his hip pocket and showed it to the curator. "It's signed by McCorkle—Gardens and Grounds."

"You can take that right back to him." Latimer glanced at the printed form. "I'm the art curator here. I want that statue left standing where it is."

Without comment, and with no great show of speed or concern, the workmen began untying the ropes and removing the plastic as Latimer watched.

"Mr. Latimer hasn't been here long," Archie confided to Andrea in a low, apologetic voice as they neared the scene. "He's a bit high strung. Mind you, he never puts a foot wrong, and seems devoted to his job. You can see the light burning in his office at all hours."

Andrew knew something of Latimer's background. He had come to the Huntington from the Amon Carter Museum in Fort Worth. Prior to that, he had conducted a Renaissance Art Studies program for an Ivy League college. She was not sure which one.

His stay at the Amon Carter had been brief, less than a year. He left by mutual agreement as the result of a quiet controversy over artistic differences. The story was that Latimer, no great admirer of western art, had removed a Frederic Remington bronze statue of an Indian scout from the main gallery. In its place, he had insisted on displaying his own personal favorite from the Carter collection, a six-teenth-century French reliquary statuette of an obscure saint.

That was the official reason for the parting of the ways. But Andrea had heard from a colleague and former class-mate at Harvard that something more substantial was the reason for the curator's departure. The "artistic differences" might have been smoothed over had that been the only problem Latimer had had with his Fort Worth employers. But when, at the insistence of the board of directors, the Remington was to be returned to its original location, the discovery was made that the statue had been

damaged beyond repair. The Indian scout's feather head-
band had been broken, the pony on which he sat was missing a foot, and worst of all, the side of the Indian's face was
caved in and totally distorted.

No guilt was ever ascribed. The damage was considered
to be accidental, possibly done by a careless warehouse em-
ployee. But as curator, it was Latimer's responsibility to see
that the works of art belonging to the museum were properly cared for and preserved. Andrea wondered if his painful previous experience was the reason for Latimer's
panicked response to the treatment of the statue in the
Huntington's garden now.

Andrea and Archie had stood by silently as Latimer ordered the plastic covering removed from the statue and sent
away the maintenance-department workmen in their truck.

"The paint removal can be done right here in the garden," he said by way of explanation to Andrea. "No need
to cart this anonymous dandy off and chance chipping the
stone."

"Anonymous dandy" had been said almost as a sneer.

Andrea found the curator's attitude offensive, but agreed
mildly, "I suppose you're right." Even if it took Latimer's
crew several days to restore the jacket of the Italian myth-
ological figure to its original limestone, there seemed to be
no reason why the work could not be done outside. December in California was considerably different than in England, where she had been yesterday. The weather was
warm, the sun was shining, and there was no hint that a
wind, rain, or snow storm lurked beyond the San Gabriel
Mountains.

Still, she would have insisted that some sort of screen or
barrier be erected around the statue. There was something
so undignified about leaving a work of art in that condition
and unprotected from public view, no matter for how short
a time. It made the statue—as well as the unknown artist—
appear comic.

Her gaze traveled down the stately line of statues and stopped at one near the fountain. She was surprised to see that no attempt had been made to repair the other vandalized statue. The splotches of red paint that had been discovered the same morning as the dead body were still there for all to see. Trying to give Latimer the benefit of the doubt, she supposed that the police might have requested that the stains be left intact for some reason.

"We'll be able to restore the statue to its former grandeur where it stands." Latimer added with a smirk, "Though I'm not sure that the green jacket isn't an improvement. This is hardly the handiwork of Michelangelo." As though sharing a tidbit that only another expert could appreciate, he added, "Henry Huntington was not exactly Lorenzo de' Medici. Instead of being a patron of the arts, he was a usurper of other people's collections."

To hell with the benefit of the doubt, Andrea thought. This guy's an obnoxious snob. She had met people like Latimer before. They did not limit themselves to the world of paintings and sculpture. They also snickered at Mozart and professed to appreciate only Bach. They called Shakespeare soppy and insisted that he was only an actor at any rate, and that the plays and sonnets were really written by Ben Jonson. The art world was full of people like Latimer.

Wanting to escape as quickly as possible, she said, "Harvey, I know you have more important things to do than to take me to lunch."

He protested, politely. She insisted, firmly.

"Well, if you're sure." He smiled apologetically. Then, with the voice of authority, he said, "Archie, accompany Miss Perkins to the main gallery so she can make some preliminary decisions on how she would like to proceed with our *Blue Boy*." And to Andrea, "I'll confirm your plans with you later."

Though he had not said so, Andrea got the distinct impression that he was telling her to keep her hands off until he gave his approval.

Harvey Latimer was in for a surprise. Her contract was with the board of directors, and she had made her own terms clear before agreeing to theirs. And though she hoped there would not be a clash of wills between Latimer and herself, she was determined to carry out this assignment as she did all her others, using her own experience and expertise in the way she saw fit.

"Space has been cleared for you in the workroom, Miss Perkins," Archie said when they reached the main gallery in the mansion. "And the lighting equipment and collapsible ladder you had shipped have been set up for you there."

"Thank you, Archie." She stood silently in the doorway a moment and surveyed the rectangular gallery that had been designed specifically to house Henry Huntington's extensive collection.

Here, in one room, were at least two dozen full-length portraits by British artists, more than were to be found in one room anywhere else, including England. Gainsborough, Reynolds, Romney, and Lawrence were all represented. At the far end was an eight-foot-tall canvas on which Sir Joshua Reynolds had portrayed Mrs. Siddons—the most renowned British actress of the eighteenth century—as the Tragic Muse in somber shades of brown. Karl Friedrich Abel, a distinguished musician of the same era was represented in like size and elegance, as were the countesses of Winterton and Harrington, the Duchess of Devonshire, the Viscountess Crosbie, and a number of other wealthy and notable citizens of the day who could afford to pay the lavish fees required to be immortalized by the premiere portraitists of that era.

With the exception of the painting that Andrea had been hired to restore, the portrait that drew the most attention from the visitors to the gallery was a work by Sir Thomas Lawrence titled *Pinkie*. The painting, so named because of the subject's pink satin hat with long flowing ribbons, was of a lovely young girl with tousled brown hair named Sarah Barrett Moulton. The gentleness that shone in her large dark eyes apparently was not equally inherited by her brother. He was immortalized as she had been, but in literature rather than on canvas. In later years, he was the tyrannical father of the poet Elizabeth Barrett Browning.

"Shows you what money can do, doesn't it?" Archie Chambers had been standing just in back of Andrea's left shoulder.

"What?" She had forgotten he was there.

"I'm afraid Mr. Latimer is right."

"About what?"

"About Henry Huntington. We've chatted about it, Mr. Latimer and I." The guard was proud of having discussed art with the curator of the museum. "Because I spent my youth in England, Mr. Latimer has said to me more than once, 'What *must* your country think about America, Archie?' "

"I'm afraid I don't understand," Andrea said.

"He was alluding to the fact that old Henry Huntington didn't go about collecting the way the original owners did." Archie spoke with a hint of disdain, as though by virtue of being born in England, he was entitled to be disapproving of an upstart American tycoon who bought up British art treasures. "He made his millions the first half of his life, then, in a matter of about ten years, he set out to buy up whole libraries and immense collections of art that had taken the original owners several generations to accumulate."

"Thank heaven there *were* people like Henry Huntington." Andrea whirled around to face the astonished guard. "At least he built a library where the books could be used, and a museum where the paintings could be seen. It seems to me far better than leaving them to molder in some decaying country estate or selling them off piecemeal to collectors who would probably have locked them away and brought them out only to impress their friends."

Archie had taken a step backward and his eyebrows were climbing toward his hairline.

"And as to those statues out by the fountain. Can you imagine what Henry Huntington would have to say about that?" As long as she was started with all this, she added, "Spray paint is bad enough. Let's hope that *sometime* it will be removed. At least the museum has provisions for maintenance and repair. In too many other places in the world they would be just left the way they are. You should see the condition of some of the statues in Italy. They're covered with bird droppings, they have initials carved in them, and they're being destroyed by smog." Andrea stopped herself. She realized that her anger was at Latimer but she was taking it out on Archie. "Sorry," she said.

"No. No, I'm sorry if I said something—"

"It's not your fault. You just struck a nerve." She smiled reassuringly at him and, in her best professional manner, entered the gallery and glanced up at the portrait she had been hired to restore. "Now then, Archie, do you think we could get that spectator's bench moved and cordon off about ten feet around *The Blue Boy*?"

"I'm sure we could," he answered tentatively. "But I understood that Mr. Latimer gave instructions to clear space for you in the workroom."

"No, I think I'll work in here."

At least she and Latimer agreed on one thing, if for different reasons. She suspected that his decision not to move the statue was only partly for fear it would be damaged. He seemed to get some obscene pleasure from letting it be exposed to ridicule. For her part, her method was always to avoid disturbing a work of art as much as possible. Moving a canvas that was almost six feet tall created the possibility of stretching or tearing. Damage could even be done by exposing the paint to different temperature or light for only a brief period. Then, too, she always enjoyed talking to visitors in the galleries where she worked. She felt she was demonstrating something positive, that a painting was a living thing that needed care and protection.

"Archie, tell me how to find the workroom." Andrea left the gallery and started toward the mansion's exit with the intention of locating her equipment and giving instructions on where and how she wished it assembled.

"I can take you there."

She noticed he glanced at his watch. "That won't be necessary. I suppose it's about time for you to go on duty."

"The gates open in just a few minutes, but I could get someone to cover for me."

After assuring the guard that she was capable of finding the building on her own if he would give her directions, Andrea thanked Archie for his help and left him at his post on the loggia.

The first of the afternoon visitors were on the sidewalks carrying cameras and consulting guidebooks. The out-of-state visitors were easy to spot. They wore woolen slacks and carried wraps, already having discovered that their coats or sweaters were too warm to wear in the afternoon sunshine.

Andrea averted her eyes and hurried past the statuary garden where two young couples stood speculating on why the jacket on one of the statues had been painted green.

SIXTEEN

BETWEEN RACES, in the paddock area outside the grandstand, the amplified voice of the Santa Anita track announcer droned above the noise of the crowd. Bored-looking thoroughbreds, in stalls with numbers above them that corresponded to the numbers on the starting gate, were being saddled and in some cases outfitted with blinders to make the animal believe that he or she was the only horse running.

Nearby, at the walking ring, a throng of eager race goers were pressed three and four deep around the waist-high whitewashed fence or stood on benches to catch a glimpse of the daily favorites, the longshots, and their owners. The owners waited in the center of the ring and were as popular an attraction as the horses. This was because the owners were often recognizable movie or TV personalities. With them stood the jockeys and trainers. The trainers chatted with their employers reassuringly. The jockeys, in brightly colored silk shirts and caps, tight white pants, and shiny black boots were, for the most part, silent and expressionless. Like any athlete, they were more concerned with the race than the preliminaries. Then, too, in many cases, they understood very little of the language that was being spoken.

When the thoroughbreds had been led around the circle for inspection, the moment came when the jockeys were boosted onto the tiny saddles on their horses' backs. In the order of the numbers attached to the saddle blankets, the racehorses were shepherded by hot walkers through a narrow passage in the grandstand, where their entrance was heralded by a hornblower in a formal red hunting coat and black top hat.

Lopez and Roberson, on their way to the parking lot, dodged and sidestepped the onlookers.

The race fans were serious and expectant as they crowded around trying to read the gait of a horse, the tilt of a jockey's head, or the smile on an owner's face before hurrying off to place a bet on the next race.

"Hey. Isn't that—oh, what's her name..." Eduardo stared at the curvy back view of a woman in a short pink wool coat with long, straight blond hair that hung past her shoulders leaving the owner's ring. "You know, the one that was on that dumb TV show for so long."

"That narrows it down." Tina pushed through the crowd in front and motioned for Eduardo to follow.

"Then she went on one of those talk shows and told about how scummy her folks were—"

"Could be any one of your well-known favorites."

"No," Eduardo hurried to catch up, "it can't be who I was thinking of. Her legs are too skinny."

Once outside the gates, Eduardo unlocked the trunk of the LAPD unmarked car and stowed the sealed plastic bag containing the tattered clothing retrieved from the drainage ditch. Tina handed him a second, smaller bag with the contents of the pockets and the well-worn Gucci shoes.

"I'll drive," Eduardo said. "You just concentrate on figuring this mess out. First off, since this stuff in the sack was found here at the track, and Goochie's body was discovered at the Huntington, how did he get from here to there without his clothes?"

Tina climbed in the passenger seat and fastened her seat belt. "I think we can rule out that he took the bus."

Eduardo grinned as he put the car in reverse and started to back out of the parking space.

"Fasten your seat belt." Tina turned toward the side window avoiding the pained look she was sure to get from her partner. Seat belts were made mandatory for police cars—after a string of police officer deaths in high speed chases—before the law that affected all legal drivers was passed. It was one of the more unpopular LAPD regulations—and least observed. There were those on the force who argued that being strapped in the car put them at a disadvantage when they had to reach for their guns and get out of the car in a hurry. But, as always, to Tina, a rule was a rule.

"With your fixation on seat belts," Eduardo said, not kindly, "you'd have made one hell of an airline stewardess." But he pulled the strap across his chest and clicked the metal lock in place.

At the exit to Huntington Drive, Eduardo speeded up to catch the last second of the yellow traffic light before it turned red. Making a sharp right turn, he headed for El Sereno and the Hollenbeck Division headquarters. Tina sat with her feet braced against the floorboard, as she usually did when Eduardo was driving.

Eduardo settled into the outside traffic lane. "Tell me again everything that Rainbow told you about Goochie."

"Not much, really." She tried to remember. "There were the shoes; he said Goochie was particular about them."

"Where did he get those shoes? Did he steal them or find them—"

"No." Tina turned sideways in the seat toward her partner. "Rainbow said Goochie was particular about his shoes because they were all he had left from before."

"Before what?"

"Before he landed on the street! Sometime, before he made the City Hall mall his place of residence, he could afford to buy Gucci shoes."

"Okay. What else?"

"Goochie knew about horses and made imaginary bets. He went through the alley behind the Times building every morning and collected a discarded copy of the sports section to check out the daily lineup when the thoroughbreds were running. And, the day he was killed, he had ten dollars some guy from a film company gave him."

"What else?"

Tina thought for a moment. With a sigh, and a shake of the head, she said, "Nothing. Nothing else I can think of."

"Where did he live before he came to L.A.?"

"Rainbow didn't know."

"Did he have a family?"

Tina shrugged.

The two detectives rode on in silence for the next few miles. Each of them tried to build a scenario for murder from the meager information they had.

"Okay, here's what we know so far," Eduardo said, finally. "Forensic says Goochie was shot in the chest at a range of about five feet, between ten and eleven P.M.—a good five hours after the last race at Santa Anita. If the murderer was someone he met at the track—or someone who followed him there—where had the two of them been before they ended up in the statuary garden?"

Tina said, "We don't know for sure that Goochie even went to Santa Anita. But let's say he did. It's possible that he and the murderer weren't there together, or that they split up for some reason, and agreed to meet later on the grounds of the Huntington." She thoughtfully tapped a fingernail against her teeth.

"Stop biting your nails," Eduardo said, "I can't stand to see someone bite their nails."

"I'm *not*," she protested, but she locked her hands together in her lap. "Obviously," she continued, "the clothes were dumped to prevent an easy I.D. of the body. The perpetrator shoots Goochie, strips him, takes his clothes, jumps in his car, and heads for the nearest place he can think of to dump them where they're not likely to be found. Or even if they are found, there's the chance that they won't be connected to the murder victim, and, even if they're connected, the perp has bought some time."

"There's one thing I don't get—" Eduardo interrupted himself to say something under his breath in Spanish to a teenager in a Toyota pickup who cut in front of him. "Why did he turn left?"

"Who?" Tina glanced through the rear window for an offending automobile.

"Who are we talking about? The perp." Eduardo put his hand on his partner's head and turned her face back toward him. "Say it was premeditated."

"It couldn't have been *very* premeditated. Goochie didn't have the money to go to the track until that morning."

"Let's assume the guy had at least enough time to decide what he was going to do and how he was going to do it. So he parks his car in the Huntington parking lot, as close as he can get to the statuary garden," Eduardo said. "After he shoots Goochie and strips him of anything that might be identifiable, he exits and drives through the residential area. He knows he needs a public place to get rid of the clothes. He wants to hide them in something like one of those big Dumpsters they have behind business buildings—and in a place where a pile of ratty clothes are not likely to get noticed right away, or at all. He comes to a stop sign on Huntington Drive. If he continues in the direction he was going and crosses Huntington, he's just in another residential area. So, he turns left toward Arcadia, where the racetrack is—instead of turning right, toward L.A. Why?"

"Why not? He's got a choice, left or right. Flip a coin—he turned left," Tina answered impatiently.

"Just hang on. Our murderer wants to get out of San Marino and jettison the evidence as quickly as possible."

"I'm with you."

"Now, if he hasn't already done so, he has to decide where he's going to dump the clothes. It's late, and dark," Eduardo said. "San Marino rolls up the sidewalks at ten o'clock, so if he goes driving through the alleys looking for a Dumpster, he'd call attention to himself. One thing those high-rent-district police are good at is keeping suspicious characters off the street and away from the vacuum-sealed residents."

"Okay, so he heads for Santa Anita." Tina still did not see the significance of which direction he turned. "Santa Anita is the closest place he can think of that handles a lot of refuse and where he can just zip off Huntington Drive, drop them in the drainage ditch, and keep on going."

"Good. That's what we think he did. Now, suppose that instead of turning left on Huntington Drive, he had turned right and driven the same distance. Where would he have been?"

Tina thought for a moment. "Right about here. In El Sereno."

"Exactly!"

As Eduardo had begun to explain his theory, they had driven through the last few blocks of the tidy communities of San Marino and South Pasadena, with their glass-fronted banks and vine-covered realty offices. As Huntington Drive narrowed into El Sereno, the well-ordered street deteriorated into a string of taco stands, concrete-slab car lots, and single-story stucco buildings with wrought-iron grating covering the doors and windows.

"So, why didn't he come this way? A car driving aimlessly around here after ten o'clock would not be suspicious. Some of the cantinas are open most of the night. There's no trouble finding a place to dump trash. He could have dropped Goochie's old clothes in the middle of the sidewalk and they might not have been noticed for days. This is where *I* would have come if I were under pressure to get rid of something. But that's because I grew up here. I know this neighborhood," he said. "Maybe the perp didn't."

"Got it," said Tina.

"If he had come this way," Eduardo continued, "he would have been taking a chance on scouting an area he knew nothing about. So he turned left toward the upscale neighborhood that *was* familiar to him—that he knew as well as I know El Sereno. We're not looking for a small-time thug. This guy has bucks!''

"*Oh* yeah." Tina was thoughtful a moment. "So you're saying the local cops were wrong—that the murderer wasn't just someone off the street or from down our way."

"It makes sense, doesn't it?"

Tina did not answer.

"Well, doesn't it?"

"Yes, except"—she was thoughtful, still considering—"what about the damaged statues? The paint?"

Eduardo laughed. "One thing we can be sure of is that Goochie wasn't shot by any graffiti artist."

"Why do you say that?"

"Look around you." Eduardo took his hand from the steering wheel and waved out the open window at the defaced buildings on each side of the street. "Some kid with a can of spray paint might have written his name—or 'fuck you'—or a gang symbol, but he would never have carefully painted a statue's jacket green."

"Umm," Tina said in concession. "But that first statue, the one they found damaged the same morning they found Goochie's body, was just splotched with red."

"Maybe he heard the guard coming. Or maybe he just got scared and left."

"Then why did he come back last night and do his number with the green paint?"

"I don't know. Maybe he's an art critic," Eduardo shrugged. "Or maybe it wasn't the same guy at all. Just a copycat." Then, after a moment, "We need to talk to Rainbow again."

"Yeah. If we can find him."

"When we know who Goochie was, it will be a hell of a lot easier figuring out why someone killed him."

"We know he didn't always live on the street. Maybe there's a missing persons out on him," Tina said. Then, before Eduardo could shoot down her suggestion, she did it herself. "But we don't have a name. And we already know his fingerprints are not on file." The fingerprints had been run through the central computer shortly after the body was delivered to the forensic laboratory. There was no record of arrests, and if he had ever had a driver's license, the DMV did not have him in their files.

Tina asked, "What's the life span of a pair of men's shoes?"

"I've never owned an expensive pair of leather shoes like that. But I'd guess it could be ten years. Longer."

"Well, bless old Goochie. I'm glad he decided to hang onto them. Otherwise, we wouldn't have a single lead."

The rest of the afternoon, Eduardo and Tina were at their desks making telephone calls, trying to chase down their one solid clue; the manufacturer's identification number on a pair of well-worn brown leather Gucci shoes. By early evening, they knew the year the shoes had been manufactured, the state where they had been shipped, the warehouse where they had been stored, and the specialty store that had sold them. This information had come to them as the result of persistent routine work. But that night they got an unexpected bit of luck. Later, when an arrest had been made, Eduardo called it an omen. Despite the weather forecast for continued warm temperatures and sunny skies, it rained.

SEVENTEEN

THERE HAD BEEN no hint of rain that afternoon. It was a typical Southern California winter day when the air was still, the sky was bleached and faded, and the sun had grown pale with boredom from the monotony of making the only contribution to the weather.

Andrea had made a side trip to the Huntington's art department workroom to check on her equipment, and as she was leaving, she noticed a few ill-defined clouds to the north. But they were thin to the point of translucence and seemed to be there more as a visual effect to highlight the rounded contours of the San Gabriel Mountains than as a threat of rain.

The sidewalk she took toward the exit curved beside the rose garden and led through pergolas and arches laced with climbing roses in full bloom. To her left was an herb garden, and beyond that, the tea room. As she passed, she glanced through the open latticed windows. Victorian floral-print wallpaper gave the room a cozy look. A dozen or so small tables were occupied by groups of four or six—mostly women in knitted dresses or Chanel-type suits. In the center of the room on a large round table, trays of scones, dainty crustless sandwiches, and fruit tarts surrounded a tall china urn filled to overflowing with winter roses in reds and pinks. The centerpiece was so large that from the sidewalk it blocked the view of most of the back of the room. There seemed to be a large rectangular table where twenty or so people were seated. Suddenly, over the tinkling sounds of silver and crystal, china and chatter, there was polite applause, and a man at the head of the long table stood and nodded in response. Andrea immediately recognized Harvey Latimer with his smirk of a smile as he took a bow.

She congratulated herself on her luck at having missed lunch with him. No doubt he had been the featured speaker or the recipient of an award from some local art or civic group and wanted her there to witness the esteem (real or polite) in which he was held.

"Miss Perkins!" Archie Chambers hurried down the sidewalk toward her.

"Yes, Archie. Hello." She went to meet him, not wanting to be seen by Latimer if he should look away from his audience.

"I found a docent to take my place by the front door, so I can help with whatever you need done in the main gallery."

"There was really no need—"

Archie waved away her objection with a flutter of fingers. "I tried to find Mr. Latimer to check with him about the, you know, about the cordoning off in the main gallery that you wanted, but he's speaking at a luncheon for the San Marino Garden Club."

They had been walking side-by-side at a moderate pace when Andrea stopped and gently took the surprised guard's arm. "Archie, I want to emphasize that there is no need for you to check with Harvey Latimer about anything I do while I'm here. If any problems arise, I'll deal directly with the board of directors."

Archie stammered. "I'm, I'm sorry. It's just that Mr. Latimer is always so insistent on knowing everything that goes on, from what cleaners we send our uniforms to—to who is on duty when, and the route we take when we're patrolling the grounds."

"It's all right," Andrea reassured him, "I just wanted you to understand my situation." She started again toward the exit with Archie keeping pace. "If you'd like to help, since you've arranged for someone to take your shift, you could oversee the arrangements I discussed with two young men from the workroom who will be bringing my equipment to the gallery."

"Of course," Archie said quickly. "I'd be pleased to be of any assistance."

"My ladder is lightweight tubular aluminum, and it fits together to make a sort of library set of stairsteps. I want the top of the stairs on a level with the bottom edge of *The Blue Boy*. There are trays that fit on each side of the top railing where I spread out my equipment. If you would see to it that they attach everything carefully and cordon off the area we talked about, I'd be very grateful."

"I'll see that it's done exactly the way you want it, Miss Perkins."

"Thank you, Archie." Andrea smiled at him.

Before heading in different directions—Archie back inside the museum and Andrea to the Dodsons' house to change clothes—they stopped a moment beneath a mammoth mesa oak that was the focal point for the entire Huntington estate. Its huge rugged branches stretched to the museum's loggia on one side and to the corner of the library and the tip of the statuary garden the opposite way. In all, the dense foliage of the ancient oak shaded an area the size of a small shopping mall.

"I'm going to get into my work clothes and pick up the rest of my equipment," she said, "but I should be back in about forty-five minutes."

Archie nodded curtly, and strode off with purpose to the museum.

At the sound of laughter, Andrea turned instinctively in its direction. Harvey Latimer, with his pack of ladies from the garden club, was crossing the lawn of the statuary garden. His head turned toward his followers, he gesticulated lavishly toward the statue in the green jacket, and said something that his audience seemed to find hilarious.

Andrea hurried toward the gate. It was not often she took such an immediate dislike to someone. But Harvey Latimer made her want to kick something—preferably his behind. In its absence, she spotted a respectable-sized rock that—with no consideration for her black leather pumps—she sent rolling a fair distance down Euston Road.

EIGHTEEN

A CAR WITH A rental company tag was parked in the circular drive of the Dodsons' house. It had not been there earlier when Andrea left to go to the Huntington. Her first thought when she reached the front sidewalk was that Sarah had out-of-town guests.

Not wanting to intrude, Andrea veered off to the flagstone path that led to the side door of the kitchen.

Georgene Dodson had given Andrea keys to all the doors of the house the day they had had tea at the Savoy in London. Andrea had a clear memory of the beautiful Mrs. Dodson with the strangely formed hand and the silvery fingernails tossing the key ring on the table. She had insisted that Andrea was to use the house and everything in it as she liked for as long as she cared to stay.

Still, Andrea could not help feeling like an interloper. She was not a friend of the family. She was a business guest— which was the way she preferred to keep it.

Her enthusiasm for California had evaporated when Aldo was not at the airport to meet her. What was supposed to be a working vacation was now merely work. Work that she planned to complete as quickly as possible. Certainly, she had no intention of getting involved in the lives of Georgene Dodson's family.

For that reason, she chose to avoid going through the entry and past the living area where Sarah would undoubtedly feel obliged to introduce and "explain" Andrea to her guests.

The flagstone path led past a free-form pond where scattered lily pads with lavender flowers floated and iridescent koi fish swam just beneath the surface. Bamboo as dense as a jungle stood opposite and provided a background for neatly spaced acacias full of soft puffs of golden winter blooms.

The tranquility of the scene was suddenly broken by the sound of Holly—"the happy housekeeper"—speaking in a very angry voice from the direction of the back terrace by the swimming pool.

"Nikki, you snot, I'm warning you!"

As Andrea reached the corner of the house, the tirade continued.

"If you so much as lay a hand on Benjamin while I'm gone," Holly added convincingly, "I'll show you what a Kentucky knuckle-buster is when I get back."

Nikki Yamaguchi laughed as though he were accustomed to Holly's threats, but it was an uncertain little laugh.

When Andrea entered the kitchen, she could see Holly and the two boys on the terrace through the sliding glass door.

Benjamin and Nikki were seated at an umbrella table. Benjamin, unconcerned, was bent over a sketch pad and a box of pastels, picking up one color stick and then the other, blending them on the paper with the heel of his hand.

Surprisingly, Sarah was there, too. She stood behind her small son watching the progress of his drawing.

"Sarah, I left some notes and the emergency telephone numbers on a pad next to the wall phone in the kitchen." The level of Holly's voice dropped as she spoke to her employer, but none of the authority was gone. "The riding instructor from the Bradbury Stables will come by in the morning to take Benjamin for his lesson—"

"I don't want to go," Benjamin said.

"My God! They fly in from Mars to take riding lessons there. What kind of a kid are you?" Holly made a funny face at the little boy. He grinned back at her. "You can endure it, right?"

"I guess." He concentrated on his drawing again.

"And, Sarah, don't forget to call a cab at least an hour before your appointment with the psychiatrist—the number is on the pad—or you'll never get there on time. Cabs in California are scarce as hen's teeth. Everybody out here drives their own car."

"Holly, I can't drive here. I just *can't*," Sarah said with a sigh.

"I know."

"It's not only that it's Georgene's car. These freeways terrify me."

"I know. I'm just saying call early for a cab."

Andrea thought there was something amusing and rather touching about this college girl in her bulging blue jeans and long-tailed striped shirt taking the responsibility for the small group.

Obviously, the rental car in the driveway was for Holly. Andrea felt disappointed. She liked the girl better than anyone she had met in San Marino and hoped she was not planning to be gone long.

Starting for the back stairs, Andrea spotted a large wooden bowl of polished fruit on the breakfast table. She suddenly remembered that she had not had lunch and took an apple.

Later, she would tell herself that she could not have missed seeing the unfinished letter lying there on the table between her and the fruit bowl. If it had been partially hidden, if it had been folded and fallen open, if there had been any attempt to conceal it, she never would have read a word. But there it was, as though it had been thrust in front of her. It was written in a large childish scrawl with a wide-point pen and Andrea had read it before she even realized she had.

Dear Mother, was at the top of the page. There was no date.

Indented, on the next line down was: *I hate you!*

One line below that was:

I've always hated you. I might as well not have been born for all you ever cared. You'd have been happier with just one child. I heard you say that! Once, upstairs when you thought I was asleep, I heard you tell Dad that. I know which one of us you could do without. Not once, not even once did you tell me that you loved me or that

The letter was unfinished.

Andrea felt furtive and embarrassed. She hurriedly started for the back stairs.

"Hey, Andrea." The sliding glass door opened and Holly came in. "I'm glad you came back before I left."

"You're leaving?" Flustered, Andrea turned her back to the letter on the table. "Where are you off to?"

"A guy I know at the University of San Diego invited me down for a fraternity Christmas party."

"That sounds like fun."

"He's just a friend. His steady just broke off with him, so he called me."

Andrea searched for something encouraging to say. "I hear San Diego is nice."

"Yeah. That's mostly why I'm going. Just a chance to see a little more of California while we're here." Holly allowed herself a fragment of youthful excitement. "You think I should leave my hair braided, or not?"

"It looks cute braided, but it would be beautiful if you let it hang loose."

"Yeah. Well, I think I'll do that. I'll just be gone a day, or two at the most."

"Have a good time." Andrea dropped the apple into an outside pocket of her shoulder bag. "I'm glad you have a chance to see your friend." She doubted that Holly took many days off.

"Andrea—"

"Yes?"

"I know I shouldn't ask you this"—Holly hesitated—"especially since you're just staying here as a matter of convenience while you're working at the Huntington. But would you mind sort of keeping an eye on Benjamin and Sarah while I'm gone?"

"What do you mean?" Andrea was puzzled and a little annoyed that Holly would ask.

"I guess I'm overprotective." The statement would have seemed ludicrous coming from this girl with the braided hair who was barely out of her teens had it not been for her look of genuine concern. "Benjamin is so fragile—oh, I know he looks healthy enough. I've *made* him eat. But he's like one of those Chinese puzzle boxes. There's no way to get inside—"

Andrea wondered if Holly had read the letter on the table. A child who hated his mother and resented his brother or sister—wherever he or she might be—had a larger problem than just a sluggish appetite.

"—He doesn't talk much, and he spends too much time with that damn bully, Nikki. That's why I'm pushing him into taking a riding lesson tomorrow. He already rides better than John Wayne, but at least this will get him out of the house. Nikki was Georgene's contribution. She hired him before we got here. Frankly, I can't stand the little sneak, and sooner or later I'm afraid he's going to get Benjamin in trouble."

Andrea was beginning to feel exasperated, not only for herself but also for this young girl. Holly had introduced herself as Sarah's cook, but apparently she had fallen into—or been coerced into—the role of protector for a mature woman and her ten-year-old son. It was not hard to see how it could happen. Holly had probably spent most of her young life mending broken dolls, rescuing wounded birds, and getting friends out of trouble. "Surely Sarah is capable of handling things while you're gone—"

"That's just it. I don't think she is. She's been seeing a dopey psychiatrist who prescribes too many pills and who hasn't helped at all as far as I can tell. Seeing him was an-other one of Georgene's bright ideas.'' Holly tugged at a strand of blond hair that slipped out of the loose braid. ''I thought coming back home to San Marino would be good for her. She and Georgene grew up here.''

''Are there other members of their family still around?'' Andrea wondered hopefully if there might be some assistance from that quarter.

''No. And Sarah doesn't seem to have any friends who still live in the area, either. As for Georgene, her darling sister—we hadn't been here a week when she suddenly decided to go to England—'' Holly cut short what she was saying with a furtive glance toward the terrace.

Sarah, who until now had continued to watch the progress of Benjamin's drawing, bent and kissed him on the top of the head, then came into the kitchen.

Even on such short acquaintance, Andrea could see the resemblance between the sisters. Sarah had none of Georgene's manufactured glamour, but their features were much the same, though Sarah's were more delicate. Sarah could have been considered truly beautiful if it were not for the deep worry lines in her forehead and around her mouth, and the light makeup she wore did nothing to hide the pallor of her skin. Also, she seemed taller than her sister. Or it might have been just that she was so thin. The full, gauzy peach-colored skirt and blouse she wore hung loosely on her. Her clothes looked as though they had been purchased when she was a size or two larger.

''Andrea. Well, hello again.'' Sarah slid the door closed behind her. They had not seen each other since the night before, when Andrea was clutching at her raincoat to hide the bikini underneath. ''You don't show any signs of jet lag. After an hour in a plane it takes me days to recover.'' She openly appraised Andrea's sleek light-woolen dress and neatly combed hair tied back in a matching green scarf. ''It's such a shame your boyfriend couldn't have been here to meet you.''

"I should be used to it by now. Transoceanic romances aren't easy." Andrea knew she sounded more accepting than she felt. The fact that Aldo Balzani had allowed his duties with the Italian police to keep him in Florence when they had planned a vacation was becoming a source for more than just disappointment. She was beginning to feel angry. Never mind that it was her *own* work that had determined that the vacation should be in California.

After a pause, when Sarah seemed reconciled that Andrea was not going to be more forthcoming about her personal relationship, she said, "Has Holly told you about her Christmas dance?"

"Yes." All that Andrea could think to add was what she had said before. "I hear San Diego is very nice."

"I suppose she's been telling you we can't possibly manage without her."

Before Andrea could respond, Holly, unperturbed, said, "There's stew in the fridge—you can stick it in the microwave in the same bowl. And there's a half-gallon of pecan crunch ice cream in the freezer if you can't get Benjamin to eat anything else." She looked at Andrea, as though the instructions were meant for her.

"Be on your way, Holly," Sarah said. "We'll do fine."

"My bag is already in the car." Holly took a quick look around the kitchen. "I told you about the food— And, Andrea, there are more cinnamon rolls in the bread box—"

Andrea smiled. "There may not be any when you get back."

"Emergency telephone numbers by the phone"—she pointed to the wall next to the side door—"including the cab company. Remember, Sarah, call at least an hour before your appointment—" Looking directly at Andrea, she said, "I left a telephone number where you can reach me in San Diego. There's an answering machine if we're not there—"

"Good-bye!" Sarah said.

Holly gave Sarah a rough hug and a kiss on the cheek. "This will be the first time you've been alone," she said, and Andrea could have sworn there were tears in the girl's eyes.

With a noisy sniff, Holly went to the terrace door and tapped on the glass to get Benjamin's attention. When he looked up, she blew him a kiss, then hurried toward the front of the house, where the car was parked.

Andrea was equally in a hurry to be gone. "I just came back to change clothes," she said to Sarah, who had not moved and was staring at the floor. "I want to get started at the Huntington this afternoon."

Sarah managed a smile that seemed a degree too bright to be genuine. "Yes, I imagine you'll be glad to be out of here as quickly as possible." Suddenly her glance fell to the letter on the table.

To Andrea's surprise, Sarah casually picked up the sheet of paper, tore it in quarters, and stood holding two pieces in each hand.

"Although I wouldn't tell Holly," Sarah said, "I'm going to cancel my appointment tomorrow afternoon with the psychiatrist. All he has done so far is ask me questions about the past. I don't know how you can get rid of everything that's happened before, do you? It seems to me you should just leave the past alone. Don't you think so? I don't know. But I can't *bear* to hear that man use the word 'closure' one more time."

Andrea watched as Sarah tore the letter into smaller pieces and dropped them into a wicker waste basket. Had she read the letter from her son? Was she simply dismissing it?

"I don't know. The doctor said it would help. But I don't feel any better. What do you think?"

"About what, Sarah?" Andrea felt as though she were questioning a child.

Sarah laughed. "I'm sorry. I must sound totally dopey— to use Holly's word. The psychiatrist I've been seeing suggested that I write letters—just for myself, not that they would ever be mailed—to the people with whom I have an unfinished relationship. He says it's the only way I'll ever be able to achieve 'closure.'" She shook her head rapidly as though she were shaking off a buzzing insect. "'Write to all the significant people in your life, no matter whether they're alive or dead,' he said. 'Dead or alive.'"

She wrote the letter, Andrea suddenly realized. It wasn't Benjamin writing to her. She was writing to her own mother.

"It seems to me," Sarah said, "you never finish a relationship. If I wrote a letter to all the people with whom there had not been…'closure'…that would be everyone I've ever known. People are not wiped out of your memory because they're out of sight—or dead. You don't just say to someone, 'Okay, that's it, you're gone, I'll never think about you again—I'll completely forget what you looked like, what you were to me, how much you hurt me, how much I loved you. You're finished. You never existed.'" Her darting eyes looked helplessly into Andrea's for an instant. "Don't you think so? I don't know."

Then, as quickly and fervently as Sarah had denounced her psychiatric treatment, she launched into an apology. "Andrea. I'm sorry! There's no excuse for unloading all this on you." With a sad little laugh, she said, "I'm not completely nuts. It's just that this has not been a good year for Benjamin and me. Thank God for Holly and her down-home common sense—and cinnamon rolls."

"Yes, it must be very pleasant to have someone like Holly around." Andrea knew that was an inadequate response, after everything Sarah had said, but she was determined not to ask any questions that would involve her in the problems that billowed and swirled around this woman like her loose-fitting clothes.

Still, she would not be normal if she were not curious. She *had* read the letter. She had not meant to, but she had.

It was Sarah's letter, not Benjamin's. Sarah had written to her own mother that she hated her. She was the one who had always felt unwanted—because of the favored child. Georgene.

"This is the only thing I can thank my psychiatrist for." Sarah picked up a handbag that she had left in a chair by the breakfast table and took out a small bottle with a pharmacist's label on the side.

Andrea must have looked slightly alarmed, because Sarah added, "They're only mild sleeping pills. I didn't sleep very well last night."

"I can take part of the responsibility for that," Andrea said, "there was really no need to meet me at the airport. I could have taken the shuttle."

"When your nice Mr. Balzani called and I could hear the disappointment and concern in his voice all the way from Italy— Well, I couldn't let you arrive with no one there to meet you." Sarah smiled and the lines around her mouth and between her brows disappeared. For a moment, there was a glimpse of girlish sweetness that seemed to belong on her face, but then, instantly, the lines came back. "I think I'll go take a nap." She winced as though she had a headache. "Nikki will be here with Benjamin until dinnertime." She started toward the sliding doors that led to the guesthouse off of the patio.

Andrea glanced out the window at the two boys. Benjamin was still working on his drawing. Nikki had changed into swimming trunks and was thrashing about in the pool, deliberately splashing water toward the younger boy. Benjamin moved his chair back. Nikki splashed harder and laughed when drops of water landed on the sketch pad.

"Sarah," Andrea said impulsively, following after her. "I'm just going to be doing some preliminary work this afternoon. Would you mind if Benjamin came with me?" The invitation was out of her mouth before she thought about it.

"You mean, go with you to the Huntington?"

"Yes. He seems so interested in art, I thought he might like to see the kind of thing I do. I might even put him to work."

She felt guilty, she supposed. First, because she had read the letter. Second, because she had jumped so quickly to the conclusion that Benjamin had written it.

And there was Nikki. Like Holly, Andrea thought he was a sneak and a bully. It seemed intolerable that he was the only companion for a young boy away from home with no other friends.

"I know he'd love to go with you." Sarah's wonderful smile was back. She tried to protest, but it was a feeble effort. "I'm afraid he'd be in your way."

"It's all right. Really."

"If you're sure, I'll go down and tell him." She smiled again.

In her room, Andrea dropped her handbag on the bed and picked up the apple when it rolled out. She bit into it, holding it in her teeth as she rummaged in her suitcase for her jeans and plaid shirt.

When she was dressed, she hurried back downstairs and into the kitchen holding the ravaged apple by its stem. She scanned Holly's spotless chrome and tile domain for a garbage can. Kitchens were not her area of expertise, and it took some scouting to discover the trash compactor and figure out how it worked.

It did no harm to take Benjamin with her just this one time. Holly said she would be back tomorrow—or the next day—so there would never be a need again. Holly would be there to keep Nikki in line and keep an eye on Sarah. God knows what her problems are, Andrea thought, but *she* didn't want to know.

As she dropped the apple core into the shiny trash compactor, she was aware that her resolve not to get involved had disappeared as quickly and completely as the apple.

NINETEEN

NIKKI YAMAGUCHI knew he was not particularly well liked. Come to that, he was aware that most people, once they got to know him, couldn't stand him. He took pride in that.

He was the youngest of three children. His brother had always excelled in the biological sciences and was now near the top of his premed class at Stanford. His sister, even as a small child, had uncomplainingly practiced the violin several hours a day and had steadily gained recognition for her virtuosity. Nikki, minus a scientific or musical bent, discovered that being obnoxious assured him of an equal amount of attention.

It was not that he was neglected or unappreciated. His parents tried to encourage all three of their children in whatever endeavors they took an interest. Early on, they recognized in Nikki what they took to be a spark of artistic ability. The first and most consistent praise he could remember was for his deft touch with crayons. He always made the skies in his coloring books blue, the trees green, the sun yellow. There was no experimentation with purple-faced children, orange dogs, or black stars—and he always, always stayed inside the lines.

As he grew older, his parents encouraged the one unique trait they thought they had found in their youngest child: they shepherded him through the Getty, the Norton Simon, the Los Angeles County, and the Huntington art museums. They enrolled him in art-appreciation classes and sent him to a three-week camp for young artists on Catalina Island each summer from junior high through high school.

By his sophomore year he was exceedingly knowledgeable about techniques and equipment, consistent with his delicate brush strokes, and painstaking with details. If he had been asked to copy *The Last Supper* on the back of a matchbook, he would have given it a try—and come close. But by the time he had progressed to this point, to his great disappointment, he was able to recognize his unique ability for what it was. Sadly, what his parents considered his artistic talent, he knew was merely excellent small-muscle coordination.

Nevertheless, because of his skill and training, he was at the top of the San Marino High School list of art tutors. This made his parents proud, and, on the whole, was satisfying to Nikki. Most of his charges were pubescent females who were content to draw Barbie-doll-like figures in bizarre outfits. These girls looked upon Nikki as an eccentric genius. With his occasional male students, he found they, too, were most interested in drawing the female form, but without the weird clothing and in greater anatomical detail. (The exception to this was the one preteen boy who was more interested in Ken's missing parts than Barbie's.) For the boys, at the end of a session, Nikki would sketch an airplane or a sailboat and help them watercolor the background, so they would have something to take home and show their parents.

Nikki knew that what he was doing was little more than baby-sitting rich kids whose parents were willing to pay twenty-five dollars an hour for time to themselves. He found it amusing. He thrived on the feeling of superiority that it gave him.

When he was hired to tutor Benjamin Anderson, he asked the boy if there was any particular subject matter he was interested in drawing. Benjamin shrugged in what seemed to be boredom.

Nikki, in turn, had sketched a basic sailboat, then dipped the brush in a clear blue watercolor and handed it to the boy with instructions to "fill in" the water. Benjamin did. Then, with no help from Nikki, he rearranged the palette of chalky colors in front of him and selected two additional brushes.

Mixing a myriad of delicate shades, he added a stormy sky and roughed in a rocky coastline. On the crest of a cliff, he placed a lighthouse, and with a minimum number of strokes, the suggestion of two small figures materialized. One was clearly a man on the boat waving to shore, and the second, a child on the beach with reaching, outstretched hands, watching the boat sail away. All of this was done with exquisite shading and an extraordinary blending of colors. It was like a brilliant extemporization on a pedestrian melody.

As Nikki watched, dumbfounded, a bitter taste filled his mouth, and his long, lean fingers clenched and unclenched in fists. He wanted nothing so much as to grab the drawing and tear it to bits: without a word, apparently without even caring, this ten-year-old had demonstrated an innate artistic talent that Nikki had come to realize did not reside within his own breast.

In his sudden surge of overwhelming envy, Nikki might actually have destroyed the watercolor if Sarah had not come out on the terrace that first day to monitor her son's progress. As she watched Benjamin complete the picture—he added the figure of the child last—her eyes filled with tears.

Probably because Benjamin would not fight back, Nikki made the boy the repository of his own frustration in competing with his doctor-to-be brother and virtuoso-to-be sister. Heaped on top of the frustration was resentment against his parents for encouraging him to take a path for which they supplied the guidebook but where he had no natural sense of direction.

But most of Nikki's taunting and shoving and general meanness (always out of Sarah's sight, though Holly was not so easy to avoid) was the result of a corrosive jealousy that burned and shriveled him inside. His passion might have been less consuming if Benjamin had responded. But the boy seemed to place no value on the extraordinary gift he had been given. Thus, if his work was threatened, he

seemed to feel it was no great loss. Once, when Nikki sur-
reptitiously spilled a glass of iced tea on a half-finished
pastel of the lily pond—a remarkable rendering done entirely in shades of green—Benjamin had merely stopped a
skittering ice cube on the flagstone patio with his foot and
half-heartedly kicked it at his tutor. What Nikki had found
truly maddening was that though the boy had every right to
jump on him with pounding fists, he merely picked up his
equipment and moved to the opposite side of the pool and
started over—this time experimenting with shades of lavender.

Benjamin, with only ten years on earth, had already decided, it seemed, to make himself invulnerable to disturbing emotions. He refused to show anger or pleasure or pain.
It was as though his allotment for each had already been
used and could not be replenished.

That afternoon when Holly had driven away in the rental
car, Sarah had taken her bottle of pills and gone to the
guesthouse to rest. Andrea—changed into jeans and a plaid
shirt—started off with Benjamin to the Huntington art museum. Nikki, it was supposed, returned home.

He started walking in that direction. His family lived in
an estate only a quarter of a mile away. Suddenly, though,
he stopped and watched the retreating figures of Andrea and
Benjamin as they took the curved sidewalk around the perimeter of the Huntington gardens toward the entrance to
the grounds. Prompted again by jealousy or frustration,
curiosity, loneliness, or any one—or all—of his boiling
emotions that were as puzzling to him as to anyone who
knew him, Nikki decided to follow. There was no need to
make his presence known or to take time with the sidewalk.
He could be at the art gallery and waiting before Andrea and
Benjamin even got there.

Actually, he had never had the nerve to go over the fence
in broad daylight before. But with a quick look in both directions of Euston Road to make certain there were no people or automobiles in sight, he ducked behind a broad

eucalyptus tree next to one of the high metal posts. Spurred by fear of being caught and the excitement of intrigue, he was over the top and onto the grounds in seconds.

Nikki ran up the slope toward the gallery, not sure what he would do next, just pleased with the success of his endeavor so far. When he reached the sidewalk in front of the statuary garden, he laughed out loud at the sight of the statue still wearing the green jacket. He was surprised to see that no one had even tried to remove the paint yet.

TWENTY

EDUARDO AND TINA checked out at Hollenbeck and stopped by El Fenix to compare notes. Their afternoon spent on the telephones had garnered a meager amount of information about Goochie's mysterious background, but nothing they learned gave them a clue as to why he ended his days shot through the chest in the statuary garden of the Huntington, wearing only the accumulated grime of the streets of Los Angeles.

The two detectives took a booth in the corner. Eduardo waved to the bartender and ordered a draft beer for himself and the usual tonic water with lime for Tina. It was just past four-thirty P.M. and the El Fenix cantina was almost empty. By five, during the daily Feliz Hora Fiesta, customers would be three deep around the bar and buffet table. Dishes of salsa and guacamole dip, baskets of chips, trays of tiny tacos and tostadas, and warming pans filled with bite-sized tamales and enchiladas would all be set out as an inducement to the afterwork crowd to buy more drinks and, oftentimes, to stay on for dinner.

"Ah, my friend Eduardo!" Armando Estrada, the proprietor, carrying a large tray, backed into the cantina from the kitchen, using his ample backside to push open the swinging door.

"Hey, Armando."

"You and your lady"—Armando never referred to Tina any other way, although she had explained to him more than once that she and Eduardo were both detectives and worked together as partners—"the two of you must try my chicken *taquitos*." He set the tray on the long buffet table, then took a small plate from a neat stack and piled it high with rolled and fried tortillas filled with a spicy chicken mixture. "Still almost too hot to touch."

"Thanks, Armando." Eduardo frowned at the plate that had been set in front of him. "But it's too early."

"¿Como?" Estrada looked puzzled.

"The sign over the bar says 'Feliz Hora—five P.M.'" Eduardo made a production of checking his watch. "It's already a quarter till."

Tina rolled her eyes.

Armando laughed and went back to the kitchen.

"I can see where it would all lead." Eduardo was deeply disapproving. "I mean, even though we're off duty, it's a matter of appearance. First, you accept free *taquitos* fifteen minutes before happy hour, and the next thing you know you're walking out of Winchel's without paying for a doughnut—"

"Oh, for God's sake, *eat* the damn things!" Tina grabbed one of the crispy rolls and bit into it, sucking in air with the bite to cool her mouth. "I wouldn't know how to write it up, anyway."

"I'm sure you could find something in the manual that would cover it."

When the plate was empty, Tina wiped her fingers on a paper napkin from a nearby plastic holder and reached into her handbag for a notepad. "Where do we start?"

"You begin. Just tell me everything we know so far." Eduardo motioned to the bartender for another beer and a second tonic and lime for Tina.

"The victim was called Goochie by his street pal, Rainbow, because of his Gucci shoes. The shoes that were found with the victim's missing clothes in a drainage ditch at Santa Anita Race Track were part of an order shipped to the Lexington Stables Silks and Bootery, a specialty chain with outlets at the major racetracks that catered to stable owners and their personnel, especially jockeys."

"Because of Goochie's size, we can rule out that he was a jockey, and because of the price of the shoes, he was al-

most certainly more than just one of the stable hands."
Eduardo took a drink from the frosty beer mug. "Go on."

"This part is supposition. Okay?"

Eduardo nodded.

"Suppose Goochie was maybe even a stable owner—because of where he bought his shoes. He could have found the same brand a number of different places, but he was familiar with a shop that supplied racing silks and boots and clothing for folks associated with the racetrack. So, since he wasn't a jockey, and because he had that kind of money to spend on his feet, let's at least assume he owned a thoroughbred. That takes lots of bucks. Meantime, it's not unlikely he was also a gambler. Maybe he got in over his head. And believe me, after all those afternoons I spent at the track with my dad, I know that between the time it takes to say 'And they're off!' and 'The winner is—!' a life's savings can disappear. So, let's say Goochie loses everything and hits the street. We know he'd probably been there several years because of the condition of his beloved shoes. But he never lost his interest in racing. Rainbow said he checked the daily lineup every day. Then, suddenly, he comes into a small windfall—the ten bucks the TV guy gave him for breaking up the fight. But once you're a habitual gambler, you don't ever really lose the desire. Gambling's like drinking."

"Or sex."

"Huh?"

"Go on," Eduardo said.

"So, we know he at least started for Santa Anita. Suppose he got there and really did win a bundle. There's no faster way to make a new friend than with someone who's seen you standing in line at the pay-out window.

"Or it's not impossible that he ran into someone from his more prosperous days who still had a grudge against him— maybe Goochie had run out on a debt, or something. Naturally, in either case, it would be hard for the perp to do him in right there at the track. So he gets Goochie drunk and lures him away in a car to a place he knows they're not likely to be seen or heard. Shoots him, and removes his clothes—hoping the body can't be identified. And as you so cleverly pointed out, he turns left on Huntington Drive—back toward Santa Anita—to an area he knows well, and dumps the clothes in the drainage ditch where he thinks they won't be found. At least, there's a fair chance they won't be connected to Goochie—" Tina leaned back in the booth with a deep sigh, her animation dissipated. "But why—"

"But why the statuary garden at the Huntington?"

"Yeah."

"Yeah," Eduardo echoed. "It makes no sense. There had to be a better place than that. The Huntington was closed and patrolled—not very well, I grant you. But the only way Goochie and his killer could have gotten onto the grounds was to come over the fence. How do you convince a drunk to climb a six-foot fence?"

"And what about the statue?" Tina squeezed the last drops of juice from the lime wedge into her tonic water and plopped the rind back into the glass. "I mean, the red paint on the statue the next morning. What was that all about. And then the green paint on another one today?"

"That's something else—nothing to do with Goochie's murder. I'm convinced of that," Eduardo said. "And it sure as hell was not the work of a graffiti artist."

The two of them sat silently for several minutes—Eduardo staring into his empty beer mug, Tina stirring her drink with a straw clockwise for several revolutions, then counterclockwise.

"So, what do we do next?" Tina asked.

"We've got to get a positive I.D. on the body."

"How do we do that?"

"Tomorrow morning we take the racing page that was in Goochie's pocket and call all the stable owners who had horses running the day he was murdered and tell them what we've got. We'll see if one of them can give us a lead."

"Hey! Yeah, I see." The excitement was back in Tina's voice. "Maybe it wasn't just *any* horse that was running that day, but a *particular* horse—"

"It's a longshot."

"As they say in racing circles."

Eduardo grinned at his partner, then turned to survey the cantina that had quickly become crowded and noisy. A mariachi trio in tight black pants and jackets with silver studs and wearing wide sombreros had stationed themselves at the far end of the bar and launched into a lively rendition of "El Rancho Grande."

"Unless there's something else we need to talk about," Tina scooted to the edge of the booth and stood up. "I'd like to put on my running shoes before it gets dark."

"Sure. Go on ahead."

"What do you mean, go on ahead? Aren't you going to take me back to Hollenbeck to pick up my car?" They had driven to El Fenix in the unmarked LAPD automobile that Eduardo usually took home with him.

"Leave your car at the division tonight, and take the monster outside home with you."

"What?" Tina was incredulous. He had never suggested that before.

"Look. I've had a beer."

"Oh." She felt chagrined. It was usually Tina who kept track of the number of drinks her partner had. But one beer—even she wouldn't complain about that. "I'll take you home if—"

"No, no. You go ahead. I'll get a ride."

"If you're sure," she said, but he seemed adamant. "Okay then. I'll catch up with you in the morning."

At the door, still surprised at her partner's behavior, Tina turned back for a final look.

Opposite Eduardo, in the booth where Tina had sat, was the sexy waitress in the short red skirt who had so pointedly waited to talk with him the last time they had been in the El Fenix.

"*Oh* yeah," Tina said, reaching in her handbag for the duplicate keys to the unmarked police car.

TWENTY-ONE

LATE THAT afternoon, the rain descended from heaven with the timing of a deus ex machina in a Greek drama. Like an ancient god lowered on stage to untangle the problems created by mortals, the rain arrived with a bolt of lightning and a clap of thunder and altered the paths of the players.

IN THE GUESTHOUSE of Georgene Dodson's quiet home on Euston Road, the lightning was so close it seemed to sear the closed eyelids of the woman who lay on the satin coverlet half sleeping. Instantly awakened by the flash, Sarah was upright in a sitting position before the thunder cracked like a gunshot.

It sounded exactly like a gunshot to Sarah. She hugged her knees to her chest and dropped her head to her arms, sobbing.

Thunder. That was all it was. It was only thunder this time, she told herself, but she could not stop crying as the memory of the time before came back in horrible detail.

ANDREA HAD NOT realized the rain was coming. There were no windows in the main gallery at the Huntington, which had closed to the public at four P.M. Only she and Benjamin remained, oblivious to the unexpected storm clouds that were swirling in a south-easterly direction from the Pacific.

Before the first clap of thunder, the boy had seemed perfectly content to sit with his feet dangling over the edge of a polished-oak bench in the center of the gallery as Andrea began to examine the painting of *The Blue Boy*.

Benjamin had watched, expressionless, as she climbed the library-type ladder and pulled on a pair of sterile gloves like the ones worn by surgeons.

Starting in the top left corner, she began to draw her fingertips across the surface of the painting. Methodically, she felt her way, inch-by-inch, across the face of the canvas.

She had completed a tactile examination of the top third of the painting before Benjamin asked, "Why are you doing that?"

"Sometimes the eye misses things that the fingers find," she said. "I want to know if there are any tiny cracks in the canvas or lumps of varnish that I'm going to have to consider before I start."

That seemed as basic an explanation as she could give. She hoped it might prompt another question from the little boy, but none came. The only sound was the crackling of cellophane as he unwrapped a piece of hard candy and put it in his mouth.

After many more moments of silence, a faint shuffling noise filtered through the closed door to the hallway. For an instant, Andrea was afraid that Benjamin had left the gallery. But with a quick glance over her shoulder, she saw that he was still there on the bench, holding his feet straight out in front of him, apparently engrossed in studying the multicolored shoelaces in his dirty high tops. With raised eyebrows his eyes met hers. Wordlessly, they both acknowledged the sound, and Andrea dismissed it with a slight shrug as . . . nothing.

It must have been the guard. The officious uniformed female with the sturdy build and tightly permed gray hair had introduced herself earlier. She was a retired executive with a supermarket chain, she had told Andrea when she came in to announce that it was closing time and she was locking up, but that she would be making rounds.

Andrea was accustomed to the silence of working alone, but with Benjamin there she felt she had to entertain him in some way.

"Benjamin, would you like to see something interesting?" Andrea turned and pointed to a place on the hardwood floor about six feet in front of the portrait, and a bit to the left. "Go stand over there."

The boy lifted his head and looked at her suspiciously, as though he expected a trick or a punishment.

I'm not doing this right, Andrea thought. Then smiling, she said, "Just go stand there. I want to see how good your eyes are."

Obediently, Benjamin stood where she pointed.

"Now. Look at the portrait."

He frowned at the painting of the boy in the unlikely blue satin knee britches and lace-trimmed jacket, and then at her.

With one finger, Andrea touched the painting just above *The Blue Boy*'s head. "Does the background here look different to you than anywhere else in the painting?"

"It looks like a dark blob."

"Yes, at first glance. Actually, if you look very closely, you can *almost* tell it's a second face." She saw a spark of interest and hurried on. "This picture is really quite mysterious. When the painting is X-rayed, you can see clearly that Gainsborough painted over a portrait he had started of someone else. And even without X-ray eyes, you can nearly make out a man's collar and chin from where you're standing."

Benjamin moved his head to the left, and then to the right as he studied the painting.

Encouraged, and with no other topics of conversation rushing to mind, Andrea went on to explain that when the artist was commissioned to paint a portrait of a wealthy patron, he always started with a fresh canvas. The fact that in this case he used a discarded one suggested that he painted *The Blue Boy* just because he wanted to.

"No one knows for sure who the boy was." Andrea added that the model was probably the son of the artist's friend—an ironmonger named Brutall—who lived in London. And the reason Gainsborough asked the boy to pose in the blue satin suit was to settle a long-standing argument about color. Other artists of that period maintained that *blue* was not vivid enough—too cold—to be the dominant color in a painting. "And as you can see, Gainsborough proved them wrong."

"There's *still* too much blue," Benjamin concluded. He stood studying the picture of the adolescent boy a minute or two longer, then sat again on the bench. Andrea thought she had lost him until he asked, "How long ago was that picture painted?"

"A little over two hundred years."

"Did boys really dress like that?"

"No, it was like a costume," Andrea said. "It was kind of like when you were little. Your mom probably took a photograph of you wearing a cowboy suit or a Batman cape. Same sort of thing. Gainsborough kept a trunkful of costumes for customers—grown-ups, too—who wanted to be painted in 'fancy dress.' In several of his portraits, the people are different, but the clothes are the same."

This was going pretty well, Andrea thought. She was considering how to describe the controversy of whether the Venetian artist Titian was the greatest influence on Gainsborough, or whether—as she believed—it was the Flemish artist Van Dyke.

"Most great painters have been influenced by the work of someone else—" she began. Suddenly she felt the ladder move and looked down to see Benjamin standing with his hand on the railing.

"I heard someone again," he said in a hushed tone.

"What?"

"I heard someone out in the hall." There was no fear in the boy's face. He was simply reporting something that was unexpected.

Andrea had heard only the sound of her own voice. "There's always a guard on duty." She looked in the direction of the closed door. "She's probably just making a routine check."

"Maybe," Benjamin said, but he seemed unconvinced.

Though she had heard nothing, Andrea decided to investigate. She took off the gloves and laid them on the equipment tray at the top of the ladder. As she turned with one foot poised above the top step, the gallery was suddenly plunged into darkness.

With no windows to look through, Andrea had not seen the lightning as it slashed across the sky and struck a power pole near the entrance to the Huntington. In the next moment, when a crashing clap of thunder seemed to rattle the walls and reverberate throughout the building, she realized what had happened.

"Benjamin. It's just a thunderstorm. Are you okay?"

The sound of crashing metal and an astonished cry came from the direction of the hallway.

How could he have gotten that far so quickly? "Benjamin?"

"That wasn't me." The sound of the boy's calm voice came from the foot of the ladder where he had been standing when the electricity went off.

"Stay there. Stay where you are." Andrea carefully felt her way on the stairs until her hand found his on the railing, and she grasped it tightly. Leading him blindly to the bench that she knew was only a few feet away, she said, "Wait here until I open the door." There would be light in the hallway through the French doors. She tried to sound reassuring. "No need for both of us to bang our shins in the dark."

Without the overhead lighting panels, the room was in total blackout. Care had been taken when the gallery was designed to maintain a constant temperature. As a result, the room was sealed against outside air, dust, and the California sun. There was not even a glimmer of light beneath the door to help Andrea find her way.

Holding her hands in front, she walked carefully in what she hoped was a straight line toward the entrance to the hall. There were no obstructions in the gallery, only the row of center benches, and she consciously stayed clear of them. Quickly, she reached the door and pushed it open. Almost instantly, Benjamin was standing beside her, and she took his hand again.

After the total darkness of the gallery, the gray light of the cloud-swathed afternoon that filtered through the French doors was almost blinding.

From above, on the second floor, came the faint sound of running feet near the stairs. Closer by, at the opposite end of the hall, in the dining room of the mansion, was the crashing sound of metal as before.

Instinctively, Andrea pushed Benjamin behind her. With just a few steps she was at the doorway. Another flash of lightning through the west windows seemed to illuminate the eighteenth-century crystal chandelier. Reflective sparks of light danced across the polished surface of the long, teak-wood dining table and glinted on the British silver compotes and candelabra set there on display.

On the east wall, beneath a Gilbert Stuart portrait of George Washington, a mammoth rococo fireplace—unused for at least three decades—yawned open, unprotected. On the stone hearth, lying flat where it had fallen, was a gigantic bronze fire screen in the shape of a peacock with a spread tail. And sprawled half in, half out of the fireplace he had used as a hiding place was Nikki Yamaguchi, looking equally foolish and frightened.

The midshift guard hurried through the doorway. "Miss Perkins! Is everything down here all right?"

The eyes of the retired supermarket executive gleamed with excitement. A two-way radio crackled unintelligibly in her hand, and a baton swung from a belt loop as she strode around the room. "I thought I heard something fall!"

"We're fine. No harm done."

For the first time, the guard noticed Nikki. She watched sternly as the teenaged boy climbed out of the fireplace and righted the screen. "Do you know him?" She looked accusingly at Andrea. "I thought there was just going to be the one boy. When I came on duty, I saw only you and one boy in the gallery.''

"Yes, they're both with me. I'm sorry I didn't let you know.'' Andrea felt certain she would regret accepting responsibility for Nikki. The creepy kid had probably hidden behind the firescreen at closing time with the idea of scaring her and Benjamin later.

"What was this one doing in the dining room?'' The guard cocked a thumb at Nikki, then examined the firescreen to make sure no damage had been done.

There was another lightning flash and clap of thunder. Andrea saw Nikki's eyes get large and his shoulders tense. He was frightened! He was scared of the storm!

"We were all in the gallery when the lights went off.'' She took Benjamin's hand again. "Benjamin was amazingly calm. He stayed with me until we could see where we were going. Right after we heard the thunder, we heard the firescreen fall.''

Frowning, the guard stood waiting for a better explanation. Andrea did not blame her.

Then, confidentially to the guard, but loud enough for both boys to hear, Andrea said, "You know how being in total darkness affects some people—and then the thunder. That can be pretty frightening, too.'' She cast a meaningful look in Nikki's direction. Sweetly, but with some malice, and a great deal of pleasure, she added, "I'm sure Nikki didn't mean to knock over the firescreen. But you know how it is when you're scared out of your wits . . . It's just that he must have been in such a hurry, he wasn't looking where he was going.'' She leaned closer to the guard and let her voice drop even more. "I suspect it's some sort of phobia—like being afraid of spiders, or something.''

Andrea knew that Benjamin had missed nothing. He had seen how frightened Nikki was, and how foolish he looked climbing out of the fireplace. The tormentor was vanquished!

It was worth the lies to see Nikki's embarrassment and at last to hear Benjamin laugh—a rusty little laugh that sounded as though it had not been used in a long time.

Andrea squeezed the small boy's hand in camaraderie. Later, she was surprised to realize how vividly she remembered the feel of his little hand, and how surprised she was at its roughness, and that it scratched against her palm.

"There's no telling how long the lights will be out," the guard said, not totally taken in.

"You're right," Andrea agreed. "I think we'll leave right now before the rain starts pouring."

WHEN TINA ROBERSON left El Fenix restaurant, she took the Pasadena Freeway toward Dodger Stadium, then exited on the Academy Drive off ramp. The police academy was her favorite place to run. She knew the feel of the hard-packed earth, and the exact number of times she could circle the track in thirty minutes—more than anyone else had been able to in her graduating class.

The sky was overcast and there was no glare. It looked like a perfect afternoon for running. Even the smog that sometimes left her choking when she pushed herself too hard was gone.

As the road wound to the top of the hill, she had a view of the San Gabriel Mountains and most of the valley below.

Before she reached the parking lot, rain had begun to streak the windshield, but not enough to turn on the wipers. That was no problem; she liked to run in the rain.

When she had changed clothes, and was halfway to the track, a bolt of lightning forked across the mountaintop and flashed to earth, striking somewhere in the valley. From how quickly the rattling thunder followed, and the direction in which the lightning struck, Tina guessed it must have hit somewhere near South Pasadena or San Marino.

"Damn! That was powerful!"

She did not know whether lightning had a particular affinity for young women of color wearing lime green, nylon shorts and running shoes, but she decided against putting it to the test.

"Well, hell." She found herself using her father's phrase, "It's just not my day."

She did not want to go home this early. Her sister's kids would be having dinner. And, as usual, her sister would be gone—God knew where—and her mother would be complaining about having already raised one family and not needing another one to look after.

With her father gone, Tina spent less and less time at home. He had been dead for more than a year, but she still found it painful to see the trophies she had won on the shelves that her father had built for them in the entry.

"No need to hide your light, babe," he had said. "These trophies are not going under a bushel. Let people see the kind of champ you are." He had winked at her, "And the kind of coach I am." She had not had the heart to take them down, but she could not stand to look at them, either.

Her father had been her coach, her friend, her hero, and her greatest worry. Until his death she had never given up hope that he would end his love affair with the racetrack.

She pulled on a warm-up suit over her shorts, and bought a plastic-wrapped pimiento cheese sandwich from the dispensing machine. Might as well go back to Hollenbeck and get a head start on her report, she decided.

As she took the road back down the hill from the academy, she was still thinking of her father. She remembered a day during a sudden downpour just before the last race at Santa Anita when she had stood with him under the overhang of the grandstand.

"Let's go, Daddy." The track was turning to mud. None of the favorites would run.

"Hang on, babe." He was listening to the public address system and not to her. "Let me hear which horses have been scratched." He marked off the name of each mount that had been pulled from the race because of the condition of the track. Then, unfolding the crumpled newspaper further, he read aloud the statistics of the horses that were left, and Xed and underlined his choices. "The longshots come in on a muddy track," he told her. "This is going to be our day."

And for once, it had been. He had won more than eight thousand dollars on an Exacta in the ninth race.

As she ran through the rain to get back in her unmarked police car at the academy, she remembered the way her father had splashed around like Gene Kelly in the Santa Anita parking lot the day of his big win. There had not been many days like that.

At Hollenbeck, she shook the rain from her jacket at the entrance, then draped it across the back of the wooden chair at her desk.

The sandwich was tasteless and she hardly realized she was eating it as she looked through the notes she had made that day with Eduardo. On the second page, she had jotted down the name Rainbow.

Tomorrow, she would stop by his bench at the mall and talk with him again. At least now she had some questions to ask. Had his friend Goochie ever mentioned owning horses or training them? Were there any names of horses or stables or people that he could remember hearing Goochie talk about? What, exactly, had Goochie told him about where he was going that last day?

Tina stood to toss the dry bread crusts and the plastic into the wastebasket she and Eduardo shared. On the floor next to the basket was the small cardboard box containing the contents from the pockets of Goochie's clothes that they had collected from the grounds keeper at Santa Anita.

She had no real hope of finding anything new. Nevertheless, she laid out the items side by side on her desk. Nail clippers. Pencil stub. Racing page from the newspaper— There was something wrong there. They had overlooked something. She opened the neatly folded sheet of newsprint and examined it carefully. With an excited laugh, she picked up the phone to call her partner.

She probably would have noticed what was wrong about the paper even if, earlier, she had not been remembering the day her father won the eight thousand dollars. Just the same, she could imagine hearing him say, "You see, babe? All those days I took you to the track paid pretty good odds after all."

RAINBOW THOUGHT there had been an earthquake, and that the thunder was the sound of City Hall South cracking apart. He had been asleep. He jumped up, planning to crawl under his bench to escape the falling debris, then saw that the building was still standing. This was confusing. He was more disoriented than usual until he felt the rain.

Rain—because it was so rare in Southern California—was something the inhabitants of the benches in the L.A. Mall never took into consideration until it happened. There was some protection in the block of underground shops and restaurants after closing time. But the area was posted, and the cops came around once in a while and made everyone who was congregated there move.

There was the covered bandstand across from the federal building, but it was always overcrowded when the weather was rough. And there was room for a few people in the doorways of the government buildings and under the aboveground walkway between City Hall and City Hall East.

Of course, the Mission had room for some, but it filled up fast and latecomers were turned away when the maximum capacity number the fire department determined was reached.

Rainbow did not like being crowded. It was dangerous. You never knew who you were next to. It could be someone with a broken bottle or a pocketknife.

As soon as he understood that he would have to find some dry place for shelter, Rainbow decided what he was going to do. Goochie had made it work once. Goochie had been better at that sort of thing than he was, but it was worth a try.

Rainbow left the mall, and as he crossed in front of the L.A. Police Department headquarters, he hunched his back against the rain and hurried on toward the rear of the building. Goochie had said to really bring it off, you had to have the right setting.

How long ago had that been? Then, at the corner of San Pedro, when Rainbow saw the Christmas decorations across First Street in Little Tokyo, he remembered. Where a banner hung now proclaiming JOY TO THE WORLD, there had been one announcing Nisei Week.

Rainbow's destination—St. Godard's church—was just around the corner.

St. Godard's was a small, deserted brick church that stood almost flush with the sidewalk on San Pedro, and was diagonally across from the rear entrance of the police department. It had been saved from demolition by the L.A. Conservancy because of the four Ionic columns of the portico. Though it had not fallen to the wrecking ball, no one had come forward to refurbish it, either. So it remained in its forlorn state with grass growing through cracks in the foundation and boards covering its broken windows.

Rainbow took a stance directly in front of the plywood plank that blocked the entrance, and raised his arms to heaven.

"God! In this Christmas season, send down thy wrath!" He shouted as loud as he could, hoping the sound of his raspy voice would carry across the street to the police parking lot.

"Save us from thy wrath! Thy wrath is mighty!"

Wrath was a word Goochie had used a great deal, he remembered.

"Satan's wrath is mighty, but thy wrath is greater! Show thyself in all thy strength! Let us hear thy voice!"

The rain was falling harder, and Rainbow's ranting was punctuated occasionally by thunder and lightning. The drivers of cars slowed to look at him. Most pedestrians who had to pass stepped off the sidewalk and into the water that rushed next to the curb to avoid the crazy-looking man who was shaking his fists at the sky.

"Let loose your angels of wrath and your tigers of wrath! Behold the grapes of wrath, all ye sinners!"

His voice was giving out, and he was about to lose hope when the police car came to take him away.

He was pleased with the outcome.

Some of the people on the street would steal a bottle of wine from the liquor store to get arrested so they could spend a night in jail. But Rainbow was not a criminal. He had no desire to fraternize with thieves.

The USC County Psychiatric Clinic was different. He would be taken to the emergency ward. It was always crowded, and he might have to sleep on the floor because they ran out of gurneys pretty fast. Still, it was warm, and dry, and they had to keep him for thirty-six hours for observation.

It would probably have stopped raining by the time he was released.

To be convincing, he had to keep shouting even in the back of the police car until he was safely checked in. But he was not as loud now. He was making plans. He decided that when he got out he was not going back to the mall. He didn't like it there since Goochie was gone. Maybe he would try Union Station. He might even hop a train and go up north. He had heard Sacramento wasn't a bad place.

MICAELA HAD decided to take the evening off from waitressing at El Fenix. It was raining and business would be slow. The tips would hardly be worth waiting around for, she explained to her boss. Armando accepted her excuse and agreed to let her go. But he was not at all surprised to see Detective Lopez get in her car with her when she left.

Eduardo's apartment was in Alhambra, just a few miles east of El Sereno. It was on the second floor and had one bedroom, and a large living area with a gas-log fake fireplace, a dining alcove, and a mirrored wet bar that had a pass-through from the efficiency kitchen. His color scheme was dominated by deep red with black wrought-iron accents.

"Should I make us a margarita?" He took Micaela's plastic raincoat and hung it on one of the bar stools.

"Not for me." She was still wearing the short red skirt and white peasant blouse of her waitress uniform. "I'd rather see the rest of the apartment."

He opened the pass-through so she could peer into the seldom-used kitchen, then pulled back the drapes in front of sliding glass doors that opened onto a balcony with an umbrella table and four chairs. "That's it," he said. "The only thing left is the bedroom."

She was perched on a bar stool. When she leaned her elbow on the counter, her blouse adjusted itself downward on her shoulder. "I want the full tour," she said in a throaty voice.

EDUARDO'S BEDROOM was just large enough to hold his king-size waterbed in its elaborately carved oak frame and the matching bedside tables and still leave space to open the doors to the bathroom and the closets. Blackout curtains covered the windows—an investment he had made when he was on patrol and working the nightshift.

Eduardo kissed Micaela as they stood in the doorway. He liked her mouth. Her lips were soft and her tongue darted and flicked around his with a teasing sensuality. The rest of her was not quite as exciting. Her legs were good; the thighs might have been a bit too plump. Her hair, though long and shiny black, was coarse and stiff with hair spray. Her breasts were full, but lacked firmness and flattened against his hand. Still, he could compensate with such a willing partner and his own imagination.

In the past, in similar situations, he had pretended that he was with a girl from the Calvin Klein jeans ad, or the sexy star from the latest movie he had seen. Now, he found himself thinking of the woman with the red hair and slim body he had met that afternoon at the Huntington. Andrea. Oh, yes. Andrea.

He and Micaela had moved, without interrupting their kiss, across the room and were sitting on the side of the bed when the phone rang. He let the ringing continue. His rule was, if the caller had not given up by the seventh ring, he would answer. He knew it would be Tina before he picked up the receiver.

"*Sí?*"

"Eduardo?"

"Yeah."

"I'm at Hollenbeck."

"Go home."

"No. Listen, I think I found something."

"Go home."

"You know the newspaper that was in Goochie's pocket? He didn't make marks by any of the horses, or the jockeys, or the trainers. Did you ever know anyone who went to the track and didn't mark the horse he was going to bet on?"

"Maybe he bought a program and wrote on that."

"No. He wouldn't have spent money on a program." Tina was so excited her words tumbled over each other. "The only thing that was marked—with a faint pencil line, and I almost missed it—was the names of the people in the picture."

"What picture?"

"On the same page was a picture of two women at the Santa Anita Turf Club. Underneath, it says, 'Georgene Dodson, member of the board of the Huntington Library, played hostess to her sister, Sarah Anderson, owner of the Lexington Stables of Lexington, Kentucky,' blah, blah, blah."

Eduardo let go of Micaela's breast and stood holding the phone in both hands. Smiling, he nodded approval for his partner. "Hey! Good work, Tina. Good work."

"Lexington Stables! That's where Goochie's shoes came from!"

"Yeah! You've got a good eye, partner."

Tina laughed. "Now what?"

"Go home."

"I mean, what do I do now?"

"Go home! We can't follow it up until the morning."

"Right. Well, okay. Good night."

"Tell you what," Eduardo said. "I'll let you drive tomorrow."

Tina laughed again, and hung up.

When Eduardo turned back to the bed, Micaela was lying there in nothing but bikini panties.

As he explored her body with closed eyes, he was picturing the sunlit grounds of the Huntington, and remembering his meeting with Andrea. This was developing into one of his better fantasies. He was imagining that everything had taken place *almost* exactly as it did. Only there was no one else around. And neither one of them was wearing clothes.

Will you be in San Marino long?

He reached out and touched her hair and let his hand slide down her arm.

No, I'm just here on business.

She took a step toward him and ran a finger lightly across his lips.

Where are you staying?

He lifted her in his arms and then lay beside her on the grass. No, not the grass—the grass would be scratchy. They found a blanket. There was a blanket under one of the benches.

I'm the houseguest of one of the Huntington board members. Mrs. Dodson.

Eduardo, who had his thumbs hooked in the elastic of Micaela's panties and was gently easing them down, suddenly let go of the silky fabric and sat up. Mrs. Dodson! "*Chi*huahua!"

Micaela, surprised, and not a little angry, said, "Hey, Eduardo! What about me?"

THE FACTS THAT LED to the identity of Goochie's murderer would without question have been revealed even under the usual cloudless California skies. But looking back, Detective Lopez, who believed in such things, was convinced that the unexpected cloudburst was sent as an omen—a sign of approval—to assist him. If nothing else, it might have been some time later before the gun was found—if at all—had it not been for the rain.

TWENTY-TWO

By EARLY MORNING the showier aspects of the storm had dissipated. The thunder and lightning were gone, but the rain had settled into a steady, even pace that suggested it was out to break the previously widely noted forty days and forty nights.

A section of the Foothill Freeway between Pasadena and Glendale had been closed due to mud slides. Innumerable fender-benders had been reported involving local residents who had limited experience driving on rain-slick streets. The Los Angeles River—usually a trickle down the center of a wide, concrete-lined ditch—was challenging the banks with its swift current and acting as a dangerous magnet to the curious.

In the Australian garden at the Huntington, two eucalyptus trees that had stood for decades on a down slope had fallen across the path when the soil around their shallow roots was washed away. Archie Chambers, in his hooded slicker and rain boots—which he referred to in the British vernacular as Wellingtons—had dutifully made note of the fallen trees as he toured the grounds.

Usually, under the cloudless California skies, early mornings in the Huntington gardens were a blaze of variegated foliage and bright blossoms in a spectrum of hues. Now, with the overcast skies and the rain, the trees, shrubs, lawns, and flowering plants seemed reduced to dull shades of brown and gray-green. The lack of distracting color may have been the reason Archie noticed a silvery object beside a row where newly planted azaleas had been washed clear of their moorings. He could see something glinting in the mud as he made his last tour through the statuary garden before writing his report and checking himself out and off duty.

With a sense of foreboding, Archie squatted down to examine the metal object. Before the morning when he discovered the dead body lying only a few feet from where he was now, he would have expected to find perhaps a gardener's trowel—at the worst, a discarded soft-drink can. Now, he felt sure he knew what the rain had uncovered even before he looked more closely. He reached to pick it up, then thought better of it and hurried to the guard's office to make a phone call.

Detective Lopez's card was thumbtacked to the bulletin board. If Lopez worked a day shift, it was too early for him to be at the Hollenbeck Division, so Archie called the home number that was written in pencil on the back.

"Yeah?"

"Detective Lopez?"

"Yes. Who's this?" The voice was sleepy. There was a cough and then a noisy clearing of the throat.

"It's Archie Chambers—at the Huntington."

"Yeah, Archie." This time there was a yawn.

"Sorry to wake you, but you said to call anytime."

"It's okay." Eduardo turned on the bedside lamp.

Micaela groaned without waking and turned away from the light.

"I think I found something," Archie said.

"What?"

"Actually, I'm sure . . . I'm almost positive it's a gun."

"Where? Where was it?" The voice was wide awake now.

Archie explained in needless detail how he had first discovered the fallen eucalyptus trees and then, when he noticed the uprooted azaleas, how he had seen the silvery barrel of a gun that had been uncovered by the rain. "I didn't touch it," he said. "I thought, fingerprints and all that."

"Thanks, Archie. Make sure it's left where it is, okay? I'll be there in thirty minutes."

WITHOUT PUTTING the phone back in the cradle, Eduardo pushed the disconnect button, then called Tina's number.

"Hello." She answered brightly after the first ring.

"Jesus. Don't you ever sleep?"

"I was asleep—sort of," she said defensively.

"If you bothered to get undressed last night, put your clothes back on. Looks like the gun's been found."

"Hallelujah. Where?"

Eduardo told her quickly about Archie's call. "I'll pick you up in thirty minutes."

"I'll pick *you* up in twenty-five. I've got the car, remember? You had other means of transportation last night."

Eduardo pulled the blanket up over Micaela's bare shoulders. "Oh, yeah. Take an extra ten and stop by Winchell's and pick up two large coffees and some doughnuts."

"Okay."

"And don't forget to get a receipt."

"Huh?"

"Just to make sure you paid for them." His voice was laden with virtue. "I don't want you giving the appearance of evil."

"Go to hell."

Eduardo grinned as he hung up the phone. When he was dressed, he sat on the edge of the bed to pull on his lizard-skin cowboy boots. At the sound of the rain, he stood them again in the closet and reached for a pair of worn leather low tops instead.

Micaela gurgled in her sleep. Eduardo patted her rounded behind, turned off the lamp, left his apartment, and took the elevator to the lobby to wait for his partner.

THE OVERWORKED forensics lab never moved fast enough for Eduardo and Tina—or anyone else in the department. But with the escalating number of gunshot cases in Los Angeles and the amount of blood-stained clothing and ballistics evidence that the specialists had to examine, it was impossible to keep up.

"As soon as we can," was the stock answer the detectives were given when they filled out the request and left the gun for examination early that morning.

There was probably no hope of fingerprints after the abrasiveness of the dirt and mud. They knew that. But they needed an official matchup between the bullet that had been removed from the body and the gun that had been recovered. Still, the most important bit of new information—the registration number—they could track down for themselves.

It was almost too easy. In less than thirty minutes in front of their computer at Hollenbeck, they discovered that the gun had been purchased in Pasadena, and they had the name and address of the owner.

Before nine A.M. the LAPD's unmarked green Plymouth was headed up Huntington Drive to San Marino.

TWENTY-THREE

ANDREA POURED a glass of milk from a carton in the refrigerator and helped herself to one of Holly's cinnamon buns from the bread box. She sat with her improvised breakfast at the kitchen table and watched raindrops plop and splash into the Dodsons' swimming pool.

Her trip to California had gotten off to an unpleasant start. But she was convinced it was only because she had become involved in things that did not concern her. For the rest of her stay, she promised herself that she would not let Harvey Latimer and his phoney aestheticism, or Nikki Yamaguchi and his adolescent abrasiveness, or even Sarah Anderson and her neurotic problems—whatever they were—distract her from the work she had been hired to do.

Despite the rain, the world looked brighter this morning because Aldo Balzani had called from Florence the night before to tell her he would be arriving in Los Angeles at the end of the week.

She rinsed her glass and put it in the dishwasher. Through the sliding glass doors she could see Sarah and Benjamin across the pool in front of the guest house. They stood under an awning that covered a walkway between the main house and the guest quarters. Sarah was buttoning Benjamin's raincoat while a weathered-looking middle-aged woman in riding pants and rain gear stood waiting. Sarah gave Benjamin a little push, and he went with the woman— a bit unwillingly, it appeared—through the gate at the back to the driveway.

Sarah watched until the gate closed behind them, then turned and saw Andrea in the kitchen. She waved and hurried in to join her.

"Sorry about the rain," Sarah said, shivering a little.

"No need to apologize," Andrea smiled at her, "it's not your fault."

"I came in for one of Holly's cinnamon buns."

"You're lucky I left you one."

"Benjamin's off to a riding lesson." Sarah reached into the cabinet for a china plate, then took a silver fork from a drawer, and a linen napkin from the drawer next to that. Andrea had used her fingers and a paper towel.

Andrea could not help asking, "They're going riding on a day like this?"

"Well, no. They probably won't take the horses out unless it stops raining. But the instructor said Benjamin could help her in the stable organizing the tack and cleaning the stalls," Sarah said. In a gruff voice that must have been an imitation of the riding instructor's, she said, "'There's more to riding a horse than putting your ass in the saddle.'"

This was as lighthearted as Andrea had ever seen Sarah.

"I haven't been on a horse since I was your son's age," Andrea said. She did not add that her mother had insisted that she attend a riding academy in Boston one summer and that she had hated every minute of it.

"Benjamin *loves* horses. He already rides very well. The lessons while we're here are Holly's idea—an excuse to get him away from the house for a while," Sarah said between forkfuls of cinnamon roll. "Of course she's right. He needs to be around other people. We have a stable back home—I don't know if you knew—"

Sarah was interrupted by the melodic chime of the front doorbell.

"Ben must have forgotten something." Sarah reached for the napkin in her lap.

"I'll get the door if you like," Andrea said. "I was just going up for an umbrella, anyway."

"If you don't mind," Sarah licked her index finger and picked up the last crumbs of cinnamon and sugar.

There were wide plate-glass panels on each side of the front door. As Andrea walked down the hallway she was surprised to see a rather beat-up green Plymouth parked in the circular drive in front. When she opened the door, she was even more surprised to see the two detectives she had met the day before at the Huntington.

"Andrea. Hello, again," Eduardo Lopez said.

"Hello," she said hesitantly. She could not imagine what he was doing there. There was no mistaking the fact that he had flirted with her in a less-than-subtle way the day before, but what was he doing here at this hour—and with his partner? "Detectives Lopez and Roberson, isn't it?"

"That's right. I thought this was where you said you were staying," Eduardo said.

"Yes, but I was just leaving—"

"We're here to see a Joseph Dodson," Tina said.

"Who?" For a moment in her confusion, Andrea had forgotten the name of Georgene's husband, whom she had never met. "Oh. Joseph Dodson. He isn't here."

"Could you tell us when he'll be back or where we can find him?" Tina reached in a pocket of her unbuttoned raincoat and took out a pen and notepad. Her black leather belt with the attached LAPD badge, Rover radio, and holstered Beretta was in startling contrast to the shell-pink running suit she wore.

Eduardo stomped his feet on the wet flagstones, then wiped them on the woven mat.

"I'm sorry. Please come in." Andrea realized she had kept them standing on the doorstep. "Mr. Dodson's sister-in-law is here." She closed the door when they were inside the wide entry. "She can give you more information than I can."

"Before we talk to her," Eduardo said softly, "we'd appreciate it if we could ask you a few questions. When is Mr. Dodson expected back?"

"He and his wife are in England. I don't *know* when they'll be back, but I think you really should speak with Mrs. Anderson—I'm only a houseguest here—"

"What is it, Andrea?" Sarah stood in the glass-sided hallway from the kitchen. In the gray light behind her she looked ghostly.

"It's something about Georgene's husband," Andrea said. "Nothing to do with Benjamin." Somehow, she had felt it was necessary to reassure Sarah that her son was all right. What must she think, seeing two police officers in the hallway? Undoubtedly, her first thought would have been that something had happened to her child. Why else would she look so concerned?

"What is it you want?" Sarah asked the two detectives directly, showing no sign that she felt more at ease.

"We'd like to ask you a few questions." Tina pointedly looked down at the drops of water that had slid from the detectives' raincoats to the marble floor of the entry.

"I'm sorry," Sarah said. "Wouldn't you like to get out of those wet things?" She dispatched the coats to the stair railing and seemed to relax a bit with a hostess duty to perform. "If you'll follow, we'll go into the kitchen." Sarah turned toward the hallway.

"I'll be on my way, Sarah." Andrea, in her resolve not to get involved, started for the guest room.

"No, please! Stay with me."

The urgency in Sarah's voice stopped Andrea in her tracks. She followed the others into the kitchen.

"If you could just tell us when Mr. Dodson will be back, or how we can reach him," Tina said, as they each pulled a chair out from the table and sat.

"I'm afraid I don't know when my sister and her husband will be back, but they're staying at the Savoy Hotel in London. I suppose you could reach them there, if it's something urgent," Sarah said.

"Are Mr. and Mrs. Dodson on vacation, or is this a business trip?" Tina's question seemed no more than polite small talk.

"My brother-in-law is retired, though he does like to keep in touch with his import business. And my sister joined him to do some shopping. But, please. Tell me what this is about."

"We'd like to ask Mr. Dodson some questions about a gun," Tina said.

Eduardo watched Sarah intently.

Sarah's face was blank. "What gun?"

"Do you know if the Dodsons have had a robbery lately? Perhaps someone broke into their house," Tina said.

As his partner asked questions, Eduardo's eyes did not leave Sarah's face. He watched her expression—gauged her reaction.

This is the way they work, Andrea thought. One of them asks the questions; the other one concentrates on the answer and the physical reaction. She suddenly felt very protective of Sarah. Why didn't they just state their business? "Detective Roberson, maybe Mrs. Anderson could be of more help if you would tell her what this is all about."

Eduardo turned to answer Andrea. It was Tina's turn to watch for reactions.

"As you know," he began in a friendly, conversational manner, "we've been investigating a murder that took place in the statuary garden at the Huntington. It's been a real bear, because until yesterday, we couldn't even identify the body. We still don't have a full identification—not a legal one."

Eduardo went on to explain the discovery of the clothes, and how they were able to trace the shoes to Lexington, Kentucky.

"I believe you're from Lexington, aren't you, Mrs. Anderson?" Tina asked the question in the most casual way possible, but she had her pen poised above the notepad ready to write the answer.

"Yes, my son and I live in Lexington." Sarah's blank expression suddenly became an interested frown. "How did you know that?"

"That's one of the strangest things about this case," Eduardo laughed as though he were recounting an incident to a stranger who had asked how detectives find their clues. "In a pocket of the clothing we recovered there was a folded page from the *L.A. Times*—the daily lineup from Santa Anita. From previous information, we already suspected that the victim liked to play the horses. Anyway, on that particular day, there was a picture of you and your sister taken at the Turf Club. The odd thing was, he hadn't marked any of the horses—which is what most people do when they've decided on their favorites. But he *had* made an X next to the picture." Eduardo allowed a second of reaction time to elapse. "It mentioned in the article that you were visiting from Lexington."

"I see." Sarah leaned back in her chair, her eyes fixed on a spot in a corner of the ceiling.

"What does any of this have to do with Mr. Dodson's gun?" Andrea was growing more concerned about Sarah. She wanted the two detectives to get on with whatever they had come for, then leave.

"Well, early this morning, I got a call from one of the guards at the Huntington," Eduardo said. "The rain uncovered a gun that was buried in the statuary garden. The gun was registered to Joseph Dodson at this address."

"And that's why you asked about the robbery," Andrea said quickly. "You think someone stole it! Sarah, do you know anything about—"

Sarah put her hand on Andrea's. She might as well have put it across her mouth. It had the same silencing effect once Andrea looked in the other woman's face.

"Do you know the name of the man who was killed?" Sarah asked Tina the question.

"No, he was known around the L.A. Mall, where he hung out as Goochie."

"Goochie?" Sarah looked blank, then, astonishingly, she laughed. "It was the shoes, I suppose."

"Yes," Tina said. "It was."

"He couldn't give up those expensive leather shoes even after he gave up everything else." Sarah suddenly seemed to have found strength from somewhere. She spoke with a resolve that Andrea had never heard her use before. "I can tell you the man's name, if you want to write this down, Detective Roberson."

"Yes, ma'am. I will," Tina answered matter-of-factly.

Andrea could not believe that neither Eduardo Lopez nor Tina Roberson seemed at all surprised at what Sarah had just said. They *expected* her to tell them the name of the murder victim. "Wait, Sarah—"

"It's all right, Andrea. His name was Bryan Anderson. He was my husband."

Eduardo did not rush her with the next question, and he seemed careful to keep any hint of either accusation or sympathy from his voice. "Do you think you could identify the body, Mrs. Anderson?"

"Yes, but I'd rather not."

Eduardo followed with, "How can you be sure without viewing the body?"

Sarah seemed impatient with the two detectives. "You *are* asking me about the dead man who was found in the statuary garden, aren't you?"

"Yes," Eduardo answered.

Tina, head down, waited to write what Sarah said next.

"Well, then, I'm sure of who it was, because I shot him."

TWENTY-FOUR

FOR A LONG MOMENT, the efficient hum of the refrigerator and the rain on the flagstone patio were the only sounds in Georgene Dodson's kitchen.

Andrea felt as though she were peering through the closed window into a strange house at people she did not know. The two detectives, even Sarah Anderson, were virtually strangers. She had met Sarah for the first time only two nights before. They had spent less than an hour in conversation since then. She had no knowledge of Sarah's past. They had no shared experiences that Andrea could draw on to evaluate what Sarah had just said: that she had shot her husband.

There was no way to read the large dark eyes that stared out at the rain, or to guess why the tension had left Sarah's face and the pale mouth had grown slack and fallen partly open. Andrea could not tell whether what she saw in Sarah's expression was emotional exhaustion from telling such a horrible truth—or whether it was the estranged look of insanity.

The faces of the detectives were just as unreadable. No one but Andrea seemed surprised at what had just happened.

Sarah, it seemed, had *expected* the police to call. And they—even if they had not anticipated a cool confession—had believed before they arrived that she had shot her husband.

"Andrea, would you please call Holly? She wrote the phone number of her friend in San Diego on the pad next to the refrigerator. And I suppose I'll need a lawyer. There'll be one listed in Georgene's address book." From Sarah's abstract manner, she might have been discussing the guest list for a dinner party.

"Sarah! Listen to me!" Andrea had no advice, no admonitions, but she felt it was imperative to break through to some core of reasoning that would help this woman protect herself. "Think about what you said! Think about—"

As though she had not heard, Sarah said, "Holly will know what to do about Benjamin."

Eduardo Lopez was at the phone calling for a police car.

"I'll call London and try to get through to Georgene." Andrea wondered what other possible sources of help there might be. "Are there other family members I should contact? What about your... doctor?" She hesitated to say "psychiatrist" in the presence of the police officers, "The doctor you had the appointment with today?"

"No, don't bother with any of that." Sarah seemed impatient. "If you will just call Holly. I hate for her to have to cut her trip short, but she's so good with Benjamin. She can get through to him better than I can." For the first time, there was a glint of panic in Sarah's eyes and her lower lip trembled until she caught it between her teeth. Then, calm as before, she turned politely to Detective Roberson, to include her in the conversation. "Benjamin is my ten-year-old son. Holly is—she calls herself a cook—and she does do the cooking, but she's also a nanny." With a twitch of a smile, she added, "For both of us."

"It's nice to have someone like that," Tina said.

"Oh, yes. Holly's a treasure." Sarah stood from the kitchen table.

Tina stood, too.

"I'll need a raincoat." Sarah turned toward the sliding glass doors that led to the guest house. "I never expected to need a raincoat in California."

Tina followed Sarah beneath the covered walkway and stayed with her until she returned with her coat and handbag.

Almost before Eduardo hung up from calling dispatch, Andrea could see through the window to the street a black and white police car with two uniformed officers pulling into the driveway.

Eduardo went to the front of the house to let them in.

The two detectives had not pressured Sarah. They had explained her rights to her and they seemed willing to delay any further questions until she was in custody.

"Sarah." Andrea took Sarah's hand. It was smooth and childlike—cool, and with a tiny tremor. "If you think of anything else—"

"No. Really. But thank you." She squeezed Andrea's fingers, then released them.

Tina said to Andrea, "Detective Lopez will be back in a moment to give you some information." She nodded to Sarah and the two women walked down the hall side by side.

Andrea stayed in the kitchen. She heard subdued voices from the entry, the front door closed, and after a moment, one of the cars left. She was conscious of the sound of the refrigerator and the rain again until Eduardo Lopez spoke to her from the doorway.

"This is where she'll be taken." Eduardo wrote the address of the police station on the back of one of the cards. "She'll be all right," he said. "She'll have a chance to talk with her lawyer before we question her."

"It's just that—" She started to say that she did not think Sarah was very stable, then realized that might create an impression that would be harmful to her.

"I'm sorry about this," Eduardo handed Andrea the card. "I had hoped that the next time I saw you would be under different circumstances."

Andrea looked up in surprise, but Eduardo had already turned to go join his partner.

WHEN THEY REACHED Huntington Drive, Tina switched on the Plymouth's turn indicator with her little finger and turned right toward El Sereno and the Hollenbeck Police

Station. "I guess you can't argue with statistics," she said with a deep sigh.

"What do you mean?" Neither Eduardo nor Tina had spoken until now.

"Statistically, you know, the number-one cause of murder is domestic violence."

"It can happen in the best of neighborhoods."

They both fell silent again. There was always a letdown when they had completed an investigation. As long as they were pursuing the unknown, there was a compulsion to fit the odd-shaped pieces of information together into an interlocking whole. But when the last piece was dropped in and the completed puzzle revealed a human face looking back at them in confusion or fear or remorse, there was sometimes a desire to step back, to turn away, to deny the evidence that they had so painstakingly gathered. Of course, they did not. They had to deal with facts.

Although it was shortly after ten in the morning, some of the cars on Huntington had their headlights on in the rain. Reflections shimmered in the slick streets.

"She has a son," Tina said. "He's ten years old."

"Yeah. I heard."

That's another statistic, Tina thought, sadly. There are nearly always kids involved. One family member knocks off another, then goes to jail, and the kids are left to deal with strangers.

San Marino had become South Pasadena and now they were entering El Sereno. Eduardo stared through the window, not really seeing the familiar pastel-colored buildings with their peeling paint and wrought-iron grills as they passed by.

He was thinking of Andrea Perkins. Vaguely, until today, he had considered calling her to invite her to lunch, or maybe a Lakers game—she might like basketball. There must be some things she enjoyed besides art. His daytime fantasies were more restrained than those he had at night. He could imagine showing her Olivera Street with the Mexican restaurants and the pottery and leather-goods vendors in the center of the courtyard and the secret passageways underneath. Or maybe she'd prefer Chinatown or Little Tokyo. But you can't ask someone like Andrea Perkins "What are you doing Saturday night?" and expect her to jump at a chance to go out with you after you've just arrested her friend.

Tina pulled into their reserved parking space behind the police station.

Eduardo was not aware of where they were until his partner turned off the ignition.

At least the rain had almost stopped.

As he got out and locked the door on his side of the green Plymouth, he wondered if Micaela had to work tonight.

TWENTY-FIVE

As A MATTER OF expediency, Andrea decided to place a call to Georgene Dodson before she tried to contact Holly. San Marino, after all, was Georgene's home territory. She would know which lawyer to call, not just the name of a firm. And she *was* Sarah's sister—the *only* family member, as far as Andrea knew. There might be close friends who lived nearby who could be of help. Georgene would know who to contact.

In Sarah's mental state—whatever it was—she could not be relied upon to think clearly in this situation. And it seemed not only impractical but unfair to rely on the teenaged Holly to handle such a catastrophic situation.

Andrea talked with the local telephone operator who gave her instructions for direct dialing to the Savoy Hotel in London.

"Yes, Mr. and Mrs. Dodson are registered at the hotel," the Savoy front desk operator confirmed, "but, sorry, neither of them is in. If you would care to leave a message?"

THE TAXI PULLED to the curb near the intersection of Knightsbridge and Sloane Street. Georgene Dodson paid the fare and cut across to walk down Brompton Road. She was intent on another visit to Harrods department store. Joseph Dodson was off somewhere on business—God knew where. And if He knew, He was probably the only one who cared. Certainly, Georgene did not.

Though it was just past six P.M., it seemed much later to Georgene, who always needed a week or so in England to grow accustomed to winter's early darkness there. Beneath street lamps, in the flash of automobile headlights, and in the glow of store windows, icy crystals of snow and sleet danced and swirled. They stuck to Georgene's white mink coat and hat, sparkling like sequins.

The sidewalks were choked with Christmas shoppers. Surprisingly, few of them seemed put off by the huge white police van at Harrods' corner. "Just a precaution," Georgene heard someone say, "the store requested extra protection in case there was an I.R.A. bomb threat."

It would take more than the Irish Republican Army, Georgene thought, to keep her from shopping when she wanted to. Not that there was anything specific that she wanted to buy; it was just that she felt particularly invincible—and invisible. Feeling invisible was one of the things she liked best about being in a city where she knew virtually no one. But *invisible* was not exactly the word—*unrecognized* was better. Heads turned to stare at the stunning woman with the dark eyes and blond hair only a shade darker than the creamy white of the fur she wore. She was aware of the effect she created, though she pretended not to notice.

A small band of Salvation Army carolers and a bell ringer were positioned discreetly to the side of Harrods' front door. Without slowing her pace, Georgene took a ten-pound note from her pocket and dropped it in the kettle. She heard the "God bless you" from the young woman with the bell in her hand and saw the smiles of approval from the singers, though she did not acknowledge them.

As she entered the mammoth Edwardian showplace, the scent from a blaze of bayberry candles and the orchestral recording of "The First Noël" seemed to slam against her. The evocative scent and sound, for a moment, blotted out the display cases and the crowds. In that instant, all she could see was the mental image of the last Christmas her father had been at home. The pain of his leaving was as sharp and surprising as it had been when she was a child. Oh, how she had loved her charming, handsome, irresponsible father!

But he left.

Georgene stepped to one side to let an apologizing man with a huge gift-wrapped package pass by.

He had left her when she was twelve. He left her mother in perpetual tears that finally drained the life from her. He left Sarah tiptoeing around trying not to cause any trouble, as though if she were good enough, he might come back.

Georgene gave a reflexive shake of the shoulders, scattering pinpoints of melted snow from her coat into the heated air where they evaporated like the memory of her father's kiss on her forehead.

To escape the bayberry candles, she headed for the Chanel perfume counter. From a sampler on a mirrored tray, she sprayed a tiny drop of a new fragrance on the inside of her wrist and touched it to her nose. Too sweet, too flowery. She preferred something more exotic. This scent might do for Sarah, but who would notice? Bryan never had, she thought with a pleasant twinge of malice.

"May I be of service?" A saleswoman in a moss green smock with her hair pinned back so tightly that it pulled the corners of her eyebrows up pointedly left a disheveled customer in a cloth coat to assist Georgene. "This new Chanel is divine, don't you agree?"

"No."

Georgene crossed the aisle to men's furnishings in order to avoid the woman. She looked through the locked glass case at sterling silver shoehorns and gold-plated manicure sets in zippered Italian leather travel cases. These were the kinds of things that Bryan always liked. Anything that was showy—anything that was novel. But the cost of a gift had not seemed the important thing to him. In high school she had given him a key chain that had a four-leaf clover embedded in plastic. He was still carrying it years later. She had seen it on the hall table in Kentucky after he and Sarah were married.

Sarah had refused to recognize what Georgene had known all along. Bryan was just like their father!

She turned quickly and walked with seeming purpose toward the rear of the store.

She and Joseph did not even exchange gifts. "Just buy what you like. I'll order anything I need," he had told her early on in their marriage. It was strange, she thought, when you could afford almost anything you wanted, there was not very much you *did* want.

Her husband was the least sentimental of men. That was one of the things that had attracted her to him.

She still smiled to herself at the way they met. "I have a wealthy widower for you," a family friend had told her mother. After the divorce, their financial difficulty was no secret. "I'm bringing him over to meet you this weekend. It's time you were married again."

It had been obvious from the first that Joseph Dodson was not interested in her mother, but in Georgene.

She had never regretted the outcome of that meeting for a moment. What difference did it make who married him? Her mother's motives and her own were the same. And Joseph had not been cheated. He made very few demands. His only interest was that she remain beautiful.

That damn music! "Chestnuts roasting on an open fire..." Mel Tourme's voice filtered through the sound system and seeped in through her pores. "Jack Frost nipping at your nose..."

It was nostalgia nipping at her heels. Why was it that cheap popular music could stir up emotions you had kept buried for years?

All right. This could be a test. Unless she locked herself in her hotel room, it was impossible to avoid the sentimental music and Christmas displays everywhere she looked. She had to fight for control.

She took the turn to the Food Hall. Quickly passing the displays of Christmas cakes and tins of cookies, she crossed the tiled floor and stopped in front of the long, glass-fronted cases of seafood. Frowning with concentration, she read a hanging wooden sign that listed TODAY'S MARKET OF

SMOKED FISH—SMOKED HADDOCK, COD FILLET, COD ROE, EEL, BUCKLING, KIPPERS, SMOKED SPRAT FILLET.

"We have some excellent smoked salmon that just came in," a young man in a spotless white jacket leaned across the counter and told her confidentially.

"No. No salmon." She really must get out of here.

She turned in a different direction as she left the hall and found herself in the infants' clothing department. Lacy white christening gowns were displayed on chubby-faced mannequins. Everywhere she looked were pink and blue receiving blankets, downy sleepers and footed pajamas, crisp little dresses and wooly suits. Her heart was pounding.

"Nothing could have been changed," she said out loud, though no one heard her in the babble of shoppers. "It was the only thing to do."

She was almost running through the store now. Shoppers who saw her coming stepped out of her way, and others she bumped into turned, ready to say something rude, but were quiet when they saw her stricken face.

Outside in the cold air she felt better. She leaned against the store window where an electric train went through tunnels and over bridges, circling and recircling a twinkling Christmas tree.

She buttoned the top of her coat and went to the corner to wait for the light to change so she could cross the street and hail a taxi.

Through the street scene of moving shadows and flashing lights, she caught sight of a man in the jostling crowd who was wearing a tailored tweed top coat and a jaunty felt hat. For a moment—just for a moment—the sight of him made her stop breathing and her muscles tense, ready to run in his direction. She desperately wanted his arms around her and needed to hear him tell her that everything was all right.

When he turned, it was the same as it had been a thousand times before. She could see that the man was a stranger. He was not her father. He could not have been.

They had read his obituary in the newspaper five years ago. Her father was dead. How she hated him for that.

She looked down at the street as she crossed, careful of the patches of ice—and because her eyelashes felt heavy with freezing tears.

TWENTY-SIX

"HAS SOMETHING happened to Benjamin?" was Holly's first question when Andrea called the number in San Diego that was written on the pad next to the refrigerator. There was the sound of a single saxophone playing "Rudolph the Red-Nosed Reindeer"— badly—in the background.

"No. He's still at his riding lesson. He'll be there until late this afternoon." Andrea had seen no reason to face the problem of Benjamin until it was necessary.

"Hey! Give it a rest." Holly had turned away from the phone. To Andrea she said, "My charming date was in the fraternity's excuse for a band at the Christmas party last night. I keep telling him it's too late to learn how to play the saxophone after the party's over."

The tortured solo stopped and was followed by male laughter and a surprised squeal from Holly as though she had been pinched or swatted or kissed or something that she enjoyed. All of which made telling her about Sarah's extraordinary confession that much more difficult for Andrea.

"Oh, my God. Sarah didn't really say she shot Bryan, did she?"

"Yes, she did." Andrea reached for something reassuring to say. "I tried to call Georgene. She wasn't in, but I left a message for her to call as soon as possible. And, I found the name of a lawyer in the Dodsons' address book. He's on his way to be with Sarah now."

"Tell me again." Holly sounded unbelieving. "Why did the police come there at all?"

Andrea sketchily repeated what she had said before—that a gun had been found in the statuary garden, and that the detectives had discovered that it was registered to Georgene's husband, Joseph Dodson.

"That damn Nikki Yamaguchi!" There was unaccountable anger in Holly's voice. "I don't know why Georgene thought she was doing us such a favor by hiring him!"

"What do you mean about *Nikki?*" Andrea felt—not for the first time that day—that she was trying to communicate in a language that no one else understood.

"I'm leaving right now," Holly said decisively. "Unless there's mega-traffic, I should be able to drive back in—well, I should be there by early afternoon. Will you still be at Georgene's house, Andrea?"

"Yes, of course."

"Thanks." The line went dead.

Andrea replaced the white telephone receiver on the white desk in Georgene Dodson's white office.

The Dodsons' interior designer had obviously worked with the architect to direct the eye through the glass wall to the brilliant foliage and flowers on the terrace outside. Inside, the office had the same almost total absence of color as the master bedroom. Atop a white fleecy carpet, Plexiglas tables with crystal lamps were spaced between white leather couches and chairs that were arranged conversationally in front of a white marble fireplace. On the white wall above the mantel was the one intentional touch of color—twin portraits in sepia tones of Georgene and Joseph Dodson.

Georgene looked as glamorous as Andrea would have expected: bare shoulders, smooth skin, silvery blond hair, and dark, dark eyes. Joseph Dodson was at least twenty—possibly thirty—years older than his wife, and quite ordinary looking. But even without the flattering advantage he had undoubtedly been given by the portrait painter, he still would not have gotten lost in a crowd. There was confidence and success in his eyes and the set of his mouth. Andrea decided that he reminded her of pictures she had seen of Lee Iacocca.

Except for a wedding picture of the bride and groom in a crystal frame on a table near the window, the portrait was the only picture in the room. However, when Andrea was looking in the desk drawers for the address book to call the lawyer, she had come across stacks of photographs of Georgene. Some of the snapshots obviously dated back to high school.

While she waited for Holly, Andrea studied some of the pictures. She had no sense of prying, now. Circumstance had intimately involved her in the lives of this family she barely knew. She felt compelled to learn as much about them as she could, if not in person, then through moments they had recorded on film.

Many of the pictures were of Georgene alone. She clearly liked the camera and it liked her. Andrea sorted through the box of loose photographs until she had a half-dozen she wanted to study more carefully. She arranged them on the desk in what she guessed was chronological order.

The first in her grouping was of Georgene and Sarah in front of San Marino High School. Even then, when Georgene's hair was a natural brown, she outshone her younger sister. Next was a picture of Sarah—still as a teenager—looking adoringly at a handsome boy in a football-letter jacket who was holding her hand. He, however, was mugging for the camera instead of looking at her. Could that have been Bryan Anderson? Sarah had said they were married here in San Marino. Maybe they were high school sweethearts. The third photo was of the two sisters and the same boy. It must have been taken near the same time. At any rate, the boy was wearing the same jacket.

Andrea recognized the setting in this picture. It was just down the street from the Dodsons' house. The boy was straddling the top of the fence that surrounded the Huntington property. Laughing, he was reaching a hand down toward the girls, as though to help one of them up.

The other photographs were taken several years later. One was a long shot of a green field with horses in the background and a man standing in the shadow of a gate that had an arch above it which read Anderson Stables. This must have been the stable Sarah mentioned, where she lived in Kentucky—the one she still owned. Was the man Bryan Anderson? She was not sure until she looked closely at a medium-shot photograph of Sarah holding a baby—no doubt Benjamin—and the man beside her, wearing a more serious, grown-up expression. Comparing the teenaged face with that of this man convinced her that the boy and the man were the same.

But there was something other than youth that was missing in the adult Bryan Anderson that had been obvious in the teenager. Were the signs of alcoholism already present in the young father? Certainly he seemed concerned or disillusioned.

Suddenly, Andrea remembered another picture in the box that she had passed over too quickly. She dug through the stack of photographs until she found it again.

Dating back before the move to Kentucky, the picture was taken at Santa Anita Race Track. Andrea scooped the pictures up like an abandoned hand of solitaire and put them back in the box. She kept the last one and hurried upstairs to the master bedroom to put it in her handbag. This one, slightly blurred photograph told her more than all the others combined.

TWENTY-SEVEN

THE RAIN WAS little more than a drizzle when Holly's mud-splattered rental car pulled in front of the Dodsons' house. From the kitchen window, Andrea saw the girl bring the automobile to a reckless stop and jump out with her suit-case in one hand and a clothes hanger that held her crum-pled evening dress in the other. Before Andrea reached the end of the hall to meet her, the front door banged open.

"Andrea?" Holly set her suitcase in the entry and hung her dress on the bannister. Her tangled hair hung loose around her shoulders. She was wearing her usual blue jeans that were a size too tight, and a baggy blue sweatshirt with gold letters that said University of California—San Diego across the chest.

"Hi." Andrea smiled at her—it would have been impos-sible not to. "I see you took the shirt off his back."

"Yeah." She grinned. "It seemed only fair. He tried to do the same to me." Then her nose crinkled and she sniffed back tears. "Oh, Andrea. What kind of mess has Sarah gotten herself into?"

Andrea opened her arms. They hugged each other hard—Holly, in need of reassurance, and Andrea, in sympathy for this young girl who was so entangled in other people's lives that she did not have a chance to enjoy her own.

When they let go, Holly said, "The first thing I have to do is go collect Benjamin."

"The riding instructor will bring him home later this af-ternoon."

"No, if I'm going to get Sarah out of this, I have to talk to Benjamin, first." She lifted her chin and straightened her shoulders as though good posture alone could get her through this.

"Would you like me to come with you?"

"I wasn't going to ask, but ... yeah. I really would."

The car smelled of onions, and an aluminum soft-drink can rolled around on the floorboard of the passenger side. Andrea stuffed the can and some loose hamburger wrappers into a crumpled paper sack and dropped them behind the seat.

Holly drove the few blocks to Huntington Drive and turned left. "The stable's in Bradbury—straight on past Santa Anita, then up toward the mountains." She settled into the middle lane and rested an elbow on the window frame. "I guess I'd better tell you what this is all about."

"Yes," Andrea agreed. "I don't understand any of it."

At another time, Andrea would have been curious about the typical Southern California suburban community they were driving through. But she hardly noticed the neat single-story businesses and office buildings, and the abundance—especially for December—of leafy trees and flowering shrubs on each side of the wide street and in the median strip. Nor did she give a second look in the direction of the rounded San Gabriel Mountains to the north or snow-topped Mount Baldy to the east. Her eyes were fixed on Holly's profile as the girl spoke.

"I started baby-sitting with Benjamin six years ago, when he was four. I was thirteen. Sarah's husband, Bryan, was still at home then. They had this really nifty thoroughbred stable outside Lexington, and a gorgeous home on a lake next to it. Bryan's folks bought it all for them. Both sides of the family had money. Something to do with racing."

A helmetless motorcycle rider zipped in front of the car and ran a light that had just turned red on Rosemead Boulevard, causing a screeching of brakes in both directions at the intersection and a string of profanities from Holly.

"Bryan, as I remember him, was Mr. Charm and Mr. Who-Me, Worry? Anyway, before Benjamin was five years old, Bryan left—by popular request from Sarah and his father who had been footing most of the bills. It was all about his heavy drinking and gambling, and having to be bailed out of debt just one time too many. The old man saved the homestead for Sarah and his grandson, then delivered a never-darken-my-door-again speech to Bryan, and we haven't seen him since. We heard he went to New Orleans and hung around Jefferson Downs Race Track for a while, until he lost what little money he had left.''

"You've lived with Sarah and Benjamin since—''

"Since I was thirteen. My mom has a passel of kids—she didn't miss just one. Sarah's helped me go to school, and I've helped her with Ben and the house.''

Though Andrea did not say so, she thought Sarah had gotten the best of the bargain.

"So. There's the background. After Bryan left, Sarah hired a guy to manage the stable. I never trusted him. He was a little too free with the bottle, a little too offhand with Sarah, and a little too careless with Ben. He was just a marked-down version of Bryan Anderson.'' Holly turned her wide, blue eyes to Andrea. "Why do women do that? Why do they keep picking the same kind of idiots over and over again?''

Andrea shrugged. In a moment, she asked, "What do you mean he was careless with Benjamin?''

"There are two things that Ben has always loved—drawing or painting, and horses. You've noticed''—she nodded at Andrea—"he really has talent.''

"Yes, he seems to.''

"There's something about color that especially fascinates him. He'll hold a leaf or a flower—or a rock or a clod of dirt—in his hand and study it. Then he'll say, 'I can do that.' And sure enough he'll get out his pastels or watercolors and come up with just the right shade.''

"But about the stable manager,'' Andrea persisted.

"Well, Ben was just a little kid—still is. But when he was only six or seven, this guy would put him up on horses that were too spirited for him to ride."

The traffic had suddenly become congested as they neared the racetrack. Holly braked behind a tour bus that said Leisure World on the back.

"And he kept a gun out in the stable," Holly said. "To shoot crows, he told Sarah. I've always been nervous about guns."

Holly cut short her story. Whether she was concentrating on driving, or whether she had reached a part that was difficult to tell, Andrea was not sure. But there was more, and if Andrea was going to be able to help in any way, she had to hear the rest.

She tried a different approach. "Do you think Bryan Anderson came to Georgene's house to get money from Sarah?"

"Oh, I'm sure he came there for money."

"I suppose the shock of seeing him in that condition, and being afraid that he might want to see Benjamin was enough to make Sarah do what she did," Andrea said.

"You mean kill him?"

"Yes. That's what she said she did."

"Sarah didn't shoot Bryan Anderson."

"Holly, she admitted it. I heard her."

"I don't care what she *said;* she didn't do it."

"Then why would she confess?"

"To protect Benjamin."

"Do you think Bryan Anderson threatened his own son in some way?"

"I wouldn't put it past him, but that's not what I meant."

The bus turned into the traffic lane designated for the Santa Anita parking lot. Holly switched to the outside, passed the Methodist Hospital, and turned left toward Foothill Boulevard. "Look, Andrea, I *know* Sarah didn't shoot anybody. I remember the night that man—I guess it was Bryan Anderson—was killed. I was with her in the living room of the guest house all evening. We sat up until sometime early in the morning. Until Benjamin came home.''

''Until *Benjamin* came home?''

''Yes. That's why Sarah made that stupid confession. She thinks he did it.''

Andrea was incredulous. All she could do was repeat the boy's name. ''Benjamin?''

''Yes. You see, he, he shot a man, once—he killed him. Sarah thinks he's done it again.''

TWENTY-EIGHT

In Lexington, Kentucky, shortly after it happened, Benjamin had tried to explain. Holly came closer to understanding than anyone else.

WHEN BENJAMIN AND the stable manager were alone tending the stalls of the thoroughbreds, the stable manager would say, "We've gotta be careful of horse thieves." His words were often slightly slurred.

Benjamin, sitting on a bale of hay, would lean back against one of the partitions that separated the horses as he watched the angular man with the sun squint unsteadily climb halfway up the ladder to the loft and reach for a revolver he kept stashed on a wide beam that spanned the barn.

"I've seen 'em hanging around." Sometimes the manager would miss a rung and almost fall as he stumbled back down the ladder. "What they do is, they get a big ole horse trailer, and they pick out two or three of the best of the stock and load 'em up. Then they're off and gone before you know it."

With the gun hanging from one hand he would stand in the doorway and squint off into the distance. "But I know how to take care of 'em if they even try to come on your mom's property."

At times, the stable manager left Benjamin "in charge" and went into his small office next to the tack room. "Gotta go call the sheriff and see if they've spotted any suspicious-lookin' bad-ass cowboys around here."

The walls of the office were only thin plywood. From outside in the stable Benjamin could hear the sound of a chair being pulled back from the desk and a drawer open-ing. He could even hear the heels of the manager's boots hitting the top of the desk when he put his feet up. But he never heard him talking to the sheriff on the phone when he went to check on the horse thieves.

"They haven't been around here today. But we can't be too careful," he'd say when he came back. And after his call to the sheriff, his breath smelled the way Benjamin's dad's used to.

Sometimes, after the manager said he had called the sheriff, he'd stand in the door again holding the gun. Then, if he saw a crow flying in the direction of the barn, he would take careful aim—and wait. Even though his body some-times swayed and his knees bent when they did not need to, his hand was steady. He would get a bead on the unwary bird and wait until it was over the clearing near the corral. Usually, he could hit it with the first shot. The crow would flutter and stop in midair, then fall like a rock to the ground.

Benjamin closed his eyes and covered his ears when he saw the gun come out, and the horses would whinny and paw at the stalls when they heard the shot.

"That's what I'll do to horse thieves."

Then, he would put the gun back where it had been be-fore and take a shovel from a hook near the door to dig a shallow hole in the loose dirt between the barn and the cor-ral. "You've always gotta bury your dead," he'd say, and kick the crow into the hole with his boot. Sometimes, he would drop an empty bottle in on top of the bird before he piled the dirt back in.

"We ought to tell my mom—about the horse thieves."

"Nooo. We don't want to tell your mom. It would worry her. Besides. If those guys even thought she knew about 'em . . . Well, you see that loop of rope hangin' on the wall? They'd tie her up with that and do things to her I can't even bring myself to tell you about."

AT MOUNTAIN AVENUE, Holly turned the rental car south again to Royal Oaks, then left toward the Bradbury Estates.

"I was the one who heard the shot," Holly said.

Andrea sat silent.

"The way it happened was, Sarah had sold one of the fillies. Benjamin didn't know about the sale. There was no reason why not—he just hadn't happened to be around when it was discussed.

"He was on his way to the stable to go riding that morning, when he saw a horse trailer parked near the barn door. Because he had heard the story so many times from the stable manager, naturally, he immediately thought, 'horse thieves.'"

Holly audibly cleared her throat before continuing. Then, with determination, she told Andrea of how Benjamin had run to the makeshift office to warn the manager, but he was not there. There was no time to call the sheriff, because through the flimsy plywood walls, he could hear the filly being led from her stall. Quietly, the boy opened the door a crack, and the first thing that met his eye was the loop of rope hanging on the wall—the rope the manager had said the horse thieves would use to tie up his mother.

Benjamin was terrified. If he screamed, they would come after him. If he ran back to the house, they might follow and find his mother. The only thing he could think to do was what he had seen the stable manager do so many times before.

He crept out of the office and up the ladder until he could reach the beam where he knew the gun was stashed. He took it in his hand and climbed back down.

From where Benjamin stood in the doorway, he had a side view of the trailer. He knew that whoever the man was, he was inside securing the horse. He aimed the gun toward the back ramp where the man would come out, and waited.

Holly stopped the car and turned off the engine when they got to Woodlyn Road in front of the private gate to Bradbury. She leaned against the seat and closed her eyes.

"The man had his back turned toward Benjamin when he started down the ramp. Benjamin shot the gun. The bullet turned the man around and he fell—dead—face up to the ground. It was Sarah's stable manager. He had been loading the horse for the new owner. And Benjamin, thinking he was a horse thief, had shot him."

Andrea put her hand on Holly's shoulder. She could feel the girl's body quivering before she heard the sobs. "That poor little boy. Oh, dear God. That poor child."

It was several minutes before Holly was able to speak again. "I heard the shot from the back of the house. At first I thought it was that idiot of a manager shooting at the crows again. Then I realized it couldn't be. I knew he had gone to load the filly. I yelled to Sarah, and then started running. When I got there— Oh, Andrea. This is so hard to say—"

"Wait, if you want to." It was as hard for Andrea to listen as it was for Holly to tell her. "You needn't tell me at all."

"No. I'll finish." With a deep, ragged intake of breath, Holly said, "When I got as far as the barn—I couldn't find Benjamin at first. Then I saw him near the door with a shovel. He had started digging a hole. He knew he couldn't move the stable manager, and he couldn't dig a hole deep enough. But he had dropped the gun in the hole and was saying something about always burying the dead."

TWENTY-NINE

THE GUARD AT THE Bradbury gate called the riding instructor to verify that Andrea and Holly were there on legitimate business.

Andrea asked him, "How far is it to the academy?"

"About a half mile past the first turnoff."

"Let's walk," she said to Holly, who agreed. To the guard, she said, "We'd like to leave the car here inside the gate."

There was room for one automobile next to his truck. Holly pulled the rental car into the vacant space.

Though it was still slightly overcast, there were patches of blue between the thinning clouds that at last had come unstuck from the mountains and seemed to be moving on.

There was no one else around—no cars, not even any houses could be seen from where they walked along the tree-lined street. A chimney on a house that was built on a down slope was visible from the curving blacktop. Wood smoke drifted lazily toward them. It smelled friendly, somehow, and reassuring. The temperature was not cold—in the high sixties, Andrea guessed. In London, they would not even turn on the heat in this kind of weather.

She thought of London and the snow outside the Savoy Grill the day she had tea there with Georgene. That was less than a week—only three days ago!

Andrea finally broke the silence when they had been walking for several minutes. "Holly, do you think Sarah really believes that Benjamin shot Bryan Anderson at the Huntington?"

"Who *knows* what Sarah thinks. Especially since she's been seeing that psychiatrist. She has a whole new vocabulary. She's always talking about repressed hostility and universal guilt and God knows what else. Probably the only thing she heard the detectives say was that they found a gun that had been buried in the statuary garden. A buried gun immediately meant Benjamin to her."

They passed a large natural stone house set far back from the street with a large wooden cutout of Santa in his sleigh.

"Christmas." Holly sighed. "Christmas should be all that a boy Benjamin's age has on his mind. Not that his mother has managed to get herself put in jail."

"Are you going to be here for Christmas?" Andrea asked.

"I don't know. The reason we're here at all is that Sarah thought it would be good for Benjamin. A change of scene. That sort of thing. What I told you about happened just a few months ago."

The sound of the Foothill Freeway a few miles distant was a low, steady hum interspersed with occasional bird calls.

"One thing I don't understand," Andrea said, "when I called you, you mentioned something about Nikki Yamaguchi. What did you mean?"

"Oh, just that Nikki was the one who showed Benjamin how to climb the fence into the Huntington. Sarah knew about that. That's another reason she might have thought—Andrea!" Holly stopped suddenly and took hold of Andrea's sleeve.

"What?"

"Benjamin *might* have been there that night. He *told* us that he had just been riding around on his bicycle. But he might have been there."

"You're not saying that you believe that Benjamin actually was the one who shot that man."

"No. I'll never believe that. But if he was there, he could have seen who did."

A SMALL wooden sign nailed to a post that held a mail box read BRADBURY RIDING ACADEMY.

Andrea and Holly walked the dirt road that led to a neat wooden stable with its row of ten stalls. At one end of the building an open door revealed a large, comfortable office with bright green indoor-outdoor carpet and a rolltop wooden desk. A worn-looking, overstuffed love seat with fussy floral upholstery stood against the wall and looked as though it had seen several years of service in a bedroom before being transferred to the office next to the horses.

Andrea waited nearby while Holly went to speak with the riding instructor, who was standing in the doorway of the tack room at the opposite end of the stable. The woman listened as Holly said something to her, then nodded, and motioned to the interior of the room with a thumb. Holly went in, and, in a moment, came out with Benjamin.

She gave the little boy a hug, and kept her hand on his shoulder as they walked the length of the stable to where Andrea stood.

"We can use the office," Holly said.

"Hi, Benjamin," Andrea said.

He gave her a tight-lipped grin.

"I'll wait out here." Andrea started for a backless bench that looked out over a rolling field. In the distance, next to the far fence, three sleek horses grazed languidly.

"Come with us," Holly said. And to Benjamin, "We have some serious stuff to talk about, but you don't mind if Andrea's there, do you?"

"No. She's okay." He shrugged.

Holly and Benjamin took the love seat. Andrea sat in the desk chair.

"Ben." Holly sat sideways, facing the boy. "You know that night your mom and I were so worried about you—when you were out so late?"

"Yeah."

"You weren't really just riding your bike around the neighborhood, were you?"

Benjamin held his feet out and examined his shoe laces the way he had when he and Andrea were at the art museum.

Holly took his face in her hand and waited until he looked into her eyes. "We've gotta have some straight answers here, kiddo. It won't take long, and it won't hurt once it's over—kinda like going to the dentist. But you've got to tell the truth, and you've got to tell it to the police. Every bit of it."

The boy squirmed away from her and started for the door. Holly jumped up from the love seat and grabbed him just as he got outside, then knelt down so that their faces were level. "Look, I didn't say anything about it being easy. But you've got to do this to help your mom."

Benjamin turned his frightened face toward the girl. "Why? What about my mom?"

"Well, she kinda made a mistake. She was trying to protect you—she didn't want you to have to talk to the police—so she told them some things that weren't true, and she got herself in trouble."

"What kind of trouble?"

"It will be all right if you'll just talk to them, and tell them the truth." Holly gave him an affectionate swat on his small bottom. "You can do that, can't you?"

Benjamin did not answer. But when the kneeling girl hugged him, he buried his face in her neck.

"I'll call detectives Lopez and Roberson and ask them to meet us at the house." Andrea had already fished Eduardo's business card from her handbag and was dialing the number.

THE LAPD's unmarked green Plymouth was parked in the Dodsons' driveway when Holly drove up with Andrea and Benjamin in the rental car.

"That must be them," Tina said.

"So it is," Eduardo said. "It's easy to recognize Andrea Perkins's pretty face and red hair," Eduardo said.

"*Oh* yeah." As they got out of the car and waited for the others to join them, Tina quickly confirmed with her partner, "You'll talk to the boy first, right?"

"And if he won't open up for me, you take over."

Andrea quickly introduced the detectives to Holly and Benjamin as she used the key Georgene Dodson had given her to unlock the front door.

"Hey, guys"—Holly gave the three adults a meaningful look above the head of the boy—"would it be okay if Ben took a shower and I dug out some clean clothes for him before we get on with this? He's been mucking around in a stable and I think we all might prefer the aroma of a little Dial soap to what Andrea and I put up with in the car."

Benjamin giggled, obviously at ease with Holly's brashness.

"Sure, no hurry," Eduardo said.

"I know it's probably not the thing you do best, but do you suppose you could make some hot chocolate, Andrea?" Holly grinned. "There's a box in the cabinet next to the sink. All you have to do is add hot water."

"I'll give it a try." Andrea led the way to the kitchen. When the two detectives were settled on stools in front of the breakfast bar, she said, "We thought it would be a good idea if you heard some of the background before you ask Benjamin any questions."

Tina reached in the pocket of her jacket and set a small tape recorder on the counter. "Do you mind?"

"No. But if you need specific details about what I'm going to tell you, you'll have to ask Holly. The story she told me explains why Sarah confessed to shooting that man at the Huntington."

"Mrs. Anderson has already given us a good reason," Tina said. "We've confirmed that she was married to the victim, that he left—at her request—and has been living on the street for a number of years. She says he showed up here on the doorstep and asked for money." Tina took a notepad from her other pocket and flipped the pages until she found what she was looking for. She read aloud, "Mrs. Anderson stated, 'I went crazy when I saw the condition he was in. He was a drunk and a derelict and I didn't want him anywhere near my son.'"

"Yes. I knew she must have told you something like that. But Holly says she can swear that Sarah never left the house that night the man was shot. And the reason Sarah immediately confessed when she learned that the gun was registered to Joseph Dodson—and obviously came from this house—was that she was afraid Benjamin had taken it. She told you what she did in order to protect her son."

Andrea told Tina and Eduardo about the fatal shooting of the stable manager in Lexington, Kentucky.

When she had finished—giving as many of the details as she could recall—Eduardo asked, "Did Mrs. Anderson believe her son had killed the man intentionally?"

"I can't answer that," Andrea said. "But my guess is that when she learned of Bryan Anderson's death at the Huntington, she was afraid that there had been a second accident—"

"Hey! Where's the hot chocolate?" Holly's voice from the hallway warned of their return a moment before she and a scrubbed and shiny Benjamin entered the kitchen. "Just as I suspected, Andrea. I'll bet you've never even boiled water."

Andrea laughed. "I'm sure you can do it much better."

"Give me room. Why don't you all sit at the breakfast table and I'll see what I can do."

"Holly—" Benjamin looked at the teenaged girl with frightened eyes.

"It's okay, sweetie, I'll be right here."

Eduardo put the tape recorder in the center of the table. "We're going to just talk a little while. And so that we won't forget what everybody said, we're going to tape-record it. You don't mind, do you?"

Benjamin shrugged.

"Did you ever see a recorder this size?" Eduardo pushed the small keycase-sized mechanism across the table closer to the boy. "It's official police issue. You can carry it in an inside pocket, and it will record a conversation clear across the room. Would you like to take a look at it?"

"I'm not much interested in electronics," Benjamin said, following Holly with his eyes as she spooned chocolate powder into the mugs.

Trying a different approach, Eduardo said, "You're from Kentucky, huh?"

"Yep."

"They have some pretty good basketball teams in Kentucky, don't they?"

"I don't know."

Eduardo waited a beat. "You like baseball? Too bad the season's over. You might have gotten to go see a Dodger game. Dodger Stadium is really a neat place." There was no response. "I'll bet you're on a Little League team back home. What are you, a pitcher? Looks like you've got the arm for it."

"I think baseball's stupid. I hate baseball."

Eduardo raised his eyebrows almost imperceptibly and looked at his partner.

Tina had been closely watching Benjamin. He was like one of her sister's kids. He couldn't be conned. Whatever he was interested in, he wasn't giving anything away. You had to cut out the bullshit and talk straight to a kid like this. "Benjamin. We need you to answer some questions for us," she said almost sternly. "Will you do it?"

The boy sat silently looking at the tabletop.

"I've got an idea," Tina said. "How would it be if Holly came and sat next to you? I'll ask the questions, but you don't have to look at me; you can look at her when you give the answers. You want to try it that way?"

Benjamin did not answer.

Andrea moved her chair back from the table to make room for Holly. The hot chocolate was left forgotten on the countertop.

"In fact, I'll ask Holly some questions before we get around to you." Tina went to the kitchen bar and collected two of the steaming mugs. She set one in front of Holly, and one in front of Benjamin. "Holly, tell me about that night the man was killed at the Huntington. Tell me where you were, where Benjamin was, and where his mother was."

Holly held Benjamin's hand under the table. At first, she seemed almost as resistant as the boy had been. She took a sip of the chocolate and wiped the foam from her upper lip, and then described how she and Sarah had been watching television together and thought Benjamin was in his room asleep. When Sarah went to check on him, his bed was empty. They didn't know how long he had been gone. When he came in through the window a few minutes after they entered his bedroom, he said he had been out riding his bike.

"You weren't, though," Holly pushed the tip of the boy's nose with her finger. "Were you?"

"No." Benjamin brushed her finger away.

"Where were you, really, that night?" This time it was Tina asking the question.

"Answer her," Holly said.

"At the Huntington."

"Why did you go there?" Tina asked.

"Nikki said I'd be scared."

"Who's Nikki?"

Andrea and Holly exchanged looks.

"He's a guy." Benjamin looked directly at Tina for the first time.

"He's Benjamin's half-assed juvenile delinquent art tutor," Holly said.

Neither Tina nor Eduardo had taken their eyes from Benjamin. Tina asked, "Did Nikki go with you?"

"No. He brought over a couple of cans of paint, and said the only way I could prove I wasn't scared was to go over the

fence and onto the Huntington grounds at night—alone—
and paint the jacket on one of the statues.''

"That little bastard." Holly set the mug down heavily,
sloshing droplets of chocolate on the polished wood surface.

Andrea, too, had been watching Benjamin closely. He
flinched a little at the sound the mug made as it banged
against the table. "I don't think Nikki's very brave, do you,
Benjamin?" Andrea said. "Remember how scared he was
of the thunder and lightning when he got caught hiding in
the fireplace?"

Benjamin giggled and seemed to relax.

Tina neither thanked nor reprimanded Holly or Andrea
for interrupting, but concentrated entirely on the boy. "That
night when you were there alone—this is important, now—
tell us everything that happened."

With Tina's patient prodding, Benjamin told her of
climbing the fence with the intention of painting the jacket
on the statue red. He had just started when he heard two
other people come over the fence. He *was* frightened then,
and hid in the bushes. One of the intruders kept urging the
other one on toward the fountain. The one who lagged behind was obviously drunk, but his companion had an open
bottle and insisted that they sit by the fountain and share it.
When they had both passed by Benjamin, he at last felt safe
in leaving. He crept through the bushes and hurried back
toward the fence. Just as he climbed over, he heard a gun go
off.

Benjamin swallowed hard, and rubbed his eyes with his
fist.

Andrea watched his hands. Those talented little hands
would eventually be his salvation once he made it past the
very large hurdles that were still ahead.

She thought she understood it all, now. Probably even
better than Holly.

"All right, Benjamin. That was good," Tina said. For the
first time she smiled at the boy. "That was real good. You

don't have to talk anymore about the gunshot right now, but we'll come back to it. Okay?''

"Okay.''

Tina gave her partner a quick glance. It was his turn.

"You're an artist, huh?'' Eduardo asked.

"I don't know. I like it.''

"Me, too.''

Confidentially, to Benjamin, Tina said, "You ought to see what *he* considers art.''

Benjamin grinned.

Kidding, Eduardo said, "I know what I like when I see it. In fact, I think I've seen some of your work.''

Puzzled, Benjamin looked at the detective he had refused to talk to before.

Still almost casually, Eduardo asked, "That night you heard the gunshot. That wasn't the only time you went into the statuary garden alone at night, was it Benjamin?''

"No.''

"That's what I thought.'' Eduardo laughed and jabbed at the boy's shoulder playfully. "That's where I saw your artwork. You're the one who gave that statue of the Italian guy the bright green jacket to wear, aren't you?''

Benjamin seemed to sense that it was all right to admit it. "Yes,'' he said.

Holly looked startled. Andrea glanced at her, warning her not to interrupt.

Eduardo asked carefully, "That's not the only reason you went back, though—just to paint the statue—is it?''

"No.''

"Benjamin, your mother was very worried about you. She didn't want you to have to talk to us about those two nights when you were in the statuary garden. She was afraid it would upset you too much. You know how mothers can be. So, she told us some things that we know now weren't really true. But I think she was trying a little too hard to protect you. You seem pretty strong to me. Still, we wouldn't put you through this if we didn't have to. The fact is, though, you're the only one who can help us find out what really did happen." Eduardo paused to emphasize the importance of the next question. "Where did you find the gun, Benjamin?"

The boy looked first at Holly, whose only expression was surprise. Andrea nodded encouragingly when he looked toward her.

Tina said, "Tell us, son."

Eduardo repeated, "Where did you find it?"

"It was out by the swimming pool, under one of the steps that goes down to the guest house."

"The guest house where *we're* staying?" Holly quickly put her hand over her mouth. She still did not understand.

Eduardo gave Holly a warning glance, then nodded with only the slightest movement of his head at Tina.

"When you found it," Tina leaned toward the boy, "you wanted to get rid of it, didn't you? Like the other time."

Benjamin quickly looked at Holly.

"It's all right," Tina took Benjamin's free hand and squeezed it hard. "That time is over. It's gone. We're not going to talk about that. But when you saw that second gun, you thought it should be buried, too. Didn't you?"

Looking down, Benjamin nodded his head a half an inch.

For the benefit of the recorder, Tina asked, "Is that right?"

"Yes," Benjamin answered softly.

"Good boy. Now, Benjamin. If you think *that* was hard—the *really* hard question is coming up. Then it will be over." Tina still gripped the boy's hand. "That first night. Did you recognize those people who climbed over the fence into the statuary garden?"

"One of them. The lady."

"One of them was a lady?"

"Yes."

"And you could see who she was?"

"Yes."

"Tell me who—just tell me—and then that's all."

The boy sat up straight and leaned his head against the wooden rail of the chair. With a sigh that was more than the release of held-in breath, but also of held-in secrets and held-in pain, he said, "It was Aunt Georgene."

THIRTY

CARS LEAVING Santa Anita Race Track were filling all three lanes of Huntington Drive. Eduardo managed to squeeze the Plymouth into a space between a beat-up camper and a new Toyota and head south toward Hollenbeck.

"I never thought we'd be calling Scotland Yard to help us with this case, did you?" Tina braced her feet against the floorboard as the Plymouth came within inches of the rear bumper of the camper when it made a sudden stop for a traffic light. "Do you suppose the department will let us go bring Georgene Dodson back?"

"No. The lieutenant will probably get a nice trip to England as a reward for our hard work."

"Maybe he'll send us a postcard."

"Don't count on it. He probably wouldn't be able to find the post office."

The light changed and Eduardo pulled into the second lane.

"What do you think Goochie—Bryan Anderson—did all day? He left downtown before noon," Tina said. "What had he been doing until he got shot?"

"The way I have it figured," Eduardo said, "he saw the picture in the paper and knew his former wife was visiting her sister, so he took the bus from downtown to San Marino with the idea of hitting his ex up for some money. But the sister-in-law, Georgene, saw him first. Naturally, she didn't want some scuzzball hanging around her fancy neighborhood, so she gave him a bottle of booze and told him to get lost until after dark, and she'd meet him at the fence to the Huntington with the money.

"That afternoon, she probably got to thinking that if he showed up once, he'd probably be back—over and over again. That wouldn't fit in with her life-style. So, she decided to park her car ahead of time near the exit to the statuary garden so she could get out of there in a hurry. Then, she met him—like they'd planned—only instead of giving him the money right away, she talked him into climbing over the fence with her to a nice, quiet, safe spot where she shot him."

"I guess," Tina was a bit skeptical. "If that's the way it happened, he'd have been pretty drunk when she met him the second time. I can't figure any other way she'd have gotten him over that fence."

"By then, he probably thought he could fly over the fence."

"You think she had it all planned ahead of time?"

"Sure. She'd have already stashed a plastic bag in the car to put his clothes in. After she shot him, she stripped him so he couldn't be identified right away—if ever—and dumped his clothes in the ditch by Santa Anita."

"Then she left early the next morning for England," Tina added, "even before Archie Chambers discovered the body."

"Feel like a taco?"

"Yeah, why not," Tina said. "But let's get them to go. We've still got a lot of work to do."

Eduardo turned off Huntington behind two other cars waiting at the drive-in window of El Fenix.

"I'm convinced that Georgene Dodson was the shooter," Tina said with conviction. "I'm sure we've identified the murderer—"

"That's our job."

"But do you think it was just blackmail?"

"Why not? Money is a powerful motivator."

They had their case, but Tina was unwilling to let go. "I don't know, I just think there must have been something else between them."

"Like sex?"

Tina rolled her eyes skyward. "Does sex always have to be involved?"

"It very often is."

"It could have been about the boy. Maybe—in addition to the money—he insisted on coming back to see his son. I can't picture someone like Georgene Dodson wanting a derelict like Goochie hanging around her neighborhood. What would her San Marino friends think if they found out he was her brother-in-law?"

"Maybe. But we'll probably never know."

GEORGENE RECOGNIZED *the eyes even embedded in the grizzled layers of beard and dirt. "Bryan?"*

"It's me." The first flash of bravado was washed away by a film of drunken tears.

"What are you doing here?"

"Georgie, the God's truth is, I came here to ask you for money. I figured you all owe me. But now, all I want is to see my son."

"Bryan. You can't do that."

Hurriedly, he said, "Oh, I don't mean meet him. I just mean—hide someplace and look at him. See what he looks like."

"He looks like you."

"I hope he has his mother's eyes."

"Yes. He does." Georgene softened a little. "You have to go. I'll give you the money I have in the house now, and I'll meet you later and we can talk more."

Twenty-five dollars and a bottle of Jack Daniel's bought her enough time to make plans.

In the moonlit statuary garden he had not seemed as repulsive as he had standing at her front door. There was still something compelling about his laugh. As he lurched across the lawn toward her, for an instant he became the drunken teenage boy who loved her—whom she had loved. But then she saw—as she had seen before—the same weakness, the same possibility of regret and disappointment that she had seen in her father.

As he came closer—laughing, his arms outstretched—she shot him.

THIRTY-ONE

THE ENTRY HALL was full of luggage. Sarah, Holly, and Benjamin were going back to Kentucky for Christmas—and to stay. Andrea had found a comfortable hotel in Arcadia that would be fairly convenient while she finished her work at the Huntington.

She had even contracted to keep Holly's rental car for at least as long as Aldo Balzani would be there. She took comfort in the thought that his plane was in the air at the moment and his plans *could not* change again.

Carrying her last, and most precious, bit of equipment—her canvas bag of art supplies—down the stairs, she saw Sarah in the hallway with an overnight bag to add to her collection that would soon be loaded onto the airport Super Shuttle.

"Sarah. Do you have a minute?"

"Yes, Andrea. I've wanted to talk with you."

By silent agreement they went into Georgene's office and closed the door.

"I talked with detectives Roberson and Lopez this morning," Sarah said. "They've contacted Scotland Yard. I don't know whether Georgene is still in England, or not. What happens next, I don't know. And I don't really care." She went to the glass wall and looked at the brilliant plantings on the terrace—as the architect and the interior decorator had planned for visitors to the room to do.

"I'm sure you know what a brave little boy you have," Andrea said.

"Yes. I do know."

"It took an enormous amount of courage to tell the detectives what he had seen that night."

Though Sarah's back was turned, Andrea knew that she was crying.

"Sarah, you didn't even see Bryan Anderson the night he was killed, did you?"

Sarah took a tissue from a white dispenser on the white desk and went to sit in one of the white leather chairs. Andrea sat opposite her.

"No, as always, Bryan came to see Georgene."

"Benjamin doesn't know that the man who was killed was his father, does he?"

"I'm sure he doesn't. Bryan had changed so much, and it had been almost four years since he left. The only time Benjamin saw him was in the dark in the statuary garden. I don't think it's possible that he recognized him."

Sarah, seeming not quite as helpless as she had before, nevertheless looked to Andrea for reassurance. "I don't think he needs to know about that for a few years yet, do you?"

"No," Andrea said. "And I don't think he needs to know who his mother is, either."

Sarah's head snapped up and she fixed Andrea with a haunted look.

Andrea had realized the truth when she saw a picture that Georgene had kept in her desk. It was taken in a bar at Santa Anita Race Track. The man, she recognized from other pictures, was Bryan Anderson. The woman, at whom he was looking so adoringly, had her back to the camera. But her hand that was touching his face was the same hand Andrea had seen across the table in the Savoy Grill.

She had wondered about showing the picture to Sarah, but she realized now it would be much too painful for this fragile woman.

"It's the hands," Andrea said. "I don't have any scientific evidence, but I think I read that a deformity like that— an extra finger—is passed on through the mother. I noticed Georgene's scar when I had tea with her in London. Benjamin's is less pronounced. There's just a tiny nub and a trace of a nail on the little finger side of his right hand. I noticed it when we were at the art museum together. I took his hand to lead him out of the room when the lights went out.''

Sarah wiped her eyes, and her shoulders melted into the soft leather of the chair. "Bryan was always in love with her. I suppose she was with him. So was I. But she could see how weak he was. I never could. When he finally accepted the fact that she would never marry him—even though she was pregnant—he asked me.'' Sarah's laugh sounded painful. "And, because I had always loved him, I accepted. It didn't matter to me about the terms. That's why we moved to Kentucky. The three of us. Then, when Benjamin was born, Georgene left, and Bryan and I kept the baby. I suppose if any of us had thought it through we'd have known it wouldn't work.''

"But it did for you, Sarah.''

"Yes. I was the lucky one. I got Benjamin.''

"Your ride to the airport will be here, soon.'' Andrea stood.

So did Sarah.

"I just wanted you to know,'' Andrea said, "that your son is not only a very fine little boy, but he has an extraordinary talent. I hope you'll make sure he uses it.''

"I will. Holly will see to that.'' Sarah kissed Andrea on the cheek. "Merry Christmas.''

"Yes,'' Andrea said, "and Happy New Year.'' She thought they might have a good chance.